PRAISE FOR ZO

Baby Tee

"Unnerving and unputdownable, *Baby Teeth* will get under your skin and keep you trapped in its chilling grip until the shocking conclusion."
—Lisa Scottoline, *New York Times* bestselling author

"*We Need to Talk About Kevin* meets *Gone Girl* meets *The Omen*. *Baby Teeth* is a twisty, delirious read that will constantly question your sympathies for the two characters as their bond continues to crumble."
—EW.com

"Deliciously creepy . . . the author keeps the suspense taut . . . offering a terrifying glimpse into the inner thoughts of a budding sociopath."
—*Library Journal* (starred)

"Tightly plotted, expertly choreographed . . . Stage palpably conveys Suzette's fear, anger, frustration, and desperation while exploring the deleterious effects that motherhood can have on one's marriage and self-worth . . . Stage fuses horror with domestic suspense to paint an unflinching portrait of childhood psychopathy and maternal regret."
—*Kirkus Reviews* (starred)

"Stage's deviously fun debut takes child-rearing anxiety to demented new heights. Stage expertly crafts this creepy, can't-put-it-down thriller into a fearless exploration of parenting and marriage that finds the cracks in unconditional love."

—*Publishers Weekly* (starred)

"Zoje Stage's *Baby Teeth* is cunning, sharp, and nasty and wickedly funny until it isn't funny anymore. This intelligent, unrelenting, layered shocker can stand proudly alongside classics like *The Other* and *The Butcher Boy*, with their 'evil' children uncannily reflecting our own sins."

—Paul Tremblay, nationally bestselling author of
A Head Full of Ghosts and *The Cabin at the End of the World*

"Every time we read the premise of *Baby Teeth*, all the hair on the back of our necks stands up. Simply put, it's about a sweet little girl who wants to kill her mother. And it. Is. Bonkers. Do you have goose bumps yet?"

—HelloGiggles

"Imagine *We Need to Talk About Kevin*, only with insight into what Kevin was thinking—and if Eva had fought back. This dark, terrifying novel unfolds as a battle of wits between a struggling mother and her psychotic young daughter—and its genius is that the reader's allegiance isn't allowed to linger too long on either side. You'll be desperate to discuss the ending once you've recovered from the shock of it. A must-read."

—Catherine Ryan Howard, *USA Today* bestselling
author of *Distress Signals*

"*Baby Teeth* is electrifyingly creepy. It calls to mind the great monster children of *The Fifth Child* or *We Need to Talk About Kevin* but has a devilish tension all its own. Twisted, playful, and deeply unsettling, Zoje Stage's debut announces her as a new voice worth celebrating."

—Colin Winnette, author of *The Job of the Wasp*

"*Baby Teeth* is deeply unsettling in the best possible way. Absolutely unforgettable and unflinching, it digs right into the painful nerve of family, obligation, and dependence—it's a hell of a debut."

—Kelly Braffet, author of *Save Yourself*

Getaway

"Stage is a writer with a gift for the lyrical and the frightening . . . *Getaway* feels original and very scary."

—*The New York Times Book Review*

"You won't blink until you read the last line."

—*Publishers Weekly*

"A chilling thriller that will definitely make you lose sleep at night."

—*PopSugar*

"I've been waiting for a thriller to capture the emotional depth of women for years . . . I can't recommend *Getaway* enough."

—Tarryn Fisher, *New York Times* bestselling author of *The Wives* and *The Wrong Family*

"Tense, unpredictable, and utterly compelling, Stage's complex story of friendship and survival is a must-read."

—Karen Dionne, *New York Times* bestselling author of *The Marsh King's Daughter*

"A harrowing, heart-pounding thrill ride."

—Rachel Harrison, author of *The Return*

"Strap into your pack and step into this inky darkness with Zoje Stage."

—Stephen Graham Jones, *New York Times* bestselling author

Wonderland

MOTHERED

ALSO BY ZOJE STAGE

MOTHERED

A NOVEL

USA TODAY
BESTSELLING AUTHOR
OF *BABY TEETH*

ZOJE STAGE

THOMAS & MERCER

Text copyright © 2023 by Zoje Stage

Published by Thomas & Mercer, Seattle

www.apub.com

Amazon, the Amazon logo, and Thomas & Mercer are trademarks of Amazon.com, Inc., or its affiliates.

ISBN-13: 9781662506246 (hardcover)
ISBN-13: 9781662506239 (paperback)
ISBN-13: 9781662506222 (digital)

Cover design by Olga Grlic
Cover image: © Richard Nixon / Arcangel

Printed in the United States of America
First edition

For Deb

AUTHOR'S NOTE

When I started writing *Mothered* in April 2020, I had no intention of it being a "pandemic story." It is common for novels to take place amid a world that looks much like our own, and the longer I worked on the book—and the longer the COVID-19 pandemic lasted—the more of that reality crept into the story. I feel it's important to note, however, that while the backdrop of this novel is the early months of a pandemic, with all its confusion and uncertainty, the world that Grace and Jackie inhabit is fictitious. You may recognize certain aspects and may have encountered similar things—but I'm aware that as waves of COVID-19 moved around the country, people in different regions experienced different protocols and rates of infection at different times. *Mothered* was never meant to document a universal experience or the specific early months of *our* pandemic—but for Grace and Jackie, *their* pandemic provides a crucial catalyst for what unfolds in their lives.

Z. S.
February 18, 2022

PROLOGUE

Silas loved a good puzzle, especially if it involved the interlocking pieces of science and soul, the known and the unknown. What made a human being turn monstrous? An error in prenatal development, a misalignment of chemicals, an insufficient ability to adapt to misfortune, too much of one thing and too little of something else? As a psychotherapist he'd never utter the words *monster* or *crazy* aloud; more than ever, the world was aware of the synergy of illness—in an individual, in a society. But in truth, his path to working with the criminally insane began with a teenage passion for serial-killer movies and horror stories.

He'd once imagined a state hospital as a barbaric castle where screams echoed in shadowed hallways. Now he knew it as a more prosaic place, an office park that wouldn't look out of place in the former Soviet Union, surrounded by rolling fields of clipped grass where no one ever ran or played. Each building had harsh lighting and its own litany of rules, though one building had more locking doors than the others.

The folder in front of him carried a mystery in its thin, fresh pages. He'd met the new patient only once, and the details of her case made it all the more confounding as to how someone so frail had committed an act of such brutality. Silas pondered it as he turned his attention to the gloom outside his window. He tried to keep his office clean and bright, with framed pictures as colorful as a child's xylophone, to counter the effects of the gray clouds that invaded the western Pennsylvania skies with mournful frequency. Homicides within a family weren't that unusual, but this . . . The file didn't have enough information, but he turned back to it, looking for whatever clues it held.

Blood had dripped from the walls. The police photos revealed a chaotic scene and Silas was sure the two had fought, physically and ferociously—no quick slicing-open-the-throat while the victim lay asleep. Overkill wasn't uncommon in crimes of passion, where love and hate bred a frenzy of mixed emotions, deep and personal, but *ninety-one* stab wounds? How long had that taken? How had those thin arms had so much strength? The detectives found four knives at the scene: two had broken from repeated, forceful use; one was embedded in the skull.

Silas looked away again, this time because the murder scene was threatening to dislodge the chipped-ham sandwich he'd eaten for lunch. He could taste the salt and mayonnaise rising in his throat.

"I had to do it. She was contagious"—her greeting as she'd opened the door to let the police in. A miasma of decay had wafted out like a poisonous cloud, making the uniformed officers gag. How had she lived with the stench? And why? Most people, if they were going to report their own crime, would do it right after the fact—not wait two weeks while living with the corpse. Her excuse, given days later, was that she'd been terribly ill (too ill to make a phone call?), but the first responders had quoted her as saying, "It wasn't an emergency. I didn't want to bother anyone."

It hadn't taken anyone long to reach the conclusion that she was mentally disturbed, and she was sent to Torrance, the region's only forensic psychiatric hospital.

Silas grinned. Another's tragedy shouldn't please him, but he couldn't help it: he loved a good puzzle, especially one that looked on the surface like the gory movies he still so loved. But film and fiction weren't enough anymore; now he craved the real thing and loved his role in revealing the perpetrator's story.

From what he knew of her so far, she was communicative and expressive and quick to open up. His job, as it often was, would be to filter the drop of truth from a waterfall of magical thinking. He glanced upward at the clock; she would be brought to his office momentarily for her first full session. Silas closed the folder and slid it into a drawer, abuzz with the nervous excitement of a boy who'd mastered the art of trespassing.

1

They were all lied to. Maybe it hadn't started as a lie—maybe it started as wishful thinking. That's how easy it was to turn good intentions, uttered by powerful people, into absolute bullshit. It confirmed what Grace already knew: everyone lied, even if they started out telling the truth. It was easy for the truth to slip away. Two weeks of lockdown became three. One month became two.

Grace whirled around the "office" in her new rolly chair, angrily pushing off the wall with her bare feet. She'd never had space for an office before. At present it was a mostly empty room, with a cheap IKEA desk in the corner—one of the mix-and-match styles where you picked the tabletop and legs separately.

"Grace?" her mother squawked in her ear. After barely talking once a month for decades, Jackie had been calling every other day for weeks; her life had been upended—first by her husband Robert's mysterious illness and death, and then by her own health scare. Now she was waiting for an answer to a simple question: *What's wrong?*

It wasn't just the loss of her job; it was the loss of her *livelihood*. Grace had just found out, and she should be talking—crying, freaking out—with Miguel, not her mother. She spun the chair in a circle. The dizziness felt better than her regret for answering the phone.

"Barbara's not reopening the salon," Grace said. "She decided to retire." After two months of chaos and confusion (and lies), Barbara had seen the writing on the wall: this wasn't going to end well, and no one wanted to risk their life for a haircut. And now Grace couldn't keep saying—to Jackie or herself—that she'd be back at work soon. She knew what was coming next.

"Oh dear. I'm sorry. Well . . . have you thought anymore about my coming to live with you?"

Were the lies to blame for the predicament Grace now found herself in? She'd said no, swiftly, to this same question two times over the last six days. It was still true that she didn't *want* Jackie to move in with her. But what she wanted was becoming less relevant as the reality of the situation nibbled away at her bank account.

If her mother moved in, Grace would lose her home office but save her house.

Buying a house, even a small one in an uninspiring neighborhood, was expensive. She'd lived in a cramped apartment and saved for a down payment for *years*. The world wasn't supposed to grind to a halt six weeks after she'd signed the mortgage. The original "two-week" lockdown hadn't been so bad: she'd been able to pack and move without taking time off from work. She was ready for the pandemic to be over now, but the authorities weren't even guessing anymore. Two weeks, two months, two years—who the fuck knew?

"Grace." Her mother sounded gentler now. "I know it's not what you really want. I know you've been on your own for a long time. I also know how proud you are to finally be a homeowner"—did she over-emphasize *finally*?—"and I know you don't want to lose your house."

All true things.

"Mom . . ." Now what? Offer her mother the unfinished basement? Perhaps she could sleep in a coffin like a vampire.

It was just too weird to picture the two of them cohabitating again. They hadn't lived under the same roof since Grace was eighteen—half a lifetime ago. Jackie moved to Fort Myers and found a husband (two, technically) while Grace stayed in Pittsburgh to attend beauty school and become a hairstylist.

"I appreciate that you want to help me—"

"Most of Robert's things went to his kids," Jackie said, eagerly butting in, "but he left me enough. And with my Social Security—I'm not affected by all of this the same way you are. I can pay half of everything. And if you're ever short—the mortgage will always get paid. But it's not just that. They're telling me I can leave the hospital soon . . . but they won't let me go home if I'm alone."

Her voice turned squeaky and desperate. Was she about to cry? For the first time Jackie needed her, but Grace wasn't sure she was ready to be needed.

Of course having a roommate would provide more financial stability in uncertain times. But if Grace had really wanted a roommate, she would've asked Miguel. She rolled her wheelie chair to the nearest window. There was a postage-stamp yard in the front and a mailing label yard (ha ha) in the back.

"Isn't there, like, a senior place there? Some sort of senior community or assisted living?"

"I don't need assisted living—I'm getting my strength back. I'll be good as new soon." She spoke quickly, preempting Grace's ability to jump in and argue. Just as Grace hadn't understood the precise nature of Robert's illness, she didn't exactly understand her mother's. *Not the virus* was the only explanation she ever got. "Believe me, you'll never have to wipe my ass—I don't want that any more than you do. If it got to that point, I'd check myself into a nursing home."

Grace didn't think it worked that way, but she was glad for her mother's blessing to seek other arrangements if necessary.

"We'd have to establish *boundaries,*" Grace heard herself say. Her alter egos reared up in protest, *Stop! Don't you realize what's about to happen?* Without explicitly saying it, Grace had opened the door.

"Of course, I understand it's your house." Jackie sounded relieved now, and excited. As a child Grace had known her mother to have one mood—cranky. Grace wasn't sure she was prepared for this more mercurial, less predictable phase of Jackie's life. "This will be good for us—it's been a long time, and we're both adults now."

Grace wasn't sure how to take that. She always heard rebukes in her mother's words, and in the silent spaces too. Could Jackie possibly be implying that the problems they'd had while Grace was growing up were due to her *age*? Some inexcusable lack of maturity that ignored the reality of her having been an honest-to-god *child*? Jackie had always hated being a mother, at least that's how Grace remembered it.

"We'll be equals, roommates," she said, trying to imagine them both in new roles. "Considerate of each other's space and needs."

That was the polite way to say, "You'll stay the fuck out of my way and my life." Still, if they really went through with this, Grace envisioned a lot of closed doors in her future. Living alone, she never thought about needing privacy as she sat on the toilet or closing her bedroom door as she dressed or slept. She shuddered at the thought of such changes, suddenly claustrophobic in her nearly furnitureless room.

"Speaking of furniture—how would that work? Getting you and your things to Pittsburgh?"

"Ollie—do you remember Robert's youngest son? He's a bit of a pothead but the best of the bunch. He'll stay with me at the condo when I'm released and help me pack up. Or maybe that part's done—his brother Sam's in a hurry to move his family in. Anyway, Ollie will drive my car, and we'll rent a small trailer. My eyesight's gotten a little iffy, so I told him he could keep the car after that."

She already had this planned out?

"There's really only room in the spare bedroom." Grace gazed at her beautiful, empty office. *Goodbye, office.* So much for having a designated place to pursue her hobby.

"That's all I need," said Jackie. "I'll bring my bedroom furniture and a few personal things, that's it. Unless there's anything you need for your house?"

"No no, that's okay." She grimaced at the thought of having old lady "Florida furniture" as part of her decorating scheme. "So, um . . . when do you think this would be happening?"

———

The minute she got off the phone with Jackie, she FaceTimed Miguel.

"Hello, lovey—"

"My mother's moving into my house! In less than three weeks! I've officially lost my mind . . ."

Miguel wasn't as sympathetic as Grace had expected; he thought it was a "nice solution." Grace realized in that moment just how much she'd neglected to tell him about her childhood. *Avoided* telling him was probably more accurate. There was nothing about her life before Jackie decamped for sunnier climes that she liked to reminisce over. In many ways there was a demarcation between life Before her mother left and After—and her life was *good* in the After.

And now her mother was coming back.

2

Grace thumbed in a string of emoji. It was so easy with the younger women, who preferred the shorthand of a heart-eyed smiley to actual words. Lexis224U typed back ILU. I love you. Grace blew her a pictorial kiss and clicked off, rolling her eyes.

Things weren't going well with Lexis224U. Grace had once lived for the adoration of her virtual dalliances. When she first started experimenting with online personas as a teenager, she'd been needy for a certain kind of attention, a certain kind of rush. The thrill of feeding someone else's fantasy. But adoration wasn't what she sought anymore. She was a better-functioning adult now—and more adept at developing profiles and stealing photos. It was important to get a mix of shots— some casual, some with blurry friends at the edge of the frame—not just a handful of hot-model selfies; she wanted to seem like a real person (a *desirable* real person).

Her whole game had evolved: now she liked young women who would take her advice; she liked feeling valuable in her role of improving someone's life. Grace had watched season after season of *Catfish* but never saw another catfisher quite like herself. Her online personas were Prince Charmings who came to the emotional rescue of Damsels in Distress. Her mission: to bolster their self-esteem; to be a cheerleader until they had enough confidence to get on with their life in a more meaningful way. Being on the receiving end of a damsel's gratitude was a great place to be, especially if it was from afar—without the ugliness and entanglements of real relationships.

Lexis224U had no idea who LuckyJamison really was. She didn't even know the person she was communicating with wasn't a man. She didn't know Grace was Caucasian, not biracial, or that she was thirty-six and not twenty-five. While all her alternate personas (most of them male) had athletic bodies, Grace had the first hints of middle-age, sedentary pudge. Every detail on every one of Grace's profiles was a lie, from the hometowns to the hobbies, and she knew how to use the internet well enough to make herself nearly untraceable. She even had a special voice, deeper than her natural one, for the unavoidable phone conversations. Anyone with basic skills of their own could do a reverse-image search to discover that something wasn't quite right. But most people didn't bother. They, too, got something out of the fantasy.

She'd have to ghost Lexis224U soon. Grace couldn't always tell at first if she was engaging with someone who was having a rough time but wanted to make better choices, or someone who complained as a daily sport; the interactions often started out the same. Unfortunately, Lexis224U was one of those women who enjoyed wallowing in the drama of their shitty lives, and she wasn't taking LuckyJamison's advice. It was obvious to Grace that Lexis224U didn't stand a chance at happiness unless she moved out of her emotionally abusive mother's house, but the girl wouldn't listen. Oh well. At any given time, Grace had half a dozen other identities and just as many damsels who might be more receptive to her encouragement; without Lexis224U she'd have more time for ShyShaina.

"Gray?"

And speaking of emotionally abusive mothers . . . Maybe that wasn't fair. More than anything, Grace was annoyed. It hadn't occurred to her when she accepted her mother's proposal that she'd hear that short form of her name—Gray—barked every ten minutes, each time beckoning her away from whatever she was doing. *Do you have more hangers? Can you carry this down to the basement? Can you move the dresser over a few inches? Do you have a pair of scissors? Can you hang these pictures?*

She closed out her apps and left the phone facedown on her desk—now in the corner of her own bedroom. Her plan had been for LuckyJamison, Malcolm, Blaine, Preston, Travis, Phoenix, and all the rest of her alter egos to be confined to her home office. Confinement, she believed, would help her become more disciplined, and she'd try to stop thumbing through messages as she brushed her teeth or watched TV or halfheartedly stirred a pot on the stove. She was still determined to cut down on the time she spent online; it would be healthier for all involved. A part of her recognized it was a questionable hobby.

With her mother's invasion of the second bedroom, her new plan was that the *desk* would define the square footage where Grace could pursue her avocation. Perhaps Jackie's presence would actually prove to be helpful: Grace muted her notifications when other people were around. She was embarrassed for anyone to witness the flurry of messaging that went on for hours every morning and evening. Not even Miguel knew about her secret hobby (though she'd admitted to catfishing someone *once*, eons ago). Maybe now, with the desk and a housemate, she'd finally cut down.

"Gray?"

"Coming!"

A long-lost image started to emerge—a distorted artifact that drifted up from deep waters, growing clearer as it neared the surface. For a moment Grace wasn't sure if she was in the past or the present. Her mother had summoned her a lot, back in the day; Grace had forgotten about that during the years in which they'd lived apart. She saw herself now, a girl, running into the kitchen to fetch something for her mom—really, to fetch something for her sister. Hope needed a *lot*, and Grace had often been the go-between, the runner, doing all the small tasks so their mom could focus her efforts on other things.

No amount of dashing around or doing chores could alleviate the guilt Grace had carried (*Guilt* should have been her name) that she was able bodied and healthy, while her uber-bright twin had been severely disabled and frequently sick. Now, responding as an adult to her bellowed name, it didn't make Grace feel as purposeful as it once had. She told herself that once her mother was unpacked and settled, she'd be less needy. Jackie had just arrived the day before; they hadn't had time yet to develop any sort of routine.

To reach "Jackie's" room all Grace had to do was open her door and take three strides. Between their two equal-size bedrooms was the tiny upstairs hallway and the bathroom. Her mother's door was wide open. Grace leaned on the doorjamb, waiting for instructions.

3

"What're you so grumpy about?" Jackie sat perched on the bed, smoothing out pieces of Bubble Wrap.

"What? I didn't even say anything." She stared at her mother, still struck by how much smaller she seemed. A result of the illness, Grace supposed. The mom from her childhood was forceful and energetic, not shrunken and bony like a winter tree.

"The way you're standing. Arms crossed. The peevish look on your face."

Oh for fuck's sake. But Grace uncrossed her arms and tried to arrange a more pleasant expression. "Did you need something?"

"I'm done with the boxes, if you want to break them down and store them in the basement."

"I'll just put them out for recycling." Grace started stacking the boxes.

"We might need them."

"For what?" She didn't bother reminding her mother that she, also, had only just moved—two and a half months prior—and had no intention of packing again for a couple of decades or more. Unless she lost her house (which wasn't supposed to happen now). Unless . . . "Are you planning to move again?"

Was this a more temporary arrangement than Grace had realized?

Perhaps she shouldn't have sounded so hopeful. Her mother shot her that old look—the angry, nearly insulted expression that would cloud her face when she was befuddled, as if Jackie's confusion were the other person's fault, an attempt to mess with her. "I just got here."

Grace scolded herself with the kind of esteem-slaughtering invective that so damaged her damsels. *Stupid stupid how could you be so stupid.* She really hadn't given much thought to what it would be like *living* with her mother again. They'd never communicated well, which hadn't mattered when it was easy to hang up the phone.

Over the years, they'd only visited IRL for important events. Grace had attended both of her mother's weddings and her first husband's funeral. (She liked her mom's second husband, Robert, better; he died during a nationwide stay-at-home order, so Grace hadn't been able to go to his funeral.) It had been relatively easy for Grace to suppress any grudges or grievances and maintain an even-keeled demeanor for a few hours at a time. But now, after only two half days and one night, Grace already hated how she felt in her mother's presence.

She's taking over my precious home.

Maybe Grace should've factored in more than the well-being of her bank account. A tiny part of her had been legitimately concerned about her mother's health—and agreeing to this arrangement was something a Good Daughter would do. But was Grace a Good Daughter? For that matter, was Jackie a Good Mother? And now, with all their questionable goodness, they were stuck together in a house that felt spacious for one person but cramped for two.

It was too soon, really, to doubt herself and her reasons and all the possible outcomes—that was the exact kind of behavior that Grace urged her damsels to avoid. What would LuckyJamison say? *Deal with the NOW. You're getting ahead of yourself.*

She had no idea, yet, what her mother was like, day in, day out. Maybe the years in Florida and the husbands with grown children and grandchildren had changed her. And even if they hadn't, Grace's years on her own, with a career she was good at and enjoyed, gave her the confidence and identity she'd lacked in her youth. *The twin that lived.* There was no reason why they needed to repeat the dynamics of their past.

"The room looks good," Grace said, finally letting her guard down a little.

While she'd needed two months to get fully unpacked, Jackie had managed it in less than two days. It helped that she'd been ready, or at least willing, to part with most of her material acquisitions. Now she only owned some knickknacks and memorabilia and the bedroom furniture. Everything matched. The bed and dresser and chest of drawers. The bedspread was in the same coral and turquoise colors as the little floor rug. The lamps were a pair, as were the nightstands. One wall was nearly covered in framed artwork, mostly reproductions, but it made the room feel like Jackie had lived there for years. In contrast, Grace's furniture had been acquired piecemeal, and while she'd say it all *blended*, neither her bedroom nor her living room was as well put together as her mother's Instant Abode.

A scent lingered in the old furniture and bedding, part perfume, part aftershave. Grace could almost see Robert's imprint on the far side of the mattress. For the first time, she felt genuine sadness for her mother—that Jackie's fun-loving husband had died, that her health was ravaged, that the elder stepsons had closed in like vultures to claim what they could. Jackie lost everything. And really, she hadn't complained. But Grace saw in her mother's stooped posture that all of it had taken a toll.

Jackie looked closer to turning eighty-five than seventy. Her skin had the bluish tinge of a bruise, the soft look of an overripe peach. Her hair had thinned, and sometime in the last few months she'd given up dying it and had it chopped off. Now it stood on end, grayish white and windblown, the soft down of a baby bird.

"It looks really nice," Grace said gently, gathering the last of the boxes.

Her mother glanced around, and Grace saw her thinking of how her things had looked before, *at home*. She probably saw Robert's imprint on the bed too.

"Thank you. For letting me come here. It means a lot." Jackie smiled, as weary as Grace had ever seen her—even more tired than after she'd worked a triple shift to try and pay for all of Hope's extra therapies.

"I'll put these in the basement." She lugged as many boxes as she could manage.

"In a dry spot," Jackie insisted.

"In a dry spot. And make some supper. Why don't you rest, take a nap?"

Her mother nodded. "It was a long trip. Staying in hotels wasn't as fun as it used to be."

"I know." Grace gave her a tender smile and eased out of the room. She would've shut the door, but she didn't have a hand free, and her mother didn't seem to mind it open.

As Grace headed downstairs she heard the creak of the old mattress and box springs—*maybe Mom would like a new memory foam bed?*—and a sigh of relief. *I won't let her bring out anything but the best in me.*

But even as she thought it, Grace registered a seedy stench. It reminded her of the waterlogged stems in a vase of flowers, going to rot. The smell followed her all the way to the basement, and she told herself it was the dampness in the walls, the mildew that wouldn't go away even with the french drains and the dehumidifier. Pittsburgh basements were wet, and she lived on the *low* side of Greenfield Avenue—something she'd insisted on, as the houses on the high side had too many front steps. (She remembered a client once describing Pittsburgh's neighborhoods as "Escher-like," with the houses perched all over the hillsides.) Yet a part of her understood that the mustiness didn't originate within the fetid walls beneath her house.

The smell was strongest in her mother's tidy, perfectly decorated room.

4

It was fortuitous that she found part-time work that coincided with her mother's arrival. The last thing they needed was to be on top of each other 24/7. Many of the chain salons were still closed, but some of the privately owned ones had reopened, with new precautions: limiting capacity; taking temperatures at the door; wearing masks. A lot of stylists didn't feel comfortable going back to work yet, standing in close proximity to clients with questionable safety practices. And a lot of people weren't ready to sit in a chair with a stylist breathing down their neck, even masked. Grace had meager hours, sometimes with little to do. But she took what she could get.

For her lunch break, she left the salon. She got take-out noodles and went down to the museum and sat on the wall near the fountain. The rectangular black pool spat monotonous shoots of water, relaxing, even if artistically dull (nothing anyone would pose in front of for an Instagram story). The trickles and splashes masked some of the bus noise on Forbes Avenue, a busy thoroughfare that primarily shuttled university students back and forth between Oakland and Squirrel Hill. Grace had worked in Squirrel Hill—where her house in Greenfield was a hop, skip, and a jump away—for all her working life, until now. Oakland wasn't that much farther away, but it was far enough that she couldn't walk, and her student clientele had a lot less money.

It was only mid-June, but she already questioned what she'd do when the weather wasn't warm enough to eat outside. She couldn't afford to keep getting takeout, and there wasn't enough room to eat a packed lunch at the salon. Her new place of employment had only three salon chairs; there wasn't even space for a reception desk, let alone room where staff could take a break. Clients who arrived early had to stand against the wall near the coatrack.

She missed Barbara's, her old salon, with its fourteen stations and a bank of sinks on the main floor, and a fully finished lower floor with tanning beds, washer and dryer, a cozy employee lounge, and two small rooms where the Orthodox Jewish women—who wouldn't show their hair in public—could have their hair done in private. Even more, she missed her motley crew of old coworkers. Some of them, like Grace, had worked at Barbara's for their entire career. In many ways Barbara's staff had been a dysfunctional family, comforting and vexing, sharing the ups and downs of their lives. Grace found herself missing even the Chief of Complaining and the Gossip Director more than she'd thought possible.

Oakland had its own vibe and South Craig Street had a lot of international culinary options, but as she forked her noodles, Grace knew she had to get back on the job hunt. Tuesdays, Thursdays, and Fridays weren't going to cut it, and with the lower base price and diminished tips, this could only be a stopgap measure. The government was talking about additional unemployment compensation for those left jobless by the pandemic, but she didn't know when that might start. And Grace preferred to work. Especially now that her mother was there, sitting at home all day, every day.

She mulled over what the commute would be like to Sewickley or Fox Chapel or Mount Lebanon, quick to picture the red brake lights of traffic. With the city's narrow roads, bridges, tunnels, and constant construction, there was always a bottleneck somewhere. But if she wanted to make real money, she needed to work in a neighborhood where people had expendable income. Not that all her Squirrel Hill clients had tipped well, but most had. A few of her regulars had booked appointments with her at the Oakland salon, but Grace wasn't sure if they'd keep coming back. The ambiance just wasn't the same. No one to bring them a cup of coffee or water with lemon slices while they waited for their hair to change color.

Her noodles tangled in her gut at the prospect of more changes ahead. It wasn't as drastic as what her mother had gone through, but the pandemic had created a sediment of stress that clung to everyone in different ways. "Back to normal" just wasn't gonna happen. And now that she'd gotten used to wearing a mask, Grace expected to do so forever, at least in crowded places. There were advantages to not catching—or spreading—every bug and cold that wafted through the air. If only everyone had done it sooner.

Grace had hoped against hope that one of her more ambitious coworkers would buy the business from Barbara or that *someone* would continue using the space as a salon. But for now it was just another empty storefront on Murray Avenue. She couldn't keep waiting for her old life to magically reappear, and though Jackie would be paying her share, that wasn't a substitution for personal income.

Ugh. The last thing Grace wanted was to depend on her mother. Before departing for Florida, Jackie had financed Grace's training—and it was much appreciated—but she had been paying all her own bills since she was eighteen. More work hours would mean not only less time together in the house but fewer opportunities to succumb to the temptation of checking on ShyShaina and the others. The homebody in Grace, who enjoyed her evenings lounging about in her own queen-dom, sighed at the reality of now having to share her domain. But she was, after all, a working-class queen.

After tucking her dangling mask around her other ear, Grace threw away her empty container and headed back up South Craig Street so she wouldn't be late for her two o'clock client. In spite of her preference for living alone, she required people the way a drug addict needed a fix—but she liked her socializing to happen within controllable situations, with easy exit strategies. Her best friend, Miguel, was the only real exception. When she was online as an alter ego, she could click off at will. And at work, there was a ticking clock to every interaction. She enjoyed people, yes, but more so when they fulfilled her in some essential way.

Many of her happiest days had been at Barbara's during a holiday or wedding rush, hour after hour, client after client. She loved being in demand, being needed. Women needed her to restore their beauty, their sense of self; people needed her as an audience, someone to talk to. It was a mutually satisfying arrangement, and her online relationships weren't so different. Grace wondered for the first time if cutting back on her virtual life would make her feel lonely.

She smirked behind her mask, imagining what LuckyJamison would advise: *It's good to get out of your comfort zone—that's how you find out who you really are.*

5

"How was your day?" Grace closed the door and hung her keys on the little hook. A giant bottle of hand sanitizer now lived on the entry table and she pumped a few squirts, rubbing it into her hands with the zeal of someone trying to start a fire with two sticks.

"Uneventful," Jackie replied, eyes on the TV.

Jackie had spent her first couple of days mostly resting in her room. Grace supposed it was a sign of improvement that she was downstairs. Though, as Grace took off her disposable mask, she noticed that the living room seemed different. At first she thought it was her mom's presence, nestled on the couch, legs stretched out—exactly where Grace spent her evenings. Jackie had a bowl of popcorn on her lap and was watching a game show. It took everything Grace had not to lash out. Her mother wasn't doing anything *wrong*; she was doing exactly what everyone did after a long day. Relaxing. Snacking. (Had Jackie *had* a long day?) But it was Grace's living room, Grace's popcorn, Grace's favorite fuzzy cushion tucked in her mother's armpit.

And something had been added to the strip of wall on the other side of the television.

Grace dropped her purse atop the entry table and kicked her shoes under it. She caught herself in the mirror mounted above the table and frowned. After lunch she'd gone back to work and voiced her interest in making some changes in her life (neglecting to mention the part about looking for a better salon). Freya, a friendly wisp of a thing, barely out of her teens, had quickly offered to do her hair. (Grace had used the same strategy herself on occasion, encouraging a new look to women who were bored of their lives.)

She hadn't been able to stand in front of the mirror at the salon and scrutinize what Freya had done. Grace had always considered herself a modestly classy person; she liked nice things but not *too* nice. She dressed well but not *too* well. In many ways she was average—average height, average weight, average looks. Average intelligence, average ambitions. Grace found safety in her averageness; the assumptions people would make about her would be benign. That's how she liked it. She was neither stuck up nor stupid. She could blend in almost anywhere, from a low-end cocktail party to a cookout. Never too frumpy and not too high maintenance. She was under the impression that she came off as an ordinary person who had her shit moderately together. Did this hairstyle still portray that?

Her former shoulder-length bob was now trimmed and angled so perfectly she might have thought Freya had used a protractor. Gone was her near-natural color with its ashy-blonde highlights. An alien head had been attached to her body, with ghostly hair as fair as a rodent's, the bottom inch of it the scary pink of sightless eyes.

There was no question Freya had done a good job, but it was a style meant for someone else. The girls in the salon had gushed, but Grace was already thinking she'd redo it herself in a week or two. She sighed, wishing she didn't have to step into her living room to confront the changes that had been made there too.

Directly opposite the front door were the stairs to the second level. To the right, the square dining room with its dark wood-like floor opened into a cramped kitchen; to the left was the rectangular living room, just wide enough to accommodate a sofa on one wall and a giant TV on the other. The archway at the far end made a loop of the first floor, passing the back door into the kitchen proper. The previous owner had blown out the living room's back wall to double the size of the window that looked over the backyard. Even at dusk, it provided enough natural light to illuminate the additions to Grace's decor.

She marched between the sofa and TV. "Did you hang these?"

It was a dumb question, but it was better than "Why the fuck did you consider it okay to put nails in my pristine wall without asking me?"

While Grace inspected the photographs—as if she'd never seen them and couldn't understand what they depicted—her mother turned away from the screen long enough to say, "You didn't have any pictures up."

Not true. The wall above Grace's sofa was adorned with a triptych of Miguel's colorful, abstract paintings; his talents extended beyond his ability to delight little old ladies with his curling iron and blow-dryer. But she knew what her mother meant. Grace wasn't one to hang family photographs, and her mother had taken it upon herself to rectify that.

"Why didn't you just put these in your room?" Grace asked. There, she'd let Jackie hang whatever she wanted. This felt like a trespass.

Her show over, Jackie changed the channel. "What's the problem? You can't possibly object, she's your sister."

Grace shut her eyes for a moment, exhausted. She wanted to snatch the salty, buttery snack from her mother's hands. She wanted her regular spot on the couch. She wanted Netflix or Hulu and not whatever crap Jackie was watching. "The problem isn't that it's my sister—it's *my wall.*"

Her mother sniffled, studying her. She picked popcorn hulls out of her teeth. "What did you do to your hair?"

Neither issue was worth an argument. Grace gave up. "Are you hungry? Do you want some supper?"

"No thanks, I ate."

Grace escaped to the kitchen, where, with Jackie out of sight, she felt a tiny bit less morose. Since she didn't need to cook for two, she grabbed a Stouffer's dinner from the freezer and shoved it in the microwave. She was still all sorts of crabby and didn't fully know why.

Everything. Nothing. And the photographs bothered her just as much as the nail holes. She loved her sister, but it was complicated. To keep life simpler, Grace endeavored not to think about Hope very often—which was easier to do without having her likeness hammered onto the wall.

As if to compete with, or balance, the three paintings, Jackie had hung three photos. They were in the other room, but Grace couldn't stop seeing them. She was in one of the pictures, an enlarged snapshot where she was partially behind her sister and slightly out of focus (*running away*). The other two were professional portraits of Hope, with her trademark open-mouthed grin. Hope's cerebral palsy had been severe, affecting nearly every part of her body. She used a motorized wheelchair to get around, and her tight jaw made it difficult for her to articulate words. But the spasms and poor muscle control didn't affect her intellect; Young Grace believed her sister was a genius. Hope was mainstreamed (Grace accompanied her to school on the short bus), with an aide to help during her school day. She got straight As; Grace was lucky to get Bs.

Everyone who saw Hope in photos remarked on how happy she looked. She appeared to be grinning almost all the time, though Grace knew the darker side of her sister's personality. The smile on Hope's face was an unavoidable contortion, not constant happiness. And when her glee was intentional, it had usually meant trouble.

6

"Do you mind if I switch over to Netflix?" Grace asked as she carried in her steaming dinner.

"No, go ahead." Jackie handed her the remote and moved her feet to make more room on the sofa.

Grace sat at the other end, a foreign place where the cushion was noticeably firmer. She brought up the next episode of *Schitt's Creek*, which she'd been rewatching, and ate with her eyes glued to the screen. The combination of TV and food tended to make her spacey, but Jackie's laughter interrupted her trance. Realizing her mom was enjoying the show, Grace took a second to catch her up on the characters. They ended up watching two episodes before Grace got up to take her dirty fork and empty dish to the kitchen.

"Need anything?"

"Refill my water?" Jackie held out her glass. "Thanks, hon."

Hon? Whatever. Grace felt better. Maybe it was the starchy goodness of the fettuccini Alfredo, one of her favorite comfort foods. Or that her mother had not, in fact, hogged the TV or made Grace feel out of place in her own living room. Quite the opposite, it had been nice—really, genuinely nice—to sit together, relaxed, laughing. Had they ever done that?

Grace was starting to see her mother through new eyes. It was easier to conclude now, after years of self-sufficiency, that much of her mom's snapping and impatience had been a result of exhaustion or stress. Jackie was supposed to have been a stay-at-home mom with twin girls—that's what her fiancé had promised. At thirty-three, she'd been working for most of her life and machinist Paul No-Last-Name wanted to be the Man of the House. Everyone had a fantasy, and his might have come to fruition if Grace and Hope hadn't arrived before their scheduled C-section.

In those days, cerebral palsy was still often attributed to a birth injury rather than brain maldevelopment, so Jackie had lugged around a heavy handbag of sin, as "birth injury" was somehow always the mother's fault. Many times Grace had heard her mom mutter—to relatives, to gawking strangers at the park—"Is it my fault my vagina got the one out too quickly and the other too slowly?" Daddy Dearest apparently thought so. Or maybe Paul No-Last-Name just couldn't handle the reality of being told his second daughter would never walk. Whatever his excuse, he reneged on his promises and left when Grace and Hope were a few months old.

Jackie went back to her job as a certified nursing assistant, working all kinds of crazy hours in a nursing home, while a neighbor babysat. Hope was fairly easy to manage when she was little and easy to pick up; as she got older, it got harder. The neighbor ladies never openly accused Hope of spitting up food or peeing on them on purpose (Grace knew her sister thought such antics were hilarious). But when they stopped being available, Jackie had to accept cheap babysitting help from a trio of questionably acceptable girls. Grace hadn't thought much about it then, but leaving Hope's safety in the hands of possibly stoned teenagers was probably stressful (although their bad attitudes were a better match for Hope's bullshit). And after caring for old people who had become as needy as babies, Jackie would come home where there was always more caretaking to be done. She never had Netflix and chill.

Grace remembered the eye rolls and clenched teeth of her mother's perpetual annoyance. And she remembered her own resentment, all the laundry and cleaning Grace had been expected to do, the endless hours she, herself a child, put into entertaining or helping her sister. (At best the rotating babysitters were on the phone; at worst they made sure Hope and Grace got home from school okay, and then hung out on someone's stoop and smoked with their friends.) Grace had never given a lot of thought to the quantity of Jackie's work, her waking hours consumed by changing diapers and feeding people. No wonder she'd sought a change of scenery—populated by moderately well-off gentle-men—the first chance she got.

For so many years Grace had misdiagnosed her mother's despair and taken it personally. But it seemed possible now—likely—that Jackie hadn't been tired of being a mother; she had simply been *tired*. And maybe it wasn't completely her mom's fault that she and Grace had never had a chance to fully bond. And maybe it wasn't too late. That, in Grace's mind, was a more important thing to rectify than an absence of family photos. If the pandemic had taught her nothing else, she knew that life—*a* life, or even normal existence—could disappear with little warning.

"Another episode?" Grace asked as she returned to the living room with her mom's topped-off water glass. It was time to check on her damsels, but Grace resisted. "Or I could trim your hair?"

"Does it look that bad?" Jackie touched it gingerly, like it was made of brittle glass.

Grace laughed. "No, but I could give it a little more shape. Something sophisticated."

The stylist in her couldn't help it; Grace started fingering her mom's hair, getting a feel for its texture, thickness, the way it grew out from the crown of her head.

"It won't look like yours, will it?"

Before Grace could get insulted, she saw the smile tugging on her mom's lips. "No, I promise."

"Not that yours doesn't look nice, but I'm too old for that."

"Me too. It was an experiment. Why don't you pull out one of the dining room chairs, and I'll go get my stuff?"

"Okay." Jackie beamed, looking tickled.

Grace jogged upstairs, her damsels forgotten. She quickly changed into a pair of comfy pants before retrieving her kit—scissors, comb, nylon cape—from the bathroom linen closet. But even this innocent act of "fetching" joggled loose another moment from the past.

Mother's Day. Grace must have been eight, and she made a picture with the sun. The recollection made her smile because she still marveled at the magical paper, given to her as a precious gift from her science teacher. She'd gathered small pebbles and laid them out on the pale paper in the shape of two hearts. It stayed on the sidewalk in a direct beam of sunshine for two minutes as Grace kept vigil. From the porch, Hope called out when the two minutes were up—and then it was time to take the paper inside and reveal its magic.

Soon after being put in a pan of water, the paper turned deep blue, with white dots where the pebbles had been. When it was dry, Grace stood beside Hope's wheelchair and they presented the card to their mother, grinning in unison. They'd chosen matching outfits that day, because Mommy liked that. *It makes us seem the same.*

"Happy Mother's Day! It's from me and Hope. We're giving you our hearts."

Mommy had hugged Hope first, quick to assume the project had been her idea. (And their mother wasn't wrong; Grace had wanted to make something with the magical paper to keep for herself.) Even though Grace had arranged the stones and followed the directions just like Mr. Harrison had told her, Hope got most of the credit—the thank-yous and kisses and so-beautifuls.

"I'll keep this in my special box!" Mommy looked happy in that moment.

After Hope died, Grace continued to make cards for her mother, for birthdays and holidays. But Mommy never admired them. She never put them in the plastic tub full of cherished mementos. Everything Hope did was special. Nothing Grace did was special enough.

The memory didn't upset her: Hope *was* more admirable, spunky by nature, ambitious, and always a Mommy's Girl. Grace had only been willing to make the Mother's Day gift out of her precious paper because she knew—coming from *both* of them—that it would be preserved in the damn plastic tub.

Things were different now. Grace was different (at least she hoped so), and it pleased her that she could pamper her mom a little. Restore her beauty, her sense of self. Listen, like a therapist, if that's what Jackie wanted.

Grace hurried downstairs, eager to do what she did best.

7

No one understood Hope except Grace and Mommy, and Grace understood her best. She knew what other people heard when her sister spoke—the grunts of a wild animal whose palate and fangs were too savage to form words. (Well, maybe other people *could* understand her, *if* they gave her enough time to enunciate each word.) Hope didn't need to say much for Grace to know what she meant. She considered it likely that they did, indeed, possess the kind of twin telepathy they'd read about in books. (Grace read aloud to Hope a lot, and they especially loved stories about twins.) It was also possible that she understood her sister so well because she'd learned Hope's language from birth; Grace was fully fluent in *two* languages—English and Hope.

To Grace, when Hope barked it wasn't so different from her own voice (though when Hope took *forever* to squeeze the words out, it could be a little frustrating). They both knew that other people looked at them and thought it a shame that Hope had been *damaged*. People gazed from one girl to the other, and their pathetic faces said, *If only* . . . Because Grace was the constant evidence of who Hope could've been.

"Geh . . . da . . . goo . . . an . . . pay-per."

"Okay!" Grace might've been older than Hope by fifteen minutes, but she obeyed everything her sister said. And she knew "get the glue and paper" really meant "let's play with our paper dolls now."

Hope had the largest bedroom (because it was on the first floor—no steps—and wasn't a bedroom at all but the dining room). Pretty fabric from a place Mommy called The Hippie Store hung over both entryways—one to the kitchen, one to the living room. The fabric, even months later, still smelled like the spicy incense that, in the store, had been strong enough to give Grace a headache.

The cloth panels made Hope's room feel more like a fort. They were meant to give her a little privacy, but she was rarely alone. Sometimes the special therapists came to the house, or else Mommy or Grace was bustling in and out. Grace often snuggled into Hope's bed and spent the night spooned behind her (unless Hope was contagious with a cold or pneumonia or a stomach bug, and then Mommy made Grace go upstairs to her own room). The cerebral palsy didn't make Hope more prone to illness than anyone else, but she was doubly unlucky and her immune system was messed up too.

Grace got the glue and the construction paper and all the other stuff she knew they'd need. Crayons, markers, scissors. And the little jar of adornments. They collected the adornments—small buttons, sequins, broken bits of jewelry—and kept them safe in an old baby-food jar. Most of the stuff they found—on the ground in a parking lot, in the hallways at school—but some of it they stole.

Hope would use her wheelchair to block Grace and hide what she was doing (even if someone looked at them askance, Hope had learned that no one at Rite Aid was gonna yell at a smiling girl in a wheelchair). They considered it not *really* stealing because they didn't take *entire* greeting cards, just the pretty hodgepodge bits. A lot of cards had fabulous decorations, like little bows and lace and faceted gems that looked like rubies and emeralds—and Grace learned to tear them off superquick.

Going to Rite Aid was like a trip to a treasure chest. Mommy always let them roam around the store on their own while she waited in line to get Hope's prescriptions. And Mommy didn't give a fart about the whats and wheres of their old baby-food jar (though she did sometimes call the girls magpies). Whenever they showed her their fabulously adorned paper dolls, she'd look up from cutting coupons just long enough to flash them a zippered smile.

———

Their paper dolls were twin girls named Mona (Hope's doll) and Rona (Grace's). They were nine inches high and had been cut from the back covers of two old spiral notebooks, which were stiffer than paper and white on one side. Sometimes Grace forgot that she alone was doing the drawing and cutting: Hope always instructed her on every detail for Mona's new clothes and advised Grace on how to embellish Rona's. Hope wanted to be a fashion designer someday, and Grace would be her assistant.

Mona and Rona were always being invited to fancy balls and needed the best clothes for each one. The dolls could never look exactly alike (though their outfits had to complement each other), and they couldn't wear the same dress twice (at least not in public). Since Mona and Rona had so many ridiculously fancy frocks, sometimes they wore the older ones as nightgowns or as play clothes—even for a rough game of dodgeball with the stuffed animals.

Under Hope's direction, Grace finished coloring a new halter-style gown in a shade of pear green that she never would've picked for Rona. Mona, with her red hair, could get away with weird greens, but Grace insisted on blues and purples for her black-haired doll. (That the dolls were so-called identical twins but didn't look alike was of no concern to the girls, who also were identical but . . . different.)

"Let me see," said Hope.

Grace folded the paper flaps of the pear-colored dress around Mona's flat body and held the doll up for Hope to inspect.

"Hmm. Good. Will look nice with a mink stole."

Unsure of exactly what a mink stole was, Grace dug through the jar of adornments, looking for emeralds and bling.

"No, you have to make one," Hope insisted.

"How?"

"Cut off a piece of your hair. Drape it around her neck, and clasp it with the biggest diamond."

Grace hesitated. Now she grasped her sister's vision of a fur wrap but wasn't sure she wanted to donate a piece of her own hair.

"Why not yours?" she asked. They had the same dirty-blonde hair, shoulder length and untidy.

"Yours is prettier."

Untrue but flattering. With a sigh, Grace separated a tail of hair from the back of her head and pulled it forward (at least no one would notice the missing piece if they only looked at her from the front). She was about to cut it when Hope issued another command.

"Longer. It has to go around her shoulders."

"We could find some yarn."

"Mink is the softest fur, no itchy yarn."

"Fine," she grumped. Grace inched the scissors closer to her scalp and cut off a hunk of her hair. She glued it to her sister's paper doll, securing it at the front with the best of their diamonds.

It was a good look, Grace had to admit. The soft-green dress, the blonde "fur," the priceless gem. She held it up for Hope's approval. Hope threw back her head (probably on purpose) and clapped (or tried to) and laughed with madcap pleasure. Her joy was enough to soften Grace's irritation. Hope was such a perfectionist, and to create something to her standards was its own sort of reward.

Grace assumed that Mona was done and ready. The ball was set to start in twenty minutes and Rona was still in her underwear, so she traced the doll on a clean sheet of paper, ready to start on a new gown.

"Need one more thing," said Hope.

"What?" Grace rolled her eyes, impatient. "I don't want Rona to be late to the ball."

"A purse. The softest calfskin bag."

"Okay, I'll make one after Rona's dress."

"Make it now, so the skin stops bleeding."

"What?" Grace, sitting on the floor cross-legged, surrounded by paper scraps and the accoutrement of two-dimensional fashion design, looked up at her sister. Perched in her power chair, Hope often seemed like a queen on a throne, larger than life. Had Grace uncharacteristically misunderstood her?

"Make it *now* so the skin stops bleeding!"

"What skin?" Grace cringed, grossed out and confused.

"Your earlobe."

Grace started to feel queasy, like she sometimes did when they were in the car, going up and down too many hills.

"You're crazy," she said. Maybe Hope was joking around—she couldn't modulate her voice well enough to make it clear when she was being sarcastic. Grace fished a piece of lace out of the jar and folded it over. "I can use this, make a pretty—"

"No! Take the scissors. Cut off an earlobe. It will be soft, the perfect clutch. Do it now."

Grace gaped at her sister. How was this happening? How could her sister demand such a thing? It didn't make sense. Sure, Hope could be a little naughty sometimes, but she was never cruel to Grace.

"No." Grace jumped to her feet, ready to flee.

"Mona needs the perfect purse!"

"No! And I'm not going to play with you anymore if—"

"Grace." A monster swept through the fabric, setting loose a whisper of tangy incense. Grace looked at Mommy, almost glad she'd come to the rescue. "Why are you arguing with your sister?"

"She told me to cut—"

"Just do what she says." Mommy never seemed to understand just how bossy Hope was; then again, Grace was the person Hope liked to boss around the most.

"What?" Something throbbed in Grace's head. Mommy looked bigger than usual, like a balloon that had been inflated just a bit beyond its regular shape. Hope was growing too—or maybe Grace was shrinking? She looked from her mom to her sister, unsure what to do and on the verge of tears. Until a minute ago, she'd had a sense of déjà vu—Grace had made these same dresses with her sister once, at another time. But this part was new. New and *wrong*.

"Why are you dillydallying?" Mommy roared. "Every minute is precious. Give your sister what she wants!"

"Mona needs a calfskin bag."

"I'm not a calf," Grace pleaded.

"No, you're a selfish brat." Mommy snatched the scissors from the floor and held them out for Grace to take. "A teeny-tiny purse, it's the least you can do."

———

That's when Grace had awakened. The dream had been bothering her all day, making her slightly nauseated every time she thought about it.

It was Saturday, and Grace had stayed in her room, glued to her phone and laptop. For several hours she juggled five messaged conversations using five different aliases. She maintained a color-coded notebook for each of her personas—and the women they were interacting with—and having them in front of her was the only way she could chat with multiple damsels at once. She needed to stay on top of the important particulars: the exploits of Alyssa215's baby daddy; ShyShaina's ever-worsening home situation; the names of TaurusGirl's three children; HoneyEyed's latest weird symptoms, which she feared were early-onset Alzheimer's (HoneyEyed was a hypochondriac who'd driven all her friends away). Last but not least, IsabelZ, a food addict nearly homebound by obesity, never failed to report on the day's scheduled food deliveries, believing that with accountability, she was consuming less. For many of the damsels, their prince was the only person they trusted with the dark secrets of their lives.

For marathons like this, Grace made updates as she went along, moving from notebook to notebook, also jotting down whatever LuckyJamison, Malcolm, SunSoakedSergei, Preston, and River shared in return. Her gentlemen didn't need to be all that different from each other, but Grace prided herself on her organizational ability to keep her relationships separate and, to the degree applicable, personal. In among the broad strokes of her lies were finely rendered details of truth, lessons and experiences from her own life.

Her phone chimed, only this time it wasn't a notification from an app. It was a text from Miguel, asking if he could bring anything. They'd planned a get-together a week earlier, eager to resume in-home social visits and anticipating Grace's need for emotional support after the Mother Home Invasion. Grace hadn't forgotten, exactly, but the day had gotten away from her nonetheless.

She texted back:

Wine?

Miguel couldn't type as quickly as her fleet-fingered damsels, but his reply finally arrived:

You got it. See u later. 😊

One by one, Grace signed out of her conversations. She needed to take a shower. *Cut off an earlobe.* She shuddered. Usually her dreams dematerialized within fifteen minutes of waking up, but last night's wouldn't go away. *Give your sister what she wants!* It clung to her like a sticky film of sweat on a stifling, humid day. Maybe she should've hopped in the shower right after she got up; maybe that would've made it dissolve.

Almost worse than the horror of the dream was how familiar the rest of it felt. She and Hope had spent hours—years—creating and playing with their paper dolls, and maybe they hadn't said the exact words that they'd spoken in the dream but close enough. *Mona needs a calfskin bag.*

The familiarity of it scared her, the tolling dread that it had all happened, and it was Grace's memory that was defective. But she touched her left earlobe, and then the right. They were both there, but she did faintly recall donating a lock of hair to the cause of Mona's accessories.

Without the distraction of the internet, the slimy sensation was getting worse by the second. She hurried to the bathroom, desperate to rub it off.

8

Grace put on black leggings and a loose blush-colored T-shirt that per-fectly fell off one shoulder. Her sports bra—for style not sport—felt tighter than it once had, and she tugged it down to her ribs. She esti-mated she'd gained about ten pandemic pounds, due to insufficient activity and too much snacking. Oh well, she'd lose the weight when she was working full time again. She slipped into her flip-flops and returned to the bathroom to straighten her hair. The one flaw in Freya's handiwork was the pink tips looked like a teenager's blunder if she let her hair air-dry in its usual disheveled waves.

She left the bathroom door open as she primped, and it occurred to her that she hadn't crossed paths with her mother all day. When Grace first retreated to her room late morning (with a hefty traveler's mug of coffee), Jackie's door had been closed. Later, she'd occasionally heard Jackie moving around, up and down the stairs. Grace hadn't been sure, before Jackie's arrival, if the stairs would be too much for her. As a full-time working mom, Jackie used to function at a pace one might have described as *impatient*, her movements swift and robotic, her focus a step ahead to the next item on her to-do list. Except for her slower, more cautious footing and a slouch in her shoulders, Jackie seemed quite physically capable, which was a relief.

No ass wiping for the foreseeable future.

Her mom had a slight tremor in one hand, and her eyes were growing milky, but several nights of good sleep had put the color back in her cheeks. After Jackie arranged her bedroom just the way she wanted it, she hadn't behaved in a helpless or needy way. It dawned on Grace that her mother had possibly never lived alone, not for any appreciable time (unlike Grace), and that may have been a worry much greater than her health.

———

Grace's flip-flops slapped against the floor as she strode through the dining room. She noted the dust bunnies clustered under the table and the ghostly remains of shoe prints and added *a quick mopping* to her mental to-do list. The dining room hadn't been used yet—she ate in front of the TV or at her desk—but proper sit-down meals with Miguel were part of what she'd envisioned when becoming a homeowner. That might have led to them planning dinner parties or game nights and who knew what else. Her apartment life had never allowed enough space for entertaining, but most people were congregating more cautiously now—if they were congregating at all. And when she'd imagined chatting half the night away with Miguel or laughing around her table with friends, her mother hadn't been part of that picture.

"Hey," Grace said, taking a quick scan of the kitchen. It was clean enough, but somewhat to her surprise her mother was at the stove, stirring something soupy.

"Hey hon, did you get a lot of work done?"

Jackie had no idea about Grace's hobby, but Grace had explained that sometimes she needed to be alone in her room To Work. That was set up as a preemptive boundary so they could establish some rules for private time. The reality of that, now so casually uttered, made Grace fear that her mother might've thought she'd been holed up in her room masturbating all day. No, wait . . . Jackie wouldn't think about masturbating. Oh God, Grace was thinking about her mother thinking about masturbating.

"Miguel's coming for dinner," Grace said, quickly changing the topic.

"I know, that's why I'm making a puttanesca sauce," Jackie chirped. "Well, it's almost a puttanesca sauce—you didn't have any anchovies. But that's okay—it's less scandalous this way."

Jackie laughed at her own incomprehensible joke. Grace's hand froze on the unopened cabinet door and she gazed, bewildered, at the woman at the stove. The pixie cut Grace had given her looked as good as she'd promised: Jackie appeared both more distinguished and more youthful. There was a pep in her step as she gave her sauce a stir and sidestepped to the refrigerator to hunt for more ingredients. Grace had planned to heat up a frozen pizza, garnished with kalamata olives and mushrooms, and accompanied by a quick salad of plum tomatoes. Cleverly, her mother had turned it all into a homemade pasta sauce.

As familiar as the dream had felt, this seemed utterly foreign. This was a mother Grace didn't know. Mommy had never cooked, except for the occasional tuna casserole or Hamburger Helper. By the time Grace was eight, she'd practically managed the household alone. Young Grace had mastered the casseroles and many other favorites, like hot dogs with baked beans, and french toast, and various things she put on english muffins (usually smothered with cheese) and baked in the toaster oven. This person, determined to prepare a better supper than Grace would've made, seemed nothing like the desperate woman who'd practically wept on the phone a month ago. On the surface these were all good things, but Grace couldn't keep up with the strange feelings, the topsy-turvy, shaken-not-stirred sensations that came with her new daily encounters with her mother.

Water. Grace had subsisted most of the day on caffeine and needed to purge some of the jitters from her system. That's what had launched her migration to the kitchen, a glass of water. Still mesmerized by Jackie, Grace reached for a glass. Her hand struck . . . a can of peaches.

Had she opened the wrong cabinet door? No.

She scrutinized the contents in front of her. Her tumblers and wineglasses and mugs and reusable water bottles weren't there. Nor were there any bowls—for cereal or ramen or anything else. Instead there were tidy stacks—alphabetized?—of canned goods on the lower shelf and boxes of pasta and rice mixes and crackers on the upper shelf.

As Jackie went about chopping and humming and pretending like all was right with the world, Grace tried the next cabinet over, which used to house her plates and Pyrex and storage containers. There she found all her cereal, neatly lined up, and above that, her chips and popcorn and snack bars.

Her throat suddenly parched, her body on the verge of dehydration, Grace felt her temperature rising. Where the first cabinet had triggered a momentary disorientation, an apprehension that the kitchen was as it had always been and her memory was (again) on the fritz, by the time she got to the cereal—arranged by *size* rather than favorites—she knew with certainty what had happened.

"What the actual fuck," Grace mumbled. Louder, to her mother, she said, "Did you rearrange my cabinets?"

She hoped the tone said, "How dare you rearrange my cabinets! You've done a bad, bad thing."

"Yes, indeed, I rearranged your cabinets." Her mother sounded happy about it, as if she'd done a good, good thing.

"Why? Where are my glasses?"

Jackie left the stove long enough to pop open a cupboard and reveal their new location. It came with a game show gesture, *Ta-da!* Grace snatched a glass, filled it with water from the pitcher in the fridge. Her movements, brusque and annoyed, should have been easy to interpret. Yet her mother continued beaming with a sense of accomplishment.

"It made more sense to have all of the dishware on *that* side of the kitchen"—Jackie pointed toward the sink—"and all of the food stuff on *this* side of the kitchen, closer to the stove and refrigerator."

If it had been someone else's kitchen, Grace might have agreed that it was a sensible arrangement. The puttanesca sauce bubbled like boiling blood. Jackie turned it down and put a lid on the pan. Grace couldn't figure out what to do. Her instinct was to scream, but she'd worked on smothering her temper over the years, mindful of how scary her mother had once been. It hadn't bothered Hope—maybe the yelling had never been directed at her—but Grace had experienced her mother's raised voice as a weapon, sharp and painful, lacerating her spongy insides. In an effort to not be similarly scary, she'd practiced denying her voice the volume of anger.

And what of Jackie's complete obliviousness to the entire situation?

"Mom."

"Yes, hon?" She got three plates out of the cabinet.

Grace rolled her eyes. Who was the *hon* for? Was that what she'd called Robert or maybe the helpful pothead?

"Mom!" Louder but not too angry. (Could she call her Jackie to her face now given their years apart and advancing ages?) Her mother turned to her, innocent eyed. Fake innocence? This whole thing was a lie, a charade. Jackie knew exactly what the problem was here, yet she smiled through the salt in the wound of forcing Grace to spell it out.

"If we're going to live together," Grace said, summoning her last reserve of patience, "cohabitate peacefully, we have to respect each other's boundaries. Remember? We talked about that."

Jackie blinked, uncomprehending. Was this part of the torture? Acting like she'd lost the capacity to function in any normally accepted way?

"I'm saying you can't just change my home without asking me."

"Oh. Oh." It was like watching a festive beach toy deflate. In the dream her mother had been oversize, and now Grace watched her shrivel. "I thought I was helping. I'm sorry."

And just like that, Grace's bitterness melted into a sloshy sort of guilt. She pressed her thumb into her temple; she rarely got headaches, but she felt one coming on. Maybe her blood pressure was the problem, not her temperature.

"Okay, we're just . . . still getting used to new ways of . . . Thank you for making supper—I'm sure Miguel will really appreciate it. I'll clean up the dining room a bit and set the table."

"Okay, hon."

Jackie turned back to her cooking. Grace descended to the basement landing, where she kept an assortment of bulky cleaning products, and slunk off to the dining room to clean up her mess.

9

Grace started to feel like her old self—her prepandemic self—the instant Miguel crossed the threshold. He smelled as expensive as always, a mixture of hair products and aftershave, and wore ass-hugging jeans and a black T-shirt—his work "uniform." Today, instead of a few stray pieces of human hair, some of Coco's orange fur clung to his shirt. It made her smile; he loved that damn cat so much, even when he complained about constantly wearing or inhaling her long orange fur. She was glad some things never changed.

"Look at you, lovey!" He went in for a hug, squeezing with his elbows, a bottle of wine in one hand and a bouquet of flowers in the other. "Oops, I'm sorry, two seconds in and I've broken the social distancing rule."

"It's fine, oh my God I'm so glad to see you—in person!"

They gushed and giggled as Grace held the flowers to her chest with schoolgirl delight. "Come in come in come in."

Just as he'd done in her various apartments, he left his shoes under the little table by the door. "I've got a mask in my pocket, if you're worried about where I've been all day."

"No worries, I have the windows open, good ventilation."

"Look at this place," he said, poking his head into the living room. "So homey. Can't believe I haven't been here since you were house hunting!"

"Social isolation is the worst," said Grace. In a parallel universe, she and Miguel would have gone to Target and IKEA together to shop for new decor. Instead, she'd only been able to shop online and show off her design additions via FaceTime.

With his back to the television, Miguel admired the paintings hanging above the sofa. "Very nice taste in art, my compliments to the artist."

"I have more rooms now, which means more wall space. Hint, hint." She opened her arms reverently toward the wondrous walls.

"Oh sure, everyone appreciates the art, until they have to pay for it."

"I would happily pay you!" Grace gave him a playful jab.

"I'm just kidding—of course I'd love to bestow a masterpiece to the cause of Grace's first house."

"Thank you, lovey."

"You're welcome, lovey."

They exchanged air-kisses.

"Shall we open this?" Miguel held up the wine.

"Yes we shall, assuming I can find the corkscrew."

"How could you misplace such a thing?" He followed her into the dining room.

"Oh I didn't, but there's been a little rearranging—"

Jackie moved into the entryway, grinning like a fool, blocking Grace's path to the kitchen.

"You must be Miss Jacquelyn!" Miguel took her hand and bent to kiss it but kept his lips inches from her skin. "Welcome back to the 'burgh."

"Thank you, oh my." The wattage of her delight lit up the room. "Supper's almost ready—it's been a minute since I had a chance to cook for anyone."

"She cooks too." Miguel gave Grace a look she interpreted as *You really are so lucky.* Was he being sarcastic? Why couldn't she tell? Last night's dream resurfaced, the itchy memory of her sister's demands. "Ladies, I have to say, both of you, your hair is looking fabulous."

Grace touched her pink ends. "It isn't too much?"

"It's way too much, but you never do Extra—this is a nice change. And I assume you did Miss Jacquelyn's?"

"I love that you call me Jacquelyn. And what lovely flowers." Her greedy eyes locked on Grace's bouquet. "A real gentleman—I didn't think there were any left."

Grace glanced at Miguel and suspected they were wondering the same thing: Did her mother think this flamboyantly gay friend was her *date*?

"Let's put these in some water." Her mother lifted the flowers from Grace's hands and turned back to the kitchen.

"And find the corkscrew. Stat." She still had a lot of apprehension about introducing Jackie to her friends. Grace had shared with Miguel only snippets of her childhood, and this version of her mother, as nice as she could seem, was a bit too alien, a shade too unpredictable.

———

"Mm. This is the finest virgin puttanesca I've ever had." Miguel ate with gusto.

Jackie laughed and blushed. Maybe Grace had read it wrong— was her mom crushing on Miguel? The flowers were now beautifully displayed in a vase beside her, and sometimes Jackie reached out and touched one of the soft, delicate petals.

"If things don't work out here with Grace, you can come stay with me."

"Careful what you wish for," Grace mumbled before swallowing more wine. She appreciated Miguel's jolly mood and his efforts to be so sweet with her mom, but it was starting to seem a little over the top.

"I would like to do more of the cooking, but I don't think Grace wants me to."

Grace stopped chewing (the sauce *was* good) and looked at her mom. "This is the first thing you've made. You never mentioned doing the cooking."

"I'd be happy to do the cooking—it's something I really learned to enjoy. Glen taught me so much"—she turned to Miguel—"Glen was my first husband. First *legal* husband. I lived with Paul, Grace's father, for years and he always said we were gonna get married, but then he just *poof*, disappeared."

Miguel had given Jackie only half a glass of wine, per her request, but after his brief toast to new-houses-and-good-friends-and-moms, she'd swallowed it in one gulp. Her words were starting to slur.

"And after Glen died—prostate cancer, he just refused to go to the doctor, didn't want someone sticking a finger up his butt—"

Grace met Miguel's eyes, and they both snickered. They would never, ever admit to Jackie just how many discussions they'd had about things going in—and out—of butts.

"Well, it's not funny really." Jackie sounded wounded.

"Inside joke." Grace shook her head, clearing images and inappropriate humor from her mind.

"I loved Glen, regardless of what *you* thought of him, and he was marvelous in the kitchen. Anyway, I've been cooking ever since, and I think I could make you much healthier meals than those frozen dinners stacked in the freezer."

Miguel wagged his fork at Grace. "Processed food is very high in sodium. Not healthy."

She gave him a smirk. He knew full well that she used to eat better, that she used to get almost daily meals from the assorted Mediterranean restaurants within a stone's throw of the salon. But then she got serious about saving for a down payment on a house. And then the world gradually fell apart. Hadn't everyone gotten lazier while they were stuck at home? Miguel didn't comment on her weight—maybe it didn't look any different in real life than it did in a video chat—but Grace wondered if she was fooling herself with all her elastic-waisted comfy pants; she might have gained quite a bit more than ten pounds.

"Mom, I would be very happy for you to do the cooking if it's something you enjoy. You hadn't said anything, so I didn't know."

"I know you're afraid I'm just going to get in your way, but all I want to do is be helpful. And I know . . . I wasn't always there for you. When you were little. I didn't mother you. And maybe you don't want my mothering now, but . . . I can try, Grace."

Grace blinked, unsure if this was real—unsure if her mother was telling the truth. She'd always wanted her mother to admit such faults to her, but Grace didn't know Jackie well enough anymore to know if this was a performance. The right words, well placed—with company as a witness? At a loss for a better response, Grace simply nodded. Smiled. Slid her glass over to Miguel for a refill of merlot.

10

"And then there was that school assembly . . ." Jackie slapped her knee and laughed. She was playing it up—Grace was sure of it; she couldn't possibly be *that* tipsy. "And the kids were all in a row, taking turns stepping up to the microphone to recite a few facts about vegetables. Grace had cabbage. *Cabbage.*" She cackled so hard there were tears in her eyes, but laughter was contagious, and Miguel had been infected. "The second she got to the microphone. *Thththththth.*" Her tongue made a crude noise. "It was like she farted right into it and the fart came through the speakers! Her line woulda-coulda-shoulda been 'That's what happens when you eat too much cabbage.'"

"Hilarious." Grace couldn't have been more hollow but no one cared. They might not even have heard her over the uproarious effects of the punch line. Wine always amplified Miguel's ability to laugh, even when it threatened to put Grace to sleep.

"Poor Grace!" he said.

After supper they'd regrouped in the living room. Jackie and Grace were on opposite ends of the sofa, while Miguel had opted for her IKEA chair—*Koarp*—from where he could appreciate his paintings and crane his neck toward the photographs of Hope. Grace had always been reticent about her sister; Hope's death polluted all her childhood memories. Even once-good times came with an asterisk* (**but then she died*). Miguel knew only sketchy basics.

Given how the evening was progressing, Grace was starting to think he was taking advantage of the situation. He hadn't even asked what medications "Miss Jacquelyn" was on when she requested a teensy refill and he splashed more wine into her glass. It was a fraction of what he and Grace had consumed—she had a cheap shiraz on hand that they dived into after finishing Miguel's much better merlot—but his conversational efforts were revealing a mischievous undertone; she got the feeling he was plying her mom with alcohol.

His questions played into Jackie's worst social tendency to spin a funny tale—often at someone else's expense—to make herself look witty. Miguel made it almost too easy, focusing on Grace's awkward elementary school years; he asked what sorts of hobbies she'd had, if she'd sung in the choir or played any sports. The less drunk part of her thought he was probably hoping to hear Jackie boast about Grace's early talents, and maybe he was ready with supportive retorts, "She always loved a good karaoke night!" or "So that's how she learned to crush her opponents!" (Miguel believed she was too competitive when it came to board games.) He might also have been digging for details about Hope.

"Can we do something else now?" Grace asked, lifeless. The school assembly memory was all the more bitter for being one of the few times her mother had been in attendance. Grace had been so excited, so nervous.

Miguel blew her a kiss and she read in his expression *This will be over soon*, which made her feel a smidge better. Maybe this was good, give Miguel a hearty dose of Brassy Mommy—which was a better match to Grace's descriptions than the Jolly Chef and Carefree Hostess he'd witnessed for much of the evening. Maybe Jackie really hadn't changed as much as it sometimes seemed. Her stresses were different now and her culinary skills improved, but perhaps underneath she was still the poisonous viper from Grace's youth, waiting to lash out.

For a moment there were just the sounds from outside—a car with the radio too loud, the jarring detonation of a pre-Fourth of July firecracker. Grace hoped, in the conversational lull, that the evening was winding down. But then Jackie caught the direction of Miguel's gaze. "You've never seen Hope?"

"No."

"Gray isn't big on family photos. Hope was a dear, a little sweetheart. Difficult, but that wasn't her fault." Just as Grace thought her mother was about to slip into a more somber mood, Jackie rebounded. "Hope was smart as a whip. When they were about six, she convinced Grace that Grace was pregnant and gonna have a baby. They didn't even know the birds and the bees—at least Grace didn't!—but Hope said something to her and Grace came to me crying, said she wasn't ready for a baby. I about panicked, thinking someone had messed with her, but no, it was just her sister, playing a little trick."

Was this a funny story? No, not really. Miguel didn't look as amused as before, but he was alert and keen to pick up more clues about Hope. Jackie never knew exactly what Hope had said to convince Grace she was pregnant, but Grace remembered.

"Did you pee this morning, then poop?" Hope had asked.

"Yes."

"Did Jacob tag you when you were playing tag?"

"Yes."

"Was he sweaty?"

"I guess so."

"Did you pick your nose today?"

Grace gave her an eye roll.

"Did you put your finger in your nose? Tell the truth."

"Maybe."

"Are your knees dirty?"

Grace looked. "Yes."

"Do you feel weird in your tummy?"

"Yes." And she'd had no idea why at the time, ignorant then of the word *heartburn* but eager to gobble up everything Mommy had brought home from Taco Bell.

"Ha ha—you're gonna have a baby!"

She'd scoffed at Hope and challenged her proclamation. But Hope had sworn that Grace showed *all the signs* and had done *all the things* and that's why a baby was growing inside her.

"What did your sister tell you?" Miguel asked, probably watching the memory move in shadows behind Grace's eyes.

With her crossed leg flapping, Grace turned to her mom. "I didn't know about *indigestion* then either, in spite of how much I loved Taco Bell."

Jackie and Miguel both laughed, satisfied with her response.

"I think Hope scared you away from ever having a baby."

The room fell suddenly quiet. Grace knew that Miguel knew that her mom wasn't referring to Hope's silly trick but the lifelong aware-ness of the possibility of having a child with special needs. A child who required a lot of effort, and still might not make it through adolescence.

"That's not true." Grace spoke softly and with an earnestness she rarely showed her mother. "I think about it a lot, actually. It's some-thing I really want, but . . ." Miguel nodded. He knew; they'd talked about it before. "The right situation, the right relationship . . . it never happened. And I'm running out of time."

"Lovey, you're only thirty-six," said Miguel.

"Yup, ticktock."

"It's not like it used to be," Jackie said. "People take longer now, to decide what they want." She sounded uncharacteristically supportive, which Grace appreciated, but reality wasn't going to alter itself for peo-ple who needed a little more time.

"Yes, that's true. But unless I freeze my eggs—or adopt. I'm not opposed to that, but I don't think I want to be a single mom. I want, I need, a partner." She shrugged, looking at Miguel. They'd discussed all aspects of this. It had taken her a long time to admit to him, or understand for herself, that she wasn't attracted to *anybody*—literally, had no concept of lust at first sight. That made dating extremely hard; most of the men she'd dated were ready for sex long before Grace had determined if she felt close to them in any meaningful way.

"Alone is a hard way to do it," her mom agreed.

"I know there's someone out there for you. You just might have to *redefine* what you're looking for." He exaggerated *redefine* but didn't spell it out in front of Jackie. Miguel had helped Grace understand she was probably "ace." *Asexual* was a term she didn't especially like, but he encouraged her to be open about it. "And I know you're resistant, but if you're clear about *who you are* and what you're looking for, a dating app really might work. It's an easy way to let people know important things."

Grace snorted. "No. I don't think so."

"There are some *real* people out there, nice people, contrary to what you say."

"I don't think so." She knew so; this was her area of expertise. Everyone online was fake in some way.

"What about you?" Jackie said to Miguel.

He did that cute thing with his mouth that he often did when he got contemplative or dreamy. It wasn't quite a smile, but the tension in his pressed lips revealed a dimple in one cheek. "I might have kids someday, I don't know—I'm a couple years younger than Grace, so I have a little more time." He flashed a wink at Grace. "But then again, it's a weird world. Tiny sentient people might deserve better than whatever I could offer them."

"You'd be a great dad, Miguel." And Grace fully believed that, but she knew he was thinking about larger obstacles, more apocalyptic issues. "Oh my God, this conversation is getting way too—"

"Maybe you could have a baby together!" Jackie wore a grin that proclaimed *That's perfect, problem solved!* Miguel and Grace looked at each other and burst into the blushing laughter of middle schoolers who finally grasped how all their parts worked. "I don't mean . . . Oh good grief, come on, I'm not clueless. And I know there are alternate ways of . . . Whaddo they call it? Artificial insemination?"

"Mom!" But it was mock outrage; Grace was actually glad to have a reason to laugh and release some of her tension.

"People do that now—gay people and friends and people who want to build their own families."

"That is remarkably forward thinking of you." Grace was impressed with her mother, but afraid now to make eye contact with Miguel. Was there any chance he was mulling over the possibility too? Now that Jackie had broken the ice?

"I know you don't give much thought to it," said Jackie. "But I had two kids. And Glen had two kids. And Robert had three kids. I worked with the elderly for almost thirty years, and most of them had kids. I actually know a lot about different kinds of parents and different kinds of . . ." She shrugged. "You know what we all know? It's hardest to be a parent in the moment, when things are happening. But when you look back . . . We all know what we would've done differently."

There it was again. The olive branch. And Grace believed her this time.

"I'm just saying . . . maybe the perfect thing doesn't come along. But maybe you look at who you have, and maybe you find a way to make that enough." Jackie smiled, but there was something sad about it. She started rocking forward, ready to push herself out of the sofa's pillowy nest. Grace and Miguel jumped up, grabbing her hands to help her stand. "Thanks hon. I'll give you kids some private time. Miguel, it was an absolute pleasure, and I'm so glad Grace has you for a friend."

Miguel gave her a cordial hug. "Thank you, Miss Jacquelyn. It was so lovely to meet you, and I'll see you again soon."

Grace felt her mom's lips on her cheek as Jackie leaned in to kiss her. "Good night, hon."

Unsure how to reciprocate, she simply said, "'Night, Mom. Thanks for dinner."

Miguel and Grace resumed sitting but remained alert, listening to every footstep as Jackie made her careful way up the stairs. Finally a door closed—the bathroom door, Grace was pretty sure. Alone at last, she grinned at her best friend. He lifted an eyebrow, and his face expressed a collage of thoughts. Grace probably had just as many, but it was a long, strange moment before either of them spoke again.

11

"Well, that was a little . . . uncomfortable." As if her empty goblet were to blame for the evening's lesser moments, Grace angrily pushed it toward the far side of her midcentury modern coffee table. Her eyelids felt too heavy, and she regretted having opened the second bottle of wine.

"Worse than you feared? Better?" Miguel kept his gaze on her as she really considered how his introduction to Jackie had gone.

"Not bad exactly. Except for the humiliating stories. But . . . I get it, I see the good parts, I really do, but she's all over the place. And it's a little, it's a little . . ." She sighed and flopped back on the sofa. "She confuses me."

"I can see that. But I think she's trying—I think she means well."

"Maybe. Sometimes."

"I know I'm not really one to talk, but I can see it better with your mom." He paused and waited until Grace met his eyes. "She might not be the same person you grew up with."

Grace nodded. "That's confusing too. Because then I don't know who she is."

"Give her a chance. It's only been a week."

A door opened upstairs. And another door creaked as it was closed, though it didn't audibly click into place. Grace imagined her mother with her ear to the crack, eavesdropping. The opening and closing doors were enough to set the air in motion, and Grace caught a whiff of the fetid smell, the flowery rot that emanated from her mother's things.

Grace locked eyes with Miguel, blinking again and again as a grin tried to vandalize her face.

"What?" he asked with a laugh.

"Would you ever consider it? What she suggested?"

"Having kids together?"

She nodded.

"I don't know. Would you?"

Grace gave a lazy shrug. "I mean, if you . . . I'm not sure if I'm at that place yet, of really figuring out how—or if I should, really—have a baby." It was a noncommittal answer. And she certainly wasn't going to pursue such a thing while her mother occupied her second bedroom (a nursery?). But raising a child with Miguel . . . it wasn't the worst idea. "You're by far the longest relationship I've ever had with a man. And a great friend."

He gave her a flirty smile. "Queer Platonic Partnership? Gay man and an ace woman."

"If I'm going to be in a QPP, I don't need a man for that."

Miguel burst out laughing. "There you go! Now you're getting in the spirit of the thing!"

She gave him a smirk. He blew her a kiss. Done with the baby talk, his attention flitted back to the photographs of Hope. Openly interested now, he angled his body so he could see them better, leaning forward with his elbows on his knees. Grace imagined how he saw her sister.

The smile like a scream. The jumble of half-grown teeth. The spittle at the corners of her mouth. In the two portraits, the photographers had her sitting on something, a love seat or bench, supported with well-placed cushions. In the candid shot, her motorized wheelchair was fully visible, as were her thin, unreliable legs.

"Why were you running away?" he asked.

Caught off guard, Grace zeroed in on the picture, on herself, a slight blur behind her sister's wheelchair. No one had ever asked her that, though it seemed obvious that she was, indeed, running away. Jackie hadn't taken many pictures of them—and this one, Grace remembered, was taken by the tall boyfriend who came in and out of their lives for a year or two.

"Do you think Hope looks happy?" she asked, evading Miguel's question but genuinely interested in his assessment. "That's why Mom always liked this one, why she had it framed. She thinks Hope looks full of . . . glee."

Miguel stood and approached the photograph to get a better look. "I guess. I don't really know anything about her. You don't think she looks happy?"

"She *was* happy, I don't doubt that. But I see something else too." She glanced upstairs, worried again about the eavesdropper. When she turned back to Miguel she whispered, "Things were weird sometimes. With Hope."

In two eager strides, Miguel joined her on the sofa, pressing in close to receive her secrets. "Weird how?"

Grace recalled the dream, Hope's cruelty and her own insistence that her sister had never been cruel *to her*. But Hope, like many children, had gory fascinations. Unlike many children, Hope had taken it beyond the theoretical.

"In that picture, Mom had just announced that she'd gotten Hope a new hamster. And while what's-his-name, the boyfriend, stood by with the camera, Mom pulled the new hamster from behind her back. That's what Hope was looking at, why she looks so surprised and happy. She was really sad when Goober died."

"Goober was the hamster, I presume, not the boyfriend?"

She glared at him until he accepted that the question wasn't worthy of an answer.

He shrugged, glancing at the photo. "That sounds normal enough. Being sad over a pet."

A faint shudder made her shoulder blades twitch. Talking about her sister made Grace feel like she had earlier in the day, unsure how to handle the residue of something that seemed both too real and not real enough. Nope, she didn't like to think about Hope. But she'd come this far—

"She ran Goober over with her wheelchair."

Miguel grimaced and recoiled a little. "Oh gross. That sucks. She must've been so traumati—"

Before he could finish the word, Grace shook her head. "That's what my mom said too. Probably why she got a replacement hamster. But Hope was good with her chair. She only ran into things—or people—on purpose, for revenge at being teased or something."

"You think she did it on purpose?"

"Probably, yes."

"Did you see it happen?"

Grace nodded. "She told Mom her finger had slipped, but I never believed her."

"Why would she do that?" The grimace lingered as Miguel stole another look at the photograph, perhaps reevaluating his impression of Hope.

"I think she just wanted to see . . . what would happen. What insides looked like. We used to talk about that, what our insides looked like."

Miguel turned his attention back to Grace. "You never told your mom?"

"She wouldn't have believed me. And I wasn't a thousand percent sure—I couldn't prove it. So to answer your question, I was running away in this picture because my first thought was that Hope would do it again, run over Goober Two. And I thought that's why she was so happy."

"Did she? Run over Goober Two?"

"I don't think so . . . I don't remember how he died, so it must not have been very dramatic. But I hate that picture."

Miguel rose, determined and proud, and lifted the photograph off the wall. He laid it facedown on the coffee table and used one germophobic finger to shove it to the farthest edge.

"Don't let her push you around," he said. "You'll feel better about everything else—all the nice things she does—if you don't let your mom push you around. This is your house."

She flung her arms around his neck. "This is why I love you!"

12

Even as it was happening, the chaperoning part of Grace's subconscious registered the wrongness of it. She should not be kissing Miguel. Should not be letting Miguel grope her that way. Why was he even going along with it? Perhaps this was what happened when love needed an outlet, when two people ran out of other or better ways to express how much they valued each other. Or maybe they were both lonely. Too much time cooped up alone. Or maybe it was the wine.

Neither of them seemed inclined to stop, though Grace's brain couldn't resist offering unhelpful commentary.

Are you sure your mother can't hear? What if she comes downstairs for a midnight snack!

Which of you is planning to bring up the birth control–slash-condom situation? Or is that counter to the plan? Are we trying *to make a baby here? Did we tacitly agree to something?*

Miguel's body felt good. How long had it been since she'd been skin to skin with anyone? He knew everything she liked—had she told him? It wasn't impossible, but she couldn't recall doing so in such detail.

She orgasmed. And lay there with her eyes closed, catching her breath.

A minute or three later, she opened her eyes.

No one was on top of her, and she wasn't downstairs on the sofa. Grace was alone, in her bed, with the door closed and her nightshirt crumpled around her ribs. She tried to remember the migration from the couch to her room, saying goodbye to Miguel, changing into her sleep clothes. But she couldn't. There was just the jump cut, from the orgasm to the next morning.

They hadn't had that much to drink, not enough to make her black out.

Had it happened? Had she and Miguel had sex? Even if it was a dream, that couldn't explain the missing chunk of time. Grace pushed herself onto an elbow and grabbed her phone. Nine forty-five. Okay, that was a normal enough time to wake up on a nonworkday, after a night of drinking. *We didn't drink that much. Wait, what day is it?*

She stumbled to the bathroom. Her face in the mirror was wrinkled with misery. While peeing she tried to gauge if it felt like she'd had sex, but nothing signaled. If this episode had involved any other person, she would've called Miguel to moan and regret and half-teasingly blame him for not stopping her. But she couldn't call him, not if she wasn't positive if they . . . She slipped a panty liner into her underwear, anticipating the start of her period. Assuming she had her days straight, her period, accurate as a Swiss watch, was due in the next few hours.

Miguel would call or text later; she was sure of it. He was good about doing stuff like that after a social engagement, a quick "Thanks for supper, let's do it again soon," and she'd be able to tell by his tone if they were okay. Maybe he'd even come right out and say, "Well that was an interesting development." If he was as chill and nonchalant as ever, she'd know it was just another of those viscous dreams.

As she left the bathroom, she saw through Jackie's open bedroom door her neatly made bed. Something made Grace step into the doorway. Her eye had always been adept at catching things before her brain fully grasped what she was seeing. As a child she'd loved, and been good at, the What's Different? game, where two cluttered pictures lay side by side and she needed to find all the things that were different between them. Now she saw it right away, but in her disoriented state, it took a moment for the significance to register.

Jackie had added a framed photograph to her wall. The picture of Hope that Miguel had taken down.

That was good, right? Jackie could've just hung it back up in the living room. Still, Grace felt the queasy hollowing that came with a reprimand. *Fine, if your walls are too precious . . .*

When a morning started wonky, coffee became an even more urgent need. She couldn't recall a morning quite as through-the–looking glass as this, but she plodded downstairs in pursuit of the only cure she knew to try.

————

The kitchen counter was covered with decapitated dolls' heads. Her mother had a large butcher knife.

Grace blinked, frozen in place. No, not heads. *What the fuck is wrong with me?* Fruit—oranges and apples and peaches.

"Gray?" There was uncertainty in her mom's voice. "You don't look so good."

"Hangover." Grace tugged at the hem of her nightshirt, suddenly self-conscious of her bare legs. She headed for the cabinet with the coffee but then couldn't remember where her mom had moved it. "I need coffee—where's the coffee?"

She heard herself on the verge of panic. Jackie calmly retrieved and handed her the pouch of dark roast. Feeling sicker by the minute, Grace went to the sink to fill the pot with water.

"Hon, I don't mean to interfere, but . . . Can I make you something more nourishing?"

In her peripheral vision, Grace was fairly certain her mom looked concerned, but then the fruit turned into dolls' heads again. No, not dolls' heads—babies' heads. Juicy and bleeding where her mother had severed them at the neck.

Grace slapped a cupped palm over her mouth to keep from screaming or vomiting. Her brain was blurry. Her eyes were confused.

"Okay, I know what you need . . ." Her mom took the pot of water from her and wrapped an arm around Grace's shoulders. Jackie led her out of the kitchen and into the living room, making a beeline for the sofa.

"Ollie was such a nice kid," Jackie said, "but sometimes he smoked a little too much—and I don't think it was always pot, maybe some mushrooms too." She plumped a cushion beneath Grace's head as she lay down. After the three-day drive from Florida, Ollie had helped get Jackie's furniture into the house; Grace agreed, he was nice. But he'd fled the second the trailer was empty, with barely a goodbye. "For all I know he dropped acid and took pills. Anyway, sometimes he got all cross-eyed and needed something healthy in his system to flush it out. And you're in luck—I was just about to make a fruit shake."

"Where'd all"—*those heads*—"that fruit come from?" Her couch was so comfy, her favorite place to lounge or nap.

"I walked to the Giant Eagle."

Even half-obliterated, Grace registered Jackie's pride. The supermarket was an easy five-minute walk away, but Grace hadn't been sure if that was an activity her mother could—or would—do. "Good. That's good."

"I'll be back in a jiff." Jackie bounded away. How could she move so quickly?

Grace was starting to feel better now that she was lying down. It wasn't so bad, actually, having someone around to help her through a rough morning. From the kitchen, a blade thwacked against wood, a short, sharp percussion of *whack-whack-whack-whack*. Then the blender whirred to life.

Jackie returned with a tall glass of pastel sludge. "Apples, peaches, fresh-squeezed orange juice, and a fat dollop of plain yogurt. And wheat germ. I take mine with some brewer's yeast, but a lotta people can't stand that. And I got some veggies to make some green juices too, though I think we're gonna need a proper juicer."

"Thank you." Grace took a gulp of the fruit shake. Lumpy yet refreshing goo slid down her throat. "Mm. It's good."

"I'm glad you like it. Just what you needed." Beaming, her mother watched her drink for a moment.

Grace relaxed, soothed by the perky sweetness of the vitamin-rich fruit. Through the back window she saw blue sky and was heartened by the thought that the day could yet turn out just fine.

13

After a lazy weekend, Grace got up early on Monday and messaged some of her stylist friends to see who might know of any openings. The person she really wanted to ask was Miguel, but he hadn't called or texted, and the longer he remained at large, the more worried she became that they had, *oh shit*, crossed a boundary in their relationship.

Some people had friends with benefits, but they usually discussed such matters first and were usually of the same orientation. Grace needed to pluck up the courage to just ask him, "Are we okay?" It was all the more confounding because she hadn't gotten her period yet. She couldn't remember if it had ever been even a day late. Something deep inside her itched a little, and she didn't know how to scratch it.

When Allison suggested they get together for lunch, Grace agreed with exclamation points and smiley faces. She'd been hoping someone would propose meeting in person but hadn't wanted to come out and say it, lest it came across like she was only networking for a job. In the guise of being a prince, she was quick to give her damsels practicable advice. All her alter egos would say, in a deeper version of her own voice, *It's okay to ask for what you want.* But Grace hadn't mastered taking all her princely advice yet.

They met at a chain restaurant in the South Hills, near where Allison worked—the kind of place that put enough food on a single plate to feed an entire family. A lot of restaurants were only available for takeout or delivery, but those with the space were offering outdoor seating.

"I never wanted an outdoor table before," Allison said as they were led by a masked hostess to just such a table. "Who wants to look at a parking lot?"

Now they were grateful for the option to dine at a restaurant, even with the concrete view.

As they perused the menu, they made small talk, catching each other up on the last few months. But as soon as their orders were taken and the menus collected, Allison cut right to the chase.

"I can offer you Tuesdays and Thursdays if you can start this Thursday. And we'll have more hours available when Ebony goes on maternity leave."

"That would be perfect, thank you so much!" As Grace gushed her thanks she pictured the interior of her wallet. Her cash reserves were shrinking, but she felt obligated now to pay for both of their meals; at least she'd have leftovers to take home.

"I'm not gonna lie—business is way down. I've been doing a few home visits on the side."

"Going to people's houses?" For some reason Grace thought that sounded horrible.

"Yeah. We're not supposed to, of course. But they pay cash, and some people won't leave the house for anything. Like, *anything*."

Allison took up most of their late lunch with the long story of how she'd landed her new position. Her hair skills were competent though not exceptional, but the younger woman's confidence and ambition surpassed Grace's. LuckyJamison or River or Preston might praise her *pure determination*, but Grace thought it all sounded like a lot of humble-bragging. When Allison insisted on leaving the tip, Grace let her—after all, Grace had paid for the rest of the meal and it was obvious that Allison wasn't hard up for cash. In addition to her ascension to management, her left hand—with its gumdrop-size diamond engagement ring—was permanently poised for a photo op. While her mouth bragged about her accomplishments, her hand bragged about her rich fiancé—as she held her sandwich, sipped from her drink, dabbed at her lips with a napkin.

They said their goodbyes with air hugs, the strange but necessary successor to air-kisses. Before Grace pulled out of her parking space she called the Oakland salon. Now that she was set to start working under Allison in three days, with shifts that overlapped, Grace had no choice but to immediately quit her current job. Freya answered the phone, and she seemed neither surprised nor put out that Grace wasn't coming back; perhaps she'd always known Grace's new hairstyle was the prelude to an exit.

She barely noticed the drive home, distracted by thoughts of the fancy graphic she would create for Instagram to announce her new location. And she also planned to email all her clients, past and present, to let them know where they could find her. Some of her clients might come back now that she had a chair in a classier salon. Her two days at the South Hills salon could potentially out-earn her three days in Oakland. And soon she'd have more hours. And Allison had mentioned that Demetri was working there part time, too, so it would feel like a mini-Barbara's reunion.

By the time she got home, it was almost three o'clock and Grace was in a better mood than she'd been in in a long time. She dropped her purse on the entry table, decontaminated her hands, kicked off her shoes, and went to the kitchen to deposit her container of leftovers in the fridge.

Before heading up to her room, Grace stood at the bottom of the stairs and listened. "Mom?"

The house was quiet. How quickly she'd acclimated to coming home and finding Jackie on the couch, watching a game show or a shopping channel. Then she remembered her mother had a doctor's appointment—set up before her move so Jackie could get established with a new primary care physician. With her mother not driving anymore, Grace had installed a rideshare app on Jackie's phone and showed her how to use it. It was important that her mother maintain her independence. Slowly but surely, they were establishing how to live together, while not becoming too enmeshed in each other's lives.

Alone in her house, Grace's first thought was this would be a good time to check on her damsels. But her second thought . . .

She locked the door behind her, peering out the miniature window to make sure Jackie wasn't stepping out of a cab. The coast was clear. Her mother's appointment was at two thirty, but every doctor's office ran late. Even if Jackie was on her way home, Grace should have at least a few minutes to herself. And it was the first opportunity she'd had to do a little snooping.

14

With stealth on her mind, she tiptoed upstairs. Had Jackie done this too? Taken advantage of Grace's absences to have a little look-and-see? She stepped into her mom's room, already with a target in mind. While helping with the boxes, Grace had become familiar with the general inventory of her mother's belongings. But everyone had secret (if not naughty) things tucked away in drawers, or precious things stashed in a closet for safekeeping. That's where Grace started—the closet—as she knew her mother still had the special plastic tub full of Hope's keepsakes.

She wasn't looking for anything in particular; it wasn't as if she expected Jackie's belongings to disclose a shattering revelation. But she liked to know what made people tick and preferred to make her observations from the safe ground of anonymity. Several pairs of shoes were stacked on top of the plastic tub. Grace made a note of what order they were in before taking them off and sliding the box out of the closet. She plopped herself down on the floor and popped the lid off.

In spite of telling herself she had no expectations, Grace's first reaction upon opening the tub was disappointment. She'd thought an aroma might waft out, a spicy scent that would transport her back to Hope's bedroom-in-the-dining-room. It had crossed her mind more than once that some of her recent dreams might have been subconsciously triggered by the nostalgic smells her mother had brought with her. But the inside of the bin only smelled of old paper.

As Grace gently sifted through the keepsakes, careful not to damage or rearrange anything, she was let down again: the entirety of the tub held *only* Hope's mementos. Report cards. School photos. Scribbly drawings. Mother's Day cards—yes, including the one they'd made with Grace's magical paper.

Young Grace had known that Mommy only cherished Hope's things. Especially after Hope's death, Grace had understood the importance of preserving these last bits of her sister. But she'd always wondered if later something of Grace's had been saved too. But no.

If judging by these relics, Jacquelyn had only ever had one daughter.

At the bottom of the tub was a smooshed cardboard shirt box, the kind people used when giving a gift of clothing swaddled in tissue paper. To open the shirt box, Grace had to lift out the rest of the memorabilia. In slow motion, she placed the stack beside her, begging it not to tumble over.

She couldn't guess what might be in the box within a box but assumed it must be something important. A birth certificate? A death certificate? A precious piece of clothing from Hope's infancy? When she lifted the lid, she found Mona.

Paper doll Mona, in one of her fine dresses.

Paper doll Mona, with her crayon orange hair and big cornflower eyes. Grace searched beneath Mona's paper wardrobe, a stack of ball gowns that Grace herself had cut and colored, but Rona wasn't with her.

Grace frowned. Mona's presence made her miss Rona in a way that wasn't logical but bruised her heart nonetheless.

Unable to handle any more memories, Grace packaged Mona into her cardboard sarcophagus and returned it to the tub. Less carefully than she'd taken everything out, she dumped it all back in. This was a waste of time; this was old news. She got to her feet and shoved the tub back into the closet, replaced the shoes atop it, and shut the door.

The digital clock beside the bed said Hurry Up; Jackie would be home soon.

The dissatisfaction of the search thus far made Grace more eager to find something of genuine interest. She considered all the framed pictures on the wall, hung with Victorian abundance. People hid things in frames. Hadn't someone found an original copy of the Declaration of Independence tucked behind a painting? In movies rich people often used a painting to hide the safe where they stashed their jewelry, cash, handguns. Jackie, a two-time widow, was comfortable financially, but she hadn't sneaked a safe in with her hastily packed things—or carved a space for one in the wall. It was tempting to turn each painting over, but Grace was concerned about the time and the likelihood of leaving evidence of her snooping. If she rushed she might accidentally leave something askew.

It seemed barely worth the effort, being such a cliché, but she went to her mother's dresser next and started riffling through the drawers. And much to her delight, she found something she'd never seen before: a small wooden box, the sort of thing she imagined might hold a medal. Had it belonged to Glen? Or Robert? She knew Robert had served in Vietnam, and afterward he protested against the war. Grace had always wondered if pothead Ollie had learned his bad habits at home; Robert may have clung to youthful pleasures beyond his preference for '60s rock.

The box wouldn't open. At first Grace thought it was just stuck together, the wood swollen from years of Florida humidity. But then she saw the teeny hole where a teeny key would fit. She grinned. Held the box to her ear and shook it. Nothing rattled. She considered its weight in her hand. Light. Maybe too light to contain anything solid, like jewelry or a medal.

She drummed her fingers against the lid's dark wood and looked around the room. Where might her mother have hidden a tiny key? No one who wanted to preserve a really good secret would keep the key too close at hand.

Maybe Mom has a stash. The thought made Grace laugh. In modern times, that wasn't something that needed to be hidden away.

Downstairs, someone was pushing and pulling at the front door, but it wouldn't budge. Grace was out of time.

Smiling, she slipped the treasure hunt prize back into the careful folds of the sweater where she'd found it. Before heading downstairs, she quickly surveyed the room. It was just as she'd found it, nothing out of place.

As Grace jogged downstairs her mother was struggling with the door key, twisting it back and forth in the lock. Grace flipped the dead bolt and let her in.

"Why did you lock me out?" Jackie was in a crabby mood.

"Sorry. Old habit. How was your appointment?"

"The people here aren't as friendly." She dropped onto the sofa, exhaling as if pooped.

"Want me to get you something?"

A hopeful expression brightened her mother's face. "There's a little bit of my breakfast shake left, that would really hit the spot."

"Okay."

Before Grace reached the cutoff to the kitchen, her mom called out, "Mind if I watch some of my TV? I just need a few minutes."

"Sure, take your time. I have some work to do in my room."

Grace opened the refrigerator and grabbed her mom's sports bottle with its last two inches of fruity sludge. By the time she crossed back through the living room, Jackie had her feet up, mesmerized as two bubbly women demonstrated a gadget for slicing bagels. Jackie took the bottle from Grace's outstretched hand without even looking at her.

"It won't take long," Grace said. "I can come back and help with supper."

"Thanks hon, but I'll be better in a minute. Just need to catch my second wind." Jackie chugged from her bottle, fascinated by the state-of-the-art bagel slicer, *So easy and safe your children can use it!*

Grace headed up to her room. This time "work" didn't mean engaging in her hobby; she had to get that email out to her clients, and she needed to text Miguel before things got too awkward. After shutting her door, Grace tumbled onto her bed and scooted back against the headboard. Quickly, she typed with her thumbs.

Everything OK? Haven't heard from u

She held the phone, hoping he'd reply right back. When he didn't, she kept staring at the screen, wondering if he just needed a minute to finish whatever he was doing. The silent phone became heavy in her hand. She didn't know what it meant, that Miguel wouldn't answer her. But she didn't like it. His absence scared her.

15

What an incredible turn of luck. Grace's mentor hadn't, after all, been quite ready to retire. Barbara's new salon was a fraction the size of the old one, and she could only offer chairs to a handful of her former staff, but Grace was euphoric to be one of them. And the cherry on top was Barbara had rented a storefront in Greenfield, where the rent was cheaper. It was situated just a stone's throw from the Giant Eagle, so it took Grace only a few minutes to walk there.

The bell above the door jangled as Grace entered the salon. It wasn't quite ready to open to the public, and she was greeted by the chemical twang of fresh paint, but she was more than happy to come in and help Barbara finish setting up. Four new salon chairs were already in place, two facing each of the side walls, but boxes of unpacked supplies made an obstacle course of the narrow room. Just as Grace was about to call out a hello, Barbara emerged from behind a partial wall at the back of the shop.

Though Grace had never been anywhere ritzy like Martha's Vineyard or the Hamptons, she imagined that all the women there (of a certain age) would bear some resemblance to Barbara. Grace sometimes pictured Barbara, petite and effervescent, jockeying a horse to a Triple Crown victory, or yanking the ropes of a sailing vessel as it sped and bobbed over white-capped waves. Barbara could laugh and eat finger sandwiches with the ladies and smoke cigars while talking stocks with the gentlemen. She dripped in gold and gems—anniversary gifts from the teddy bear husband she'd been married to for forty-five years—even when she was dressed for a day of grungy labor.

Barbara held her arms open for a hug. "Grace! So good to see you!"

"I'm so glad you called me, you have no idea." It felt so good to be in Barbara's reassuring embrace. Grace didn't even care that neither of them was wearing a mask.

"With everything going on I needed to close the big salon, I really did, and Shlomo and I had been talking about traveling," Barbara gushed, almost apologetically. "But after a long stretch at home and not *doing* anything and traveling still not an option . . . I'm not ready to give it up." Barbara held Grace's chin, examining her face, her hair. "How've you been?"

"Good. Okay." But Grace heard in Barbara's voice, saw in her concerned eyes, that she already knew: Grace wasn't completely okay.

"What's going on?"

And just like that, Grace was close to tears. "A lot. I don't know. The salon closed. And I understood, but I'd just bought my house . . . Then my mom moved in. And things are weird with Miguel right now, I don't know. I've been having a lot of nightmares."

"Oh, that's a thing." Barbara gripped Grace's hands. "That's a real thing, I read about it online. It's a pandemic, brain-on-fire, nerves-on-edge thing."

Grace nodded. She'd heard about that, too, but she wasn't ready to tell Barbara, sixty seconds after seeing her again, that it wasn't so simple. Her dreams had gotten very intense during the early weeks of the quarantine order, and she'd accepted it as constant subconscious worrying. But after the stay-at-home order had loosened and she'd started reestablishing a more normal life, she'd expected the dreams to fade away, not intensify.

"I guess I'm not used to so many changes," Grace said, trying to rationalize it for herself.

Barbara looped an arm through hers and started walking her through the salon. "I should've called, checked in with you, I'm sorry. I meant to, and then I got bogged down with my own troubles. But you were the one I was most worried about."

"I was?" That genuinely surprised Grace.

"You're like a daughter to me, you've been with me since you started, and I know work was the stabilizing force in your life." She patted Grace's hand. "We're alike that way."

When Barbara smiled the lines around her eyes crinkled. With her trim stature and endless energy, it was easy to forget she was sixty-seven, though, like Jackie, Barbara had recently let her short hair revert to its natural silver.

Grace felt her cheeks pinken with a bashful sort of pleasure. Barbara only had one child, a son in DC, who didn't come back to Pittsburgh unless someone died. Many times over the years, Grace had wished that Barbara was her mom. In Jackie's absence, it had been easy for Grace to build a life for herself with Barbara as such a steady and supportive presence. Not wanting to get weepy again, Grace swallowed her emotions and turned her full attention to the new salon.

"This place is so cute." The walls were a creamy mauve with white trim, and everything looked crisp and new—the light fixtures, the flooring, the well-laid-out stations where each stylist would work. "So bright and modern."

"It's getting there. Not as fancy as what we had before—"

"We don't need fancy."

Barbara laughed. "*You* don't need fancy." They reached the area behind the partial wall. "Only two sinks. And there's a tiny back office and a bathroom. I don't want it to seem too cluttered, so I had some shelving installed in the basement for storage. It's a little gloomy down there, but everything will be off the floor."

"I love it." Something about the layout reminded Grace of the first floor of her house, but she couldn't quite put her finger on it. The proportions maybe. Grace clapped her hands together. "What do you need me to do? Unpack, set up the stations?"

"Both, yes, but first . . ." Barbara fingered the pink ends of Grace's hair. "Can I be honest?"

Grace deflated a little, certain of what Barbara was about to say. "You hate it. I know, it was a dumb idea."

"I don't hate it at all. I just don't think it's *you*."

"That's what Miguel said." Wait, he wasn't the one who said it; Grace had made that judgment on her own.

"It's a cute cut . . . Maybe I can just trim off the pink ends? And give you back a little more color?"

"What, I don't look like a natural albino?"

Barbara laughed; her teeth didn't look as pearly white as Grace remembered.

Seconds later Grace was in the nearest chair, and Barbara whipped open a black cape to drape over her shoulders.

"I'll just dry cut the ends first, and then once we get the color right I can trim it however you like."

"You don't need to do this right now—I'm supposed to be helping *you*."

"Are you kidding, I live for this. I guess I'm gonna have to work until the day I die."

It was meant to be funny, but the thought of Barbara dying bothered Grace. With sharp compact scissors, Barbara snip-snipped the blemished ends of Grace's hair. She watched her mentor in the mirror—how dexterous and quick she was with the comb and scissors.

Something red dribbled down Grace's reflected neck. Had Barbara accidentally nicked her? It happened to the best of them, and she understood if Barbara was a little rusty after a few months off. But then the pain came, a searing sting. Grace winced. She expected Barbara to stop, to apologize, to say she was mortified. But Barbara kept hacking at her hair, a demented smile on her face.

"Mona can finally have that handbag."

What?

Horrified, Grace's hand shot to her ear. She screamed when she touched it. Her fingers came back dripping blood. Warm red rivulets streamed down her neck.

Barbara dropped Grace's severed earlobe on the counter in front of her, cackling. "Your sister's been waiting a *long* time."

Grace collapsed over the chair's arm, ready to vomit. Her mangled ear dripped perfect round spatters on the salon's new floor.

———

Queasy, Grace lifted her face from the sink and met herself in the mirror. The pink ends of her hair were gone, chopped roughly, but there was no blood. Checking, she found her earlobe intact. *Oh my God, what happened?* Her right hand seemed like a foreign object as she raised it, gaping at the scissors still clutched there. Her white sink basin was furred with pink.

"Fucking hell."

She'd cut her own hair.

A part of her hated that the dream wasn't real, such was her desire to spend her days alongside Barbara again. No, her mentor had really retired, and was probably holed up in a seaside retreat with Shlomo. Still only half-awake, Grace sought a logical answer: she'd known the hairstyle wasn't right; her subconscious—in the form of Barbara—was encouraging her to fix it before she started her new job. Fine, she could accept that. But the earlobe, the *pain* she'd felt? And how had she managed to cut her hair while asleep?

Grace turned her head from side to side, examining herself in the mirror. It wasn't perfect, but it wasn't a disaster; at least she hadn't hacked it off close to her scalp. She'd fix it later, after she was fully awake. For now, she grabbed a wad of toilet paper and scooped the pink bits out of the sink.

It was earlier than she usually got up, barely past seven, but the day was already unseasonably warm. She threw on an old halter-style maxi dress and headed downstairs. Her mother, as always, was puttering in the kitchen. Grace stopped at the threshold, grabbing it for support so she wouldn't topple over.

"What are you doing?" she gasped.

Her mother was holding Miguel's wilting bouquet like an ice cream cone, eating the dying flowers. For a second the air looked hazy. Grace had the odd sensation that her brain was spinning around inside her skull. Jackie turned to her, nonchalant.

"Throwing these away." She pulled the garbage can out from beneath the sink. Petals dropped onto the floor. "They're past their prime."

"Oh."

Her mother stared at her, a what's-wrong-with-you-now scowl on her face. Sarcastically, Jackie added, "Did you want to keep them?"

More petals rained down as she held out the bouquet.

Grace shook her head, embarrassed. She was certain—in an irrational, brain-fogged kind of way—that Jackie was somehow to blame for all this. For messing up her friendship with Miguel and messing with her head. There were reasons Grace kept Hope out of sight and out of mind, and she hadn't dreamed about her sister in years, not even during the early days of the pandemic.

It wouldn't help to talk to Jackie now, this instant, when Grace's reality felt off kilter, like a camera image that wouldn't settle into focus. But soon she and her mother needed to have a talk. In that blurry state, Grace considered it highly likely that Jackie had brought a ghost with her. *Maybe it lives behind one of the pictures, or in the little box.* If they couldn't find a way to quell its unruly spirit, her mother might have to find a new place to live.

16

Grace bypassed her mom's offer of a healthy shake and went straight for the coffee. Jackie took up entirely too much space as she swept up debris from the flower arrangement, forcing Grace to step around her as she would a sinkhole. Everything felt weird, and even the coffee machine was in on the conspiracy, brewing extra slowly, teasing her with that tantalizing smell. Grace crossed her arms and stared at nothing, pretending she couldn't see in her peripheral vision as Jackie began rearranging the drawers to find room for her new kitchen gadgets. The new juicer was plugged in next to the stove, but a box from the Home Shopping Network was sitting on the counter, unopened. Jackie seemed aware, on some level, of Grace's dark mood and didn't try to engage her in further morning banter.

After a while the aroma and comforting gurgle of the coffee machine was enough to mollify the worst of Grace's crankiness, even as questions remained. What if she *had* cut off her own ear? Could she do other terrible things in her sleep?

"Gray? I think your coffee's ready."

How long had she spaced out? Grace filled her favorite mug—a silly gift from Barbara with Mister Rogers in a jacket that turned into a cardigan when warmed by a hot beverage—and retreated to the living room. For now, curled up on the couch, she didn't even care that her mother was messing up the kitchen again. And maybe she should just let Jackie have the kitchen as her domain; it wasn't as if Grace ever made proper use of it. She sipped her coffee slowly but methodically.

As her head started to clear, Grace became more aware of the growing list of things that were troubling her. The easiest one was staring her in the face. Grace never lowered the blinds on the big window that looked out over the backyard. The window let in the best light in the house, and the trees in the rear neighbor's yard, especially now that they were in full leaf, gave her sufficient privacy. But the blind was down.

She drank a good three-quarters of her coffee before she felt rejuvenated enough to get up and deal with it. Grace strode to the window and raised the blind. The view was golden, with the sun heading toward its favorite perch in the sky and dandelions sprouting happily across the small lawn. Just as she was relaxing into a smile—

"Whaddyou do that for?" Her mother abruptly appeared in the entryway, clutching a new bouquet—this one of brightly colored utensils that looked like oversize toys.

"It's a beautiful day," said Grace.

"It's gonna be hot," said the sourpuss. "If you keep the blinds down, it'll stay cooler."

"I don't want to keep the blinds down. We don't get enough sunny days."

"But you only have the two air-conditioning units."

Grace hadn't been in the house long enough to know how hot it might get inside or how well the AC units worked—one in the dining room and one in her bedroom. She'd tested them after moving in, and her first impression was they were loud and she'd rather use fans. Jackie might be used to Florida with its central AC, but she'd also been spoiled by an abundance of sunshiny days. Today Grace needed the sun more than she cared about how it was going to heat up the house.

"What are those?" Her mother looked ridiculous with her pink spatula and baby-blue ladle and lime-green whisk.

"Silicone," Jackie said, chipper and matter of fact.

"Why?"

Instead of answering, Jackie gave her a half eye roll and turned back toward the kitchen. Grace wasn't in the mood for her—what sort of person didn't want to look at a beautiful day?—but she needed answers.

"Did I ever sleepwalk?" Grace asked, before her mother could fully withdraw.

Jackie came back, the utensils lowered, concern wrinkling her face. "No. Not that I was ever aware of. What did you do to your hair?"

"Cut it. I guess. While I was more or less asleep." Grace tugged at the uneven strands.

"You did that in your sleep?"

Grace shrugged. "I guess so."

There was a silent moment while Jackie, face scrunched, considered Grace's admission. It made Grace feel squirmy inside and she took a step away, suddenly needing a larger buffer of air between them.

"Maybe you should talk to somebody."

"And who would that be?" Grace was more than ready to be done with this encounter. Her mother had nothing useful to offer, and Grace had no idea who might specialize in the hows and whys of a somnambulist makeover.

She trudged back to the sofa and her remaining coffee. Flipped on Netflix. She expected her mom to disappear into the kitchen with her neon gadgets. But Jackie followed her and perched on the other end of the sofa; Grace didn't need to look at her to know she was wearing an expression of maternal angst.

Grace didn't want her worry or pity—where had she been all those suppers ago when Grace spoon-fed her sister one slow mouthful of Tuna Helper at a time? That's when Grace would have appreciated someone to run interference. How many times had she eaten a cold, half-congealed supper because the rule was Feed Hope First?

"You're stressed, hon. If it's about finances, I don't want you to worry about—"

"It's not that." Not entirely.

"Well, the mind-body connection is very strong, and if your mind is tangled up about something, then maybe it gets your body involved too."

Grace shot her a glare. This reasonable, says-all-the-right-things mom was like a character out of a sitcom.

"It really couldn't hurt to talk to a therapist."

"I'm not crazy," Grace mumbled.

"Of course you're not. I thought that was one of those insensitive words people weren't supposed to say anymore."

Grace gave her mom a long, cold stare. She had no memory of this version of Jackie, mindful of political correctness. This woman was a collection of splinters, held together with glue, dabbed with paint in the general likeness of a person she had once known as Mommy. Grace could hear Miguel's voice, encouraging her to get to know her again.

"Hope caused a lot of stress." Grace hadn't meant to say it aloud, but perhaps it explained why the mom she knew had been so different. In her own way it was an apology, an acknowledgment that their mother had had a lot to deal with.

Jackie nodded. "It wasn't easy."

"But we never talked about it."

"There wasn't time to talk. Not for me. On any given day . . . I just wanted to lie down. Didn't get to do that either. I'm sorry. When life got easier, with the husbands, and I had time to really think . . . I know I should've gotten more reliable babysitters. I didn't appreciate how much was on your shoulders—you did a lot for her. Is that why you brought it up? Is that what's troubling you?"

"I have no idea what's troubling me." There was nothing on Netflix she wanted to watch. Grace supported her head with her hand; the caffeine couldn't eradicate an underlying weariness. "I'm just really confused. About everything."

Suddenly, seeing a therapist wasn't such a bad idea. How had she spiraled down to this place so quickly?

"Maybe we should visit Hope's grave," her mom said. "Do you still do that?"

"Not recently." In the years before Jackie moved, Grace used to go to the cemetery twice a year—in February for their birthday and again in the summer. Once on her own, the visits became yearly. Eventually that stopped too. "I'll take you there, if you want."

"When you're ready." Jackie's smile was full of sorrow.

"I'm gonna go back to bed for a bit," said Grace.

She saw deference in the way her mother walked back to the kitchen. Jackie practically tiptoed, as if a nearby rattlesnake might awaken at the vibration of her movement. In contrast, Grace's escape was defiant and she took the steps two by two, hoisting up her dress so she wouldn't trip.

Another hour of sleep, that's what she needed. And then she'd fix her hair. She couldn't leave the house before doing that, and she needed to run to the store. Her period was only four days late, but the previous evening she'd googled "How soon can I take a pregnancy test?" She'd planned to wait a few more days—most of the tests made seven days sound like the magic number. But a couple of them claimed they were accurate on the first day of a missed period (probably not meant for instances where conception and missed period coincided but whatever). Sometimes it was easy to dismiss the possibility that anything had happened that could result in a pregnancy. But other times, uncertainty nagged at her.

If only she could pee on a stick to determine if she was losing her mind.

17

Grace cursed and white knuckled the steering wheel. According to the traffic app she'd left in plenty of time, but here she was stuck in a one-lane bottleneck, late for her first day at the South Hills Village salon. She'd never been late for a day of work in her life and had wanted to make a good impression; hopefully the effort she took in getting ready would compensate for the elements she couldn't control.

Her hair had turned out shorter than she'd ever worn it, but with a bit more layering it looked full and wavy. And, per dream Barbara's advice, she'd added in some color to make it look more natural. During the weeks at home she'd gotten out of the habit of wearing earrings, but this new start was a chance to break out of her casual malaise. Her ear bling matched a necklace that had been hibernating in her jewelry box for eons, understated enough to pass as a real blue topaz—though now people were probably only going to notice her scrambling and apologizing and looking flustered.

With nothing better to do, she checked her phone. If she'd been hoping one of her damsels might brighten her day, it was a miscalculation.

"What. The actual . . ."

Lexis224U had sent LuckyJamison a message:

I miss u baby! And with it, a nude selfie.

They'd messaged many pics back and forth over the weeks, and Lexis224U had teased the possibility of such photos before. But

LuckyJamison was a stand-up guy, pragmatic and moral, and he'd advised Lexis to never send nude photos. To anyone. Ever. *It could come back to haunt you.*

See, this was the very reason Grace had been forced to ghost her: Lexis224U just wouldn't take the good advice she was given. Although now that Grace was being ghosted by Miguel, she had a tiny bit more sympathy for the damsels she'd abandoned over the years. The traffic finally started inching forward; Grace tossed her phone into her purse without replying.

———

Just as she feared, all heads—sitting and standing—turned as Grace tornadoed through the salon's door. She imagined they were all baring their teeth behind their mouth-covering masks, like territorial dogs. As well put together as she'd been before leaving the house, now she felt like a frantic mess. For once, she almost liked the anonymity her face mask gave her. She headed straight for Allison, the only familiar thing in the room.

"I'm so sorry! Construction and bumper-to-bumper—"

"I should've warned you." Allison finished the last foil on her client's head and promised her she'd be right back. Quickly, she showed Grace the layout of the salon, where they kept the extra towels, how they organized the hair color, and introduced her to the receptionist, who would cash everyone out.

There wasn't time to get properly acclimated or meet her new coworkers, as Grace's first client—one of the women she'd emailed days earlier—was glumly flipping through a magazine, waiting for Grace to get her shit together. Seeing a familiar face helped subdue some of Grace's first-day-off-to-a-bad-start jitters, though a deeper anxiety burrowed in like a tick. What if the funny feeling in her belly wasn't jitters at all but the dividing and dividing and dividing cells of a fetus growing inside her?

The pregnancy test had been positive . . . ish. It hadn't *screamed* positive (the green check mark had been shy and pale), but the red *X* she'd been hoping for hadn't emerged at all. For thirty-some hours she'd been qualmish and confused. Maybe—probably?—she'd taken the test too soon. In a few days she'd have to try again, but she was a little afraid of what an accurate test might reveal.

"I'm so sorry to keep you waiting, Marley—how've you been?"

"Good. So glad I got your email."

They made small talk as Grace washed Marley's short, punkish hair. She was a client Grace had hoped to lure back, as Marley was on the cusp of fame. She appeared at the local comedy clubs but had cultivated a national reputation for her dry-yet-congenial wit via her YouTube channel. People were calling her the Pittsburgh Hannah Gadsby, and her comedic specialty was dissecting song lyrics to prove various points about the abomination of patriarchy. Marley was a favorite client for other reasons too: she typically got her short hair trimmed every four weeks; she was a good tipper; she was nice and often funny. While Grace was dying to know the behind-the-scenes news—had Marley found a new agent or made progress toward a TV special?—she didn't want to be a nebshit.

Back at Grace's station, she carefully combed Marley's hair. "Keeping it the same? Just a trim?"

"For today. Toying with new ideas, but I haven't decided yet. I like what you've done with yours."

"Thank you." The compliment gave Grace a boost of confidence. She took out her scissors and started cutting. "It looks like the pandemic hasn't slowed you down. I love the new videos."

Marley's eyes squinted as she grinned behind her mask. "Thanks. It feels weird to be this lucky—now, in the middle of everything—but the whole world's gone virtual."

Not quite the whole world. In the early weeks of the stay-at-home order, Miguel had talked about making a series of how-to videos for people who wouldn't be going to a salon for a while. Then Grace had pointed out that it really wasn't in their best interest for people to learn they didn't need stylists anymore. She thought her mask hid any sort of grimace or doubt, but Marley must have seen something that made her realize it was a touchy subject and quickly changed the topic.

"Did you move out this way?"

"No, kind of the opposite," said Grace. "I recently bought my first place, in Greenfield."

"Nice, congrats! We moved up to Mount Washington—I'm glad you're working on this side of the river now."

They shared an insider's laugh. For a city chock full of bridges and tunnels, the locals preferred to avoid them. It was easier to be clannish about your neighborhood and skip the inevitably slower traffic that came with every approach to every bridge and every tunnel. Outsiders didn't understand what it was really like living in a city divided by *three* large rivers.

Later, when she replayed the morning in her head, Grace couldn't recall if she'd been paying proper attention. It was unlike her to let her concentration lapse, but maybe she'd let herself get distracted when Marley opened up about her exciting career updates. Somehow in the middle of the haircut, immersed in a comfortable routine—Grace with her scissors, Marley with her chatter—the comedian let out a yelp of pain.

Grace froze. She knew what was going to happen before Marley, clenching her teeth, even reached for her ear.

Of course it was her ear. How bad was it? Dear God she couldn't have cut off Marley's—

"Are you okay?" Grace asked in a panic. "I'm so sorry!"

Heads turned at the raised voices.

"It's nothing . . ." Marley pressed a finger on a spot near the top of her left ear.

"Are you sure? I am so sorry."

"I'm sure." Marley moved her finger away; her ear was pink where she'd rubbed it.

Grace got light headed, as if she'd taken too big a hit off a bong, reassured to see that it was a very minor injury. Only a tiny smile of blood. Smaller than a paper cut. She withheld the urge to overdo her relief. It was just a scratch—which was inexcusable but better than the alternative.

"I'm sure we have a first aid kit." Grace frantically looked around for Allison, but all she saw were the judgmental eyes of complete strangers.

"I don't need that, it's barely bleeding."

"I'm really, really sorry, bordering on mortified."

Marley let out a booming laugh. "Well, at least my haters can keep calling me the One-Joke Wonder rather than the One-Ear Wonder."

While Grace appreciated Marley's good sense of humor, the slipup was a bad follow-up to a bad start. Grace knew she wouldn't take a penny from this first client at her new gig—she'd never let someone *pay* her for cutting something other than hair. A free haircut was the least she could offer, but it wouldn't guarantee Marley ever coming back.

———

After her crap day was over, Grace got stuck in traffic again. The commute was proving to be worse than she'd feared, and for some inexplicable reason, every radio station was playing songs that reminded her of Hope, a vexing soundtrack of the music her sister used to love. Grace felt trapped beyond the obvious walling in of the cars around her. She wasn't a superstitious person, at least not more so than anyone else, but signs were pointing to the continuing downward spiral of her luck. The one truly good thing that had happened in recent weeks—the new job—felt like it was slipping away. She'd never had a workday where she was so off her game, and without the certainty of the thing she was really good at, Grace wasn't even sure who she was.

Her stomach rumbled. Oh right, she'd almost forgotten: more problems were brewing inside her, the very thought of which squelched her hunger.

Suffocating in the standstill, she took out her one reliable friend, her phone. For a second she considered which damsel to check on but ended up placing a call to Miguel instead. She tried to hold back the tears so her voice wouldn't sound weird. It rang and rang. He wasn't going to answer, but she didn't know why. Her voice cracked with emotion as she left a message.

"Hey. I don't know what's going on—I really need to talk to you. Are you okay? I'm shit. Just, everything's falling apart. Please call me. Miss you. Love you."

When she finally got home she felt as if, in the course of an endless day, she'd driven halfway across the country and back. And fought a losing war without proper armor or munitions. Jackie had taken over the living room, watching TV as she sorted through her latest shipment of kitchen stuff. Boxes and packing material were tossed everywhere. After kicking off her shoes, Grace went through the dining room to get to the kitchen.

"Sorry about the mess in here, I'll clean it up," Jackie called after her.

"Whatever," Grace mumbled. She filled a sports bottle with water and headed for the stairs, ready to lock herself in her room.

"You don't want any supper? I've got it all portioned out in microwaveable containers—glass, not plastic—in the fridge. Walnut and mushroom risotto with steamed asparagus."

"Maybe later, thanks." She saw now that her mother was unpacking more Pyrex, various shapes and sizes with matching lids.

"Gray?"

Instead of answering, Grace—lifeless, robotic—came down the stairs backward until she could see her mother.

"Rough day?" Jackie asked.

"Yeah. I'm just gonna . . . Need some downtime."

"I'm sorry, hon. I wish I could make everything better."

"I'll figure it out."

"Well, the food's ready when you get hungry. And I'll clean this up—it looks worse than it is."

"Okay." Her mother's shopping addiction didn't even register on Grace's list of concerns. Though she did wonder . . . "How did all this get here so fast?"

"I ordered some of it before I left Florida." She radiated pride for such foresight. "Not all the Pyrex—I hadn't realized you were still using plastic. But it seemed silly to pack up drawers full of grubby kitchen stuff. New kitchen, new start."

Grace nodded, less than impressed. She trudged up to her room and shut the door.

It wasn't hot like it had been in recent days, but Grace turned on the air conditioner before flopping onto her bed. She'd discovered that she liked the drone of the AC: it blotted out the sounds of her mother's presence in the house. With her weary body pressed against the smooth sheets, she sank into the memory foam mattress and let the cool air caress her skin.

There was a fly in her room, buzzing around. It was stuck in an unfortunate pattern, flying in a circle and then bashing itself against the window. She sympathized with it; she wanted out too.

18

Seventeen-year-old Erika sat on the sofa, painting her nails. Grace relaxed into the threadbare overstuffed chair—her favorite place in the house—and did her homework. Mommy always complained about the chair, said it wasn't fit for a junkyard but she couldn't afford to replace it. Grace loved sinking into it, and loved how the cushions always felt warm. Sometimes she imagined it was a living animal, a giant cat with a furry belly, and she was its little kitten, snuggled safely near her mommy-cat's heart.

At this time of day, the sun streamed through the windows on the other side of the house, making silhouettes of Hope and her physical therapist on the dining room's curtained partition. Grace could hear the therapist gently encouraging Hope—"just a few more" or "let's try again"—and Hope grunting as if the entire hour of manipulating her limbs was nothing short of torture. Grace loved these afternoons when a therapist came and she had a whole hour to herself. And she didn't worry that Hope was really in pain, as she always rebounded in high spirits the instant the session was finished.

Soon (too soon), the therapist pulled the curtain aside and Hope zipped out in her chair.

"Nice to see you, Grace," said the therapist on her way out. "You girls be good."

"We will," Hope and Grace said together. Erika flapped her hands, either waving goodbye or drying her nails.

With the therapist's departure, they didn't need to pretend anymore that Hope and Grace were being properly supervised. Erika got to her feet. "Later, brats. Tell your mom she still owes me twenty-four dollars."

"Okay," Grace replied as Erika let herself out.

Now that they were alone, Hope rammed her power chair into Grace's comfy mommy-cat chair.

"Hey! Stop it."

"I'm hungry." Hope sneezed, spraying Grace with spittle.

"Gross! Cover your mouth."

"I'm hungry."

"I'm busy."

Hope started to back away and Grace thought she'd head into the kitchen, but no, Hope bulldozed the chair again.

"Hope, stop it! I'm sure there's a banana in the kitchen—go get it if you're so hungry."

"Open a can of soup."

"We don't have any."

"I'm getting a sinus infection."

"Well you're not gonna die before I'm done with my homework." Grace rolled her eyes.

Per usual, Hope didn't want to wait. She kept reversing and steering her bulky chair into Grace's, again and again. Grace started to imagine how bruised her poor mommy-cat chair was going to be if this went on much longer, so she flung herself over the back of it and stormed upstairs, where her sister couldn't follow her.

"Hey!" Hope shrieked as Grace pounded up the stairs.

"Give me *ten minutes*!"

Behind her, Hope made an audible growling noise. She was getting worse, Grace thought. Worse as in an intolerable, grumpy pain in her ass. Hope wasn't quite this bad when Mommy was around, though she bossed and sassed Mommy a lot too. Grace's room was tiny, just big enough for a twin bed and a battered old dresser. But more and more, she was thankful for their two-story house. Mommy talked all the time about buying or renting something without stairs, but in their hilly city, that was a challenge, and Mommy didn't want to move farther away from her job. Grace launched herself onto her bed. Her pillow smelled like dirty hair.

From downstairs, she heard as Hope coughed and then banged her wheelchair against the screen door as she went out onto the porch. She liked to sit out there. Having recently mastered the art of humming a melody, Hope did it all the time now and was humming a favorite pop song. Grace returned to her math book but soon became aware that her sister's voice was getting quieter, as if she was moving away . . .

Suddenly Grace understood that Hope had driven herself down the short ramp to the front walk. She dashed to her window just in time to see Hope turn onto the sidewalk.

"Where are you going?" Grace yelled through the window screen. They both knew that Mommy didn't want Hope wandering the neighborhood by herself.

"To the store," Hope called back.

"You don't even have any money!"

This time Hope ignored her and kept motoring away. Grace was torn. Though Mommy insisted "anything could happen" if Hope were left on her own, they were eleven years old, not babies. And Grace often went to the store by herself or with Hope in tow. Her sister wanted to be more independent—shouldn't they let her?

"Fine," Grace mumbled. She tried to concentrate on her homework again. But when she couldn't hear Hope anymore, she got uneasy. She didn't want to be Hope's keeper, but if one of them got in trouble for her escapade, it would be *Grace*. Her heart full of hate, she tossed aside her book and went chasing after her sister.

By the time she got to the sidewalk, Hope was at the end of the block, making the left turn toward the market.

"Hope!" She bellowed as loud as she could, but Hope either couldn't hear her or pretended not to. Grace took off running again.

The Jablonski brothers—with their chronic scowls and grunge—stopped popping wheelies in the street when she raced by. They said something nasty about "Hope the Retard, running away from home," but Grace didn't have time for her usual profane reply (she knew quite a few choice words, as did the other kids on her street). Hope was about as far from mentally slow as a person could be, but in Grace's current mood she, too, was having uncharitable thoughts about her sister. Like, maybe she could sabotage Hope's wheelchair after they got home so she couldn't do this again.

If Grace flunked out of school it would be Hope's fault. Grace knew she could do better in most of her classes, but she always did her homework in a rush and barely read her assignments because Hope needed some soup, Hope needed help with the mechanics of her own homework (Why didn't Grace get some credit for *that*?), Hope needed her to get this, get that, do this, do that. Grace was about to end the pursuit and go home, let her sister deal on her own with the fallout of her dumb ideas, but then she heard a scream.

To anyone else it would've sounded like a garbled nothing: "Hellm! Grayyyhell!"

Grace heard it for what it was, "Help me! Grace, help!"

As Grace rounded the left onto the next street she saw Hope half a block away, being lifted out of her wheelchair. Beside it was a car, its back door open. Someone was trying to kidnap Hope.

"Stop! Help!" Grace cried out, but there wasn't an adult around to see what was happening. She flew forward as Hope thrashed in her kidnapper's arms. "Leave her alone!"

The kidnapper ignored Grace's demand. The kidnapper, a woman, deposited Hope in the back seat of her car and slammed the door shut.

Grace curled her hands into tight fists, ready to lunge, ready to brawl. Then the woman, smiling, turned to face her. And Grace stumbled to a halt.

She recognized the kidnapper, but her mind shuddered like an earthquake at the impossibility of it.

It was Lexis. Lexis of Lexis224U. But wait. Young Grace didn't know her . . . Yet she knew her. From within the car, Hope pounded on the window, screaming to be let out.

On some level Grace knew this wasn't happening, knew it wasn't real. But she couldn't just let Lexis drive away with her sister.

"Let her go!" Grace commanded, sounding braver than she felt.

Lexis wasn't as pretty as she'd looked in her pictures. Greasy hair hung in her face, and her skinny limbs were all bone. Her smile revealed brown teeth and gaps. "Why do you care, *Jamison*?" she snarled. "You're sick of looking after her. I'm doing you a favor."

"How did you get here?" Grace asked, dumbfounded, because Lexis lived in Phoenix (unless she'd been lying about everything too)—and they wouldn't meet, even virtually, for another twenty-five years.

"I told you secrets. About my life. Things I've never told anyone. And you're not even a *real person*!" Spit, as brown as her teeth, flew from Lexis's mouth. Grace cringed.

"I'm real," Young Grace said meekly, inching backward as Lexis advanced.

"You don't need this bullshit." Grace wasn't sure which bullshit Lexis was referring to—the catfishing or her sister. "If you're sad and lonely it's your own damn fault."

Lexis was so much taller than Grace, so much stronger (in her emaciated state, her tendons looked like steel cables). Grace stood frozen as Lexis returned to her car in one elongated stride and got behind the wheel. As Hope pleaded—slapping the window, her eyes on Grace—the car sped away.

Grace felt something tearing—her skin, unzipping from her neck down. When it was loose enough, she pulled her arms out of the skin sleeves. Freed each leg like she was peeling off a pair of itchy tights. She left the skin facade on the sidewalk, with its crumpled facial features and limbs like flesh-colored noodles. What did she look like now? Pink tissue and red blood and white bits of bone? *Like poor Goober.* She knew what she felt like: a monster.

She dragged herself home, unsure how she'd explain to Mommy what had happened. Salty tears started to fall, but she blinked and snuffled them back up so they wouldn't burn the open wounds of her newly exposed face.

19

Grace awakened to the gut punch of guilt. Hope had been kidnapped by someone Grace knew—someone she'd lied to—and Grace hadn't been able to save her. The fact that Hope hadn't been kidnapped in real life was little consolation given the real-life fact that she was dead. Before she could deep dive into interpreting the nightmare, she picked up her phone—and practically shrieked with delight as she saw a text from Miguel, sent just twenty minutes earlier.

So sorry! Let's catch up! I could pick up brunch?

Halle-fucking-lujah. And he didn't sound mad. Grace quickly replied:

Picnic in my backyard?

She waited, hoping he was still near his phone. Thirty seconds later he responded.

Pamela's the usual?

Yes!!!!!!!!!

She wanted to send him a thousand kissy-face emoji and not just because she loved Pamela's french toast. If Miguel wasn't mad at her, if he was still her friend, then she could probably survive the wreckage that had become her life.

———

Thirty minutes later she was showered, dressed, her cropped hair drying in waves. She bypassed Jackie in the kitchen and headed down the basement steps. It took her two trips, but she happily ferried the folding card table and two chairs and set them up in the middle of the backyard. She'd decided to create an outdoor café, which she thought would be nicer than a picnic on the ground.

On a mission, Grace got out plates, forks, glasses. She stood for a moment, gazing around the kitchen, tapping a finger on her lip, wondering if she still had the tablecloth-and-napkin set—and if so, where Jackie would have put it.

"Gray?"

Grace didn't look at her straightaway. "Have you come across a plaid tablecloth? It might look a little Christmassy, burgundy with green and gold."

Her mother dropped what she was doing—

Slicing a bowl of eyeballs, her cutting board crimson with gore.

Grace blinked and shook the vision away.

No, her mom was pitting cherries. The cutting board was slick with red juice.

Jackie dug through the cupboard where she'd stashed Grace's old plastic storage containers. She retrieved the linens and handed them to Grace. "They're a little damaged, looks like you got wax on them, but it wasn't my place to throw them away."

The memory came back—a Valentine's Day evening with Miguel, when they'd both been single and cranky. Wine, candles, chocolate cake. She'd dressed up her old coffee table, and they'd binged a slutty melodrama on Netflix.

"Perfect." Grace beamed and headed outside to set her card table.

If they were eating inside she might've searched for candleholders, for old time's sake, but in addition to needing the fresh air and glimpses of sun, the backyard was the only place where she could expect some privacy. She hoped her mother would conveniently disappear before Miguel arrived, but Jackie had moved on from the messy cherries and was now rolling out a flat circle of dough. When the doorbell rang, Grace dashed to answer it, determined to usher Miguel through the house before either he or Jackie, in a fit of friendliness, could alter her plans. She and Miguel *needed* to talk.

"Good morning, lovey," said Grace, opening the door.

"Morning, lovey. I come bearing food." And for proof, he held up a take-out bag.

Grace took his free arm hostage and led him through the house toward the back door—though she couldn't stop Jackie and Miguel from exchanging air-kisses and flamboyant greetings.

"Are you making a pie, Miss Jacquelyn?"

"Cherry, nice and tart."

Grace tugged Miguel out the door.

"I'll save you a piece!" Jackie called out.

"Sorry for my manners, Grace is really hungry—"

Jackie laughed, good humored, as Grace pulled the heavy door shut behind her. She imagined her mom in there alone, her laughter becoming a cackle.

"You went all out." Miguel admired the outdoor café as they approached the table. He sat with exaggerated panache and dipped into the take-out bag for the first container.

"I'm so glad you're here. I've been a mess, and I was getting so worried when I couldn't reach you." She poured him a glass of water from the pitcher she'd left on the table.

"Lovey, it's not like we talk *every* day."

"But we also don't just ignore each other's texts."

Miguel's eyes went wide with exasperation. "Well you're not the only one who's had a week. French toast . . ." He opened the carton and handed it to Grace.

Grace's mouth started watering at the very sight of the buttery, eggy french toast. She took the proffered food and slid it onto her plate.

"And bacon. Burnt."

"You're the best." She stuffed a piece of the heavenly, crunchy bacon into her mouth.

Miguel transferred a broccoli-and-cheddar omelet and Lyonnaise potatoes onto his own plate.

"Do you want anything other than water?" Grace asked, pouring syrup and licking her fingers. "I can make coffee?"

Miguel shook his head, forking his first big bite of omelet. "I'm sufficiently caffeinated. So what in the world has been going on?" He chewed as he spoke, and they both ate as if ravenous. "If you'd left a more *specific* message I could've tried to get back to you."

"Where were you? It's like you fell off the earth."

Miguel got that exasperated look again. "My sister. Carolina. Decided to have an impromptu wedding. And wanted *me* to do in five days what really needed six months. So we had a wedding on *Wednesday*. Only twentyish guests, but Carolina had some pretty elaborate ideas for hors d'oeuvres and centerpieces and flower arrangements. The one thing she didn't want my help with? Her *hair*." He snorted. "She wore a pink wig. Don't ask."

"Why the sudden rush?" Grace had met both of Miguel's sisters a couple of times, but his family lived in Philadelphia, so she didn't know them super well. Still, she knew Carolina had been with Thom for at least four years.

Miguel gave the sky a why-me shake of the head. "And good brother that I am—"

"You've been in Philly?"

"Working my underappreciated ass off. Drove home last night. And why the rush? Carolina's convinced we're all going to be in lockdown again, *forever* next time. Maybe she's afraid . . . I don't know. But it suddenly seemed like life or death, now or never, so she chose right the fuck now."

"That was good of you—you are a good brother. And I'm sure Carolina appreciated it."

He conceded with a little smile and a one-shouldered shrug. Their appetites somewhat satiated, they ate at a more relaxed pace.

"It was good to get away for a few days, see the family," said Miguel. "You look really awesome, by the way. Your hair. And I swear you've lost ten pounds since last week."

"Really?"

"Yes. Very noticeably."

Grace hadn't noticed it herself. "I think my mom's a vegetarian."

"Is that why you're so mad at her?"

"I never said I was mad at her."

"No, you just dragged me away like she was an infectious disease. Things aren't getting better between you?"

Grace slumped back in her chair. Now that Miguel had mentioned it, she *felt* thin, in a malnourished sort of way, and wished she'd asked for a double order of bacon.

"She's not the problem, really." She put her fork down, mildly nauseated now that she had to find words for what she'd been experiencing. "I've been having the worst . . . They don't even feel like dreams. I mean, they're nightmares. Scary. But also real."

"About what?" He sounded eager, but as he happily devoured the rest of his breakfast, it made Grace feel even more alone. To him, this was something *interesting*, a new thing to talk about, not a mental health dilemma.

"Hope has been in a lot of them. But I started this"—she held out a piece of her short hair—"while I was . . . sleepwalking."

"Wow. Looks very professional."

She gave him a smirk. "I didn't do all of it in my sleep—I just *started* it."

"It makes you look younger. I'm serious, you look good, healthy."

While she appreciated the compliments, it was clear he wasn't grasping that this was a problem. But she hesitated to voice just how confused she sometimes felt about reality.

"So I haven't been sleeping well. And I'm also pretty sure I'm on probation at the job I just started. And then . . . well, I feel like an idiot, but I had this fear I might be pregnant."

Miguel held the back of his hand to his mouth, as if something unexpected might come flying out. He took a second to compose a response.

"Congratulations? Or . . . ? I didn't even know you were seeing anyone."

Time stopped. Grace gaped at Miguel. This was the confirmation she'd been wanting—that they had *not* slept together—but that meant it wasn't only her head that was messed up but her body too.

The back door opened, and Jackie came out carrying a big jar full of water and tea bags.

"Sun tea!" She grinned at them—

and in that grin Grace saw Lexis and her brown teeth

and Barbara with the scissors in her hand

—and left the jar in a patch of sun and went back inside.

"Does your mom know?" Miguel asked.

"What? God no." For some reason, the idea disgusted her.

"Thought maybe that might explain all the nutritious food. Well, except for the pie."

"No, I—my period's late. It's never late, but everything's making me paranoid." So paranoid that now she didn't believe Miguel's earlier compliments. She didn't feel healthy and couldn't imagine she looked it. She even questioned the conversation they were having, where and when—and *if*—it was happening; it felt less real than the dreams.

Miguel reached across the table and squeezed her hand. "I'm sorry. You have a lot going on and I've been AWOL—against my will, but still." His grip—his flesh—helped to authenticate the present reality. "So, first things first . . . Who is this mystery man you've been hooking up with? And why am I just hearing about it now?"

Grace choked back a sob. If only she had something as easy and titillating as a secret lover to reveal. She started at the beginning, with the first dream about Hope and the paper dolls, and told Miguel everything. Well, nearly everything—she left out the part about being a professional catfisher, and referred to Hope's kidnapper as a "bitter ex."

20

A couple of hours later, Jackie came out to fetch her sun-brewed tea and offer them slices of cherry pie. She made a peppy little waitress of herself and asked if they needed anything else. Grace was tempted to request a refill of their pitcher of water, but didn't. They thanked Jackie, gushing over her pie, and she retreated to the house to give Grace and Miguel their space.

Grace had the impression that evening was coming on, that they'd been out there talking for even longer than they had. But it was just the clouds moving in, insulating the sky like a layer of foam. There were rare moments in a relationship when Grace felt like a character in a video game, ascending to a glorious level she'd previously considered unattainable. She felt like that now, after sharing so much with Miguel. For all the fun times they'd had and in all the ways they'd been there for each other, Grace rarely got vulnerable. It wasn't a place she liked to be. Miguel had been a good listener, not once falling back in disbelief or waving away her anxiety. Jackie had suggested she talk to someone, and while Grace knew she meant a professional, opening up to Miguel offered more immediate gratification.

Now that he was aware, he wanted her to keep him apprised of the dreams, as if they were symptoms of a logical malady that would yet make sense. Grace mused that her predicament was like a very obscure version of *Name That Tune*. Miguel could usually guess a song from a handful of notes, but the whys of Grace's nightmares needed a few more measures. At least she didn't have to puzzle through it alone now.

They'd been talking for so long that Grace was almost ready to eat again.

"Remember that time we went to Ritter's for lunch," she said, "and stayed so long we ended up getting dinner too?"

"I miss restaurants," Miguel replied, wistful. "Feeling safe inside. Doing normal things."

"Me too."

"As much as I'd love to stay, Coco's mad at me and needs some lap time."

"I understand." And as much as she wanted to spend the evening with him, a weariness was settling in. Maybe she'd have a snack and take a nap.

They carried their dirty dishes and garbage into the house. This time, to Grace's relief, Jackie was squirreled away in her room.

"Oh I'm so scatterbrained, I almost forgot!" Miguel grabbed her hand and practically dragged her into the dining room. "Wait here, I have a present for you."

She obediently stood there, arms crossed, amused, and waited as he dashed out the front door. She heard his car door slam shut a minute later, and then Miguel called in from the porch.

"Shut your eyes!"

And she obediently shut her eyes, exponentially more amused.

"Don't open them." He breezed past her. "Okay. Open. Look."

He was standing on the far side of the dining room table, holding an unframed canvas—large, with brilliant streaks of color—against her wall.

Grace's mouth dropped open as she gasped.

"Do you like it?" Miguel asked eagerly.

"I. Love. It." She was almost speechless and could tell how much that pleased Miguel. The painting was greater in size than most of his work, and though it was still abstract, she saw a landscape emerging through the bolts of color. "Miguel . . . I don't even know what to say. Thank you."

"You're welcome."

"You're so talented. I'm going to hang it up right now, but first, I need to give you a hug."

Miguel set the painting on the floor and opened his arms to receive her. They squeezed each other long and hard.

"Thank you. For everything," she said. "You make everything better. That's why Carolina couldn't do her wedding without you."

"Aw, thank you. And don't worry, we'll get your situation sorted. I'll bring you some Nighty Night tea tomorrow. Banish those bad dreams."

As he walked to his car, Grace blew him kisses from the porch. "Give Coco some cheek rubs from me."

"I will."

She watched him drive away, and waved, even when he was too distant to see her. "I'm becoming an old gramma in a Hallmark movie," she muttered, heading back inside. But it made her genuinely sad to see him go.

Fortunately her mother hadn't moved the tools from the utility drawer where Grace kept all the random-but-useful things. She hammered a nail in the wall, just where Miguel had displayed his painting. It looked good there and really transformed the dining room, but as she stood back and admired it, she wondered if she shouldn't put the painting where she could see it more often—the living room, or perhaps her bedroom.

She returned the hammer to its drawer and pondered what to grab for a snack. Everything in the refrigerator looked too organic and healthy. The pie beckoned to her from its place on the counter. A bowl of cereal might be a slightly better choice, but she'd only eaten breakfast food so far that day. She ignored the snarky inner critic who pointed out that she'd also already had pie, and there were a thousand ways to justify it: the pie was easy to grab and go; she was losing weight without even trying; anything freshly baked was a rare treat.

Plate in hand, her slice was half-eaten before she reached the top of the stairs. As she started to close her bedroom door, ready to hibernate for a few hours, she heard a melody coming from her mother's room. Humming.

Jackie was humming the song Grace had heard in her dream. The song Hope had been humming as she fled from home.

21

When Grace awakened, a lavender sky was visible through her window and she smelled ozone in the air. Rain was coming. She was glad she hadn't slept *too* long—it wasn't dark out yet—but she felt so off schedule she couldn't quite tell what day it was. Her laptop sulked on her desk like a neglected lover, but she wasn't quite ready to give it, or the damsels, her attention. After a protracted stretch, she stepped into her flip-flops. She should've brought the card table and chairs in right after Miguel left, but if she was lucky she could still beat the rain.

From the top of the stairs, she heard her mother's voice in the living room. Grace assumed she was on the phone, but then she heard someone else.

"Thank you, I'm glad you understand."

It was a young woman's voice. Vaguely familiar.

After hesitating near the bottom of the stairs, Grace decided it was best to give Jackie her privacy—grateful for her mother's good behavior during her picnic—and took the dining room route to the back door. A distant rumble of thunder reminded her that her mission was time sensitive.

"Gray?" Her mother drew the word out, making it two syllables. Her tone was both a warning and a rebuke, uttered the way Miguel spoke to Coco when the cat looked ready to dig her claws into the furniture.

Grace stopped, rattled. Why would her mother reprimand her while a stranger was in the house? Grace felt like a child about to get in trouble. She looked at Miguel's vibrant new painting, as if it had advice to offer. Maybe she should just dart out the back door and not respond to her mother's summons.

In the silence, she felt them waiting for her—Jackie and the young woman with the vaguely familiar voice. Grace sighed. Her mission diverted, and her curiosity piqued, she went to the living room.

Jackie was sitting on the IKEA chair, which she'd moved closer to the sofa and the proximity of her guest. The woman looked very young indeed, a teenager, and in her arms was an unmistakable bundle: a blanket-swaddled infant.

"I'm very disappointed with you, Grace."

Her mother's tone was even more severe than before. Grace didn't like the way it made her coccyx burn, and even without the details she knew she'd done something truly awful. But what? She looked to the young woman, certain she was part of the answer, but the girl gazed down at her baby and wouldn't meet Grace's eyes. The baby's face was hidden from Grace's view by the blanket. It struck her that the infant was utterly silent and the girl wasn't rocking or coddling it, just . . . gazing.

"What's wrong?" Grace asked, a generic inquiry directed at everyone.

A flash of light strobed the room, followed several seconds later by a rolling cascade of thunder. For an instant she was in an animated world where lightning was like an x-ray, making cartoon skeletons of her mother and the girl and the baby. Grace didn't want to be in this room with these people. Even getting trapped outside in a storm would be less punishing than this strange fellowship.

"Surely you remember Bethany." Jackie made a formal gesture with her hand, forcing Grace to look again at the girl on the sofa.

Bethany. A vaguely familiar name.

"I remember *you*, Paxton." Bethany made daggers of the words.

Paxton. That was a name Grace hadn't used for many years.

Bethany. Paxton.

Oh fuck.

How had Bethany unearthed her identity and found out where she lived?

"How could you tell this girl to do such a horrible thing?" Jackie asked. She and Bethany were both scrutinizing her now, with cold, unforgiving expressions. But her mother's question wasn't rhetorical, and they waited for Grace to answer.

Grace didn't remember, off the top of her head, the details of Bethany's life. She might still have Paxton's notebook, stashed in the basement with a box of other old things, but she could hardly excuse herself to go look. Suddenly she knew what it felt like to stand before an inquisition. And she couldn't even defend herself without knowing the charges.

"I'm sorry about . . . whatever—"

"What*ever*?" Jackie cut her off with a snarl. "Look what you did!"

Bethany peeled away the blanket and held her baby out for Grace to see.

It was stiff. Mangled. Its limbs askew like a poorly put together doll. Did the pale-blue blanket mean it was a boy? Its skin was blackening with rot.

"Why?" Bethany begged, shaking the corpse of her child for emphasis.

The shaking ruptured something. Dark-cherry blood gushed from a tear in the dead baby's skin. Now Bethany bounced the child, shushing its silent cries as she tucked the blanket back into place. Blood seeped through, dripping onto Bethany's lap and Grace's sofa.

"I didn't do that!" Grace lost control of a trickle of urine. She'd never been more horrified. "How could you think I—"

"You didn't advise this young girl to kill her baby?" her mother, the Inquisitor, demanded.

"Of course not!" What they were suggesting was obscene. Why—how—could they think Grace capable of such—

Oh. Now she remembered.

Bethany had been sixteen. (Though Paxton hadn't known that at first.) Bethany's boyfriend had already dumped her. Her parents were very religious, and she was afraid to tell them she was pregnant.

"I didn't tell her to . . . I advised her. Of the option of terminating the . . ." Grace shook her head. Had Bethany lied about more than her age? Paxton had reassured her that, at eight weeks, the embryo was a mindless mass of dividing cells. Had he—she—unknowingly presented the option to abort a viable baby?

"No!" Grace was suddenly furious. They had no right to think such repugnant things about her. "She was young, and alone. I was trying to give her reasonable advice, considering her situation."

"Telling someone to kill their child is never *reasonable* advice. I'm ashamed of you."

Grace wanted out—out of the room, out of the dream. She knew that's what it was, but recognizing the reality of it wasn't enough to end the scene. Half expecting a crack to form in the room somewhere, fracturing the nightmare enough so she could leave it, she gazed frantically around.

"Wake up!" she yelled.

Bethany laughed. It was an annoying, braying, too-loud sound. Grace tried to cover her ears, but her arms wouldn't move. And now that she was ready to run, her legs were frozen too.

"Wake up!" she screamed again. Her jaw still worked, and her eyes were able to dart around. She felt like an animal at a slaughterhouse, aware of a terrible danger but unable to escape it. The warm wetness between her legs spread. Tears streamed down her cheeks and she looked to her mother. "Please. Help me."

"Oh Grace." Jackie sounded so weary and defeated. "The way out is so *easy*. Just open your eyes."

22

Grace woke up kicking, bursting free from paralysis. Her throat was full of the profanity she wanted to spew at Jackie and Bethany, at their horrid interpretation of the very reasonable advice she'd once offered a teenager in trouble. Of course it wasn't lost on her that the nightmare could have been her own subconscious guilt. As with many things, offering the words was easier than following the actions. Would she have been able to go through with an abortion had she gotten pregnant as a teen? Like Bethany, she wouldn't have viewed her mother as a safe place to land.

Then it hit her. The wetness between her legs was real. She started to turn the curses on herself, disgusted that she could lose control of her bladder while dreaming. But when she pushed aside the sheet, it was blood between her legs.

"Fuck."

Her skin ignited with goose bumps and she shivered, overcome by paranoia. What if, instead of subconscious guilt, the dream had been an act of revenge? *From who?* Aside from worrying about where she stood with Miguel, the possibility of being pregnant hadn't been a bad thing exactly. Unexpected and confusing, but thrilling in its own fortuitous way. She knew this was simply her period coming on—staining the sheets in a way that hadn't happened since she was a teen—but it felt like . . . a termination. The place inside her where the blood had been felt empty.

What if the dream meant she'd never be able to have a baby, because of the counsel she'd once given while pretending to be someone else?

She rolled out of bed and stripped the mattress, stuffing the sheets into her mesh laundry tote. She left the tote just outside her bedroom so she wouldn't forget to take it downstairs, but before washing the bedding, she wanted to wash herself. The shower fogged with steam as she turned the water as hot as she could stand it, painful but not injurious. *How much would it hurt to be burned alive?* That was how they killed people during the Inquisition. She remembered feeling helpless as her mother, in the dream, made accusations. Grace felt dirty, grimy all the way through to her soul. She squeezed more bodywash onto her shower puff and scrubbed as hard as she could.

———

The shower helped a little, until she was back in her room, where her laptop sat in judgment—a big open eye, a big open mouth—reminding her that clean skin couldn't mask a sullied heart. For the first time in decades, the last thing Grace wanted to do was get online. She quickly put on clean clothes and pulled up her blinds. The sky was the one from her dream, a soft lilac with a blanket of clouds. Was she still asleep, trapped in a time loop? Would she go downstairs and find . . .

She hugged her arms, determined not to think about it. Without evidence to the contrary, she had to accept that it was evening and rain was coming, and she hadn't yet brought in the table and chairs.

As she turned away from the window, an odd sound made her go still. It had the wrong depth to be thunder, yet it had a repetitive thumping. A moment later Jackie cried out.

"Grace?" Her voice wasn't stern, but pitiful. And Grace felt a swell of panic, certain now of what she'd heard: her mother had fallen down the stairs.

Grace sprang for her door and whipped it open. The first thing she saw was her mom in a jumble of twisted fabric on the floor a flight below. The second thing she saw was her laundry tote, a tumbled heap at the bottom of the stairs.

"I'm so sorry!" She flew down the steps. For another instant the dreamworld invaded and she saw in Jackie's pose the disjointed limbs of the dead baby. She fell to her knees beside her mother. "Is anything broken? Are you okay? Do you need me to call nine one one?"

"No need to panic, hon."

"I'm so sorry, I'm just used to leaving my laundry in the hall so I—"

Jackie waved away the rest of her words. "That had nothing to do with it. I was bringing it down and my eyes played a trick on me. Missed a step. I need help getting up though."

Grace didn't quite believe that her mother was okay, but Jackie extended her hands, and Grace helped pull her to her feet. Jackie winced.

"Might've twisted my ankle."

With one arm around her mother's waist, Grace supported Jackie as she hobbled into the living room. The second Jackie was seated on the couch, Grace gently lifted her feet so she could lie down.

"Are you sure you're okay? I have this bad habit of forgetting to do my laundry unless I leave it out somewhere where I can see it, but I didn't mean for you to carry—"

"I'm fine, it's my fault, I feel stupid. My vision gets a little fuzzy sometimes, and I know better. It can be hard for me to gauge . . . depth, on stairs 'n' things. But it was just a soft hamper and it wasn't heavy and I wanted to give you a hand."

Grace sat near her mother's feet and took a second to catch her breath. They were both talking too fast, fueled on by the fear of a close call. "Do you feel dizzy? Did you hit your head?"

"No, no. I feel fine now."

"Can I get you an ice pack? For your ankle?"

"That might be a good idea." But Jackie hesitated. "Maybe . . ."

"What?"

"I don't want to be a bother, but . . . if I'm gonna lie down, I might as well settle in for the night. Maybe you could help me get upstairs?"

"Of course."

If Grace had been stronger she would've picked her mother up in her arms and carried her. *Like we used to carry Hope when there wasn't a ramp for her wheelchair.*

Grace understood better than ever why she'd spent so little time with Jackie over the years: her mother triggered memories. As she helped Jackie back onto her feet, Grace noticed a spot of blood near where her mother's head had been resting on a cushion.

"Are you bleeding?"

"Am I?" Jackie started patting her skull while Grace examined it more carefully, parting her short hair to look for blood.

"I don't see anything."

"Nothing feels swollen, except my ankle."

That should've been reassuring, except for the other harrowing possibility: the spot of blood could have been someone else's—Bethany had been sitting there, with her broken baby.

No, that was a dream.

"Gray? You okay?"

"Yeah," she murmured. But she wasn't okay. Every passing hour made her more untrusting of the solidity of the world, of time and space.

Side by side in the tight stairwell, Grace let her mom use her like a crutch—one hand gripped the handrail, and the other clung to Grace's shoulder—so Jackie could keep the weight off her sore foot. Slowly, they worked their way up the stairs. Grace spent the following ten minutes darting up and down, getting the ice pack, a large tumbler of water, an apple, a couple of ibuprofen, and finally, a deck of cards so Jackie could play solitaire on the bed.

Oh yes, this was the mother Grace remembered—quick to bark orders, unwilling to slow down to think about the full inventory of things she might need. Grace wasn't ten anymore, and she didn't love running up and down the stairs, especially when Jackie seemed to take it as a challenge every time Grace asked, "Do you need anything else?"

———

When Jackie was finally settled, Grace grabbed her phone from her room and headed downstairs for a quiet evening in front of the TV. Five seconds after she clicked on Netflix, an explosion of thunder nearly made her scream.

"Goddammit." That's when she remembered she'd forgotten to get the table and chairs.

She leaped from the sofa and hurried out the back door. The imminent storm added a tinge of green to the gloaming sky. The first beads of rain struck as Grace shuffled back to the house, hauling a chair under each arm.

Instead of dashing back out for the table, she stood in the open doorway. The rain was coming down harder, but that wasn't what made her hesitate. The light outside was eerie—dark and bright at the same time. Grace usually wasn't afraid of storms, but this one seemed different. She could imagine a monster hiding behind the curtain of clouds, sneaking along, camouflaged, waiting for the right moment to drop down from the sky.

"Fuck it." She burst out and ran across the yard. The grass was wet and slippery, and she almost went down in a split. By the time she got the table's legs all folded, she was drenched. It was a stupid rescue mission and there was no point in hurrying back.

What a weird day. She locked the back door and stood in her kitchen for a minute, dripping rainwater. And then the dream came back, and she half expected to see a puddle of blood at her feet. Wait—which dream was that? The dream where she'd been pregnant and lost the baby? The dream where an already-dead infant cried silently as its skin split apart?

Unsure of a hundred shadowy images, the sticky raw dough of nightmares and daydreams merged together.

Grace wasn't a big solo drinker, but she regretted not having replaced the wine from her dinner with Miguel. Maybe there was a little of the brandy left that she kept on hand to make hot toddies. The binge-watching would be better with a bit of alcohol. But first she needed to wipe off the card table. And start the laundry. And change into dry clothes. She snapped her fingers, inspired, and bustled through the dining room to grab the mesh tote: she'd use the stain-free top sheet to mop up the water. Then lug everything to the basement. So much hassle for what had been meant as a relaxing evening.

Netflix was cycling through its screen saver images by the time Grace got back to it. With the bedding in the wash, the kitchen floor more or less puddle-free, Grace comfy in an oversize T-shirt—and her mom asleep—she curled up on the couch, gripping a tumbler with the last few fingers of brandy. She didn't usually drink it straight, but needs must (as they say). At least one thing had sorted itself out, and maybe her periods would always be janky now. Maybe she was in perimenopause, the clock ticking faster, entering a future of deteriorating hormones.

Just as she reached for the TV remote, her phone rang.

The temptation to not answer it was strong. But Allison was technically her boss now, which made it harder to ignore her glowing name.

"Hey Allison."

"So sorry to call at such a weird time."

"That's okay."

"We've had two stylists cancel for tomorrow, and Saturdays are usually busy for walk-ins. I know it's last minute, but I was hoping you could work?" Allison sounded so hopeful.

Grace wavered. She needed the hours and missed spending her days in a salon. Under any other circumstances, she would've jumped at the opportunity, but . . .

"My mom fell this evening. I'm not sure how she's going to feel tomorrow, if she's going to need help—"

"No problem, I understand."

"I'm really sorry. I can maybe give you a call in the morning if it seems like she'll be okay on her own?"

Allison reiterated that it wasn't a problem but then couldn't get off the phone fast enough to call someone else. Grace felt like crap; she hated disappointing people, and being available at the last minute could've earned her some bonus points after her rocky first day. She took a sip of the brandy; it went down warm and spiky, like she'd swallowed a tendril of sunshine. A yummy but slightly poisonous tendril.

Rain pelted the back windows. Finally able to relax, she was glad to be inside the cozy comfort of her house. She flipped through her queue until she found the show she wanted to watch. Just as the intro started, it abruptly winked out—along with every other light and appliance in the house. Grace rolled her eyes. And waited. She expected—hoped— the electricity would come back on momentarily.

The darkness swallowed everything. The darkness was infinite, and Grace sat there, unsure what to do.

23

Grace awakened to the sound of a jackhammer . . . no, a vacuum cleaner? It took her a minute to orient herself, the when and where and why. Then she understood the racket was the blender (the juicer?) and she'd spent another night in the living room, comforted by the talking night-light—also known as her television.

A few days ago she'd been concerned that her Saturday would be spent ferrying things up and down the stairs for her mother. In fact, Jackie had been bright eyed and bushy tailed, glib about the healing properties of spinach and eight hours of sleep, and it was Grace who hadn't felt well. Miguel had dropped off the Nighty Night tea as promised—and a quart of hot and sour soup—and Grace had accepted the lethargy as a temporary situation, a physical reminder that she hadn't had an untroubled night of sleep since her mother's arrival.

As the lazy Saturday turned into a lazy Sunday, Grace heard River, a smashingly handsome alter ego, in her head. *You deserve it, the downtime will be restorative, you'll be good as new.* But here she was on Monday morning, still on the couch, and the bright light indicated that it might be closer to noon. Her eyebrows felt bruised, the lingering evidence of the headache that just wouldn't go away. A pocket of pain gurgled in her stomach and she remembered her mother warning her to take it easy with the ibuprofen or her intestines were going to bleed.

She tilted her body into a sitting position, as stiff as if she were encased in plaster. A groan escaped her mouth and she shut her eyes, pressing her thumb and middle finger against her eyebrows, trying to loosen the ache.

The grinding noise stopped, but Grace knew the routine. Jackie would flutter in in another forty seconds, offering solutions by way of the "earth's bountiful harvest!" Grace didn't have the energy to charge upstairs before her mother arrived with a fresh glass of pulverized vegetables. Grace had spent the majority of her daylight hours holed up in her bedroom on the computer, but the nights were more tolerable with the TV lullaby and the kitchen near at hand; she was always thirsty. The consequence of sleeping downstairs—out in the open—meant she was more vulnerable to her mother's mothering, and it didn't seem fair that Jackie was on a trajectory of good health while Grace was on the decline.

"Any better this morning, hon?"

"Maybe," Grace lied, forcing herself to stand. Jackie held out her basil-green concoction. "Thanks, but I'm gonna start with water. And take a shower."

"You sure? You don't look any better, hon."

"I'll feel better if I don't lie around all day like a useless blob."

"Okay, well let me know if I can fix you something to eat."

"'Kay. Thanks."

Once in the bathroom, Grace stuck her mouth under the faucet and drank savagely. When she caught her reflection in the mirror she was surprised by the face that looked back at her. It was a younger face. With the tousled hair and muddy eyes and defined cheekbones, she could've been looking at herself at twenty-one, hungover from a night out and high on her independence. It was a fortifying thought, at least, even if Grace knew on some level that the reemergence of her cheekbones was a sign of atrophy.

———

Determined not to waste another day, Grace put on half-decent clothes (a step up from the ragged loungewear she'd worn all weekend) and a little makeup. She planned to run errands: stock up on some slightly *less* healthy food (Jackie's weird diet might work for her, but Grace needed more substantial meals), pick up some wine (and maybe a little more brandy), and make a quick stop at Rite Aid (to treat herself to some new cheap cosmetics).

Her head was finally recovering after its weekend mutiny, and the weather was cooperative enough that she thought she might eat breakfast on the porch. Wasn't fresh air a cure-all? She hadn't stepped foot outside in days—since her picnic brunch with Miguel. Speaking of whom . . .

"Hey lovey." She answered the FaceTime call and headed for her closet, in search of the wedge heel sandals she'd gotten on sale last fall and had almost forgotten about.

"Are you going out?" Miguel asked.

"That was the plan. Ooh, found them!" She held up the sandals for Miguel to see.

"Cute! New?"

"Newish. Haven't worn them yet." She sat on her bed to fasten them on.

"I'm glad you're feeling better, and I don't mean to rain on your parade, lovey, but I have some news and we need to have a little talk."

Grace had an instant twinge of worry and stopped what she was doing to give Miguel her undivided attention. She'd been trying to force herself into a productive, all-better-now sort of day but his words—his tone—made her feel like a bumblebee who'd lost her buzz.

"Are you okay?" She really wanted to ask if she'd done something wrong, as that was almost the greater concern. *What did you fuck up now, Grace?*

"Yes . . ." But the word was a lie.

"What's wrong?"

He was sitting at his kitchen table and Coco walked in front of the camera, a giant orange fur ball. Miguel moved his iPad over, but Grace could still see Coco's tail, undulating like a fishing lure. "I don't want you to freak out," he said.

"Words that never stopped anyone from freaking out." Moments ago Grace had been ready to go, but now the weariness was returning. Her thighs fused to the mattress; she couldn't get up even if she wanted to.

"Seriously, there's nothing to panic about." *Oh God.* "But Carolina's maid of honor tested positive, and she's been hospitalized."

Grace just gazed at Miguel, blinking, stupefied. They were common words, words she heard every time she turned on the news—*hospital, test, positive*—but they'd never been applied to her own circle, or extended circle, of friends.

"Is she okay?" Grace asked. "She's young, isn't she? Carolina's age?"

"Yes, thirty. But . . . it sounds serious."

Grace recalled more words: *next wave, mutations, variants. "Fuck."*

Miguel nodded, as somber as she'd ever seen him. "I'm so sorry, Grace. I should've worn a mask when I was over."

It took her a second to grasp what he was saying. "Are you sick?"

"No, but I was around her for days—I could easily have been exposed. And even with having the wedding outside . . . we were in and out, not really social distancing, only wearing masks in the car or in public. We all have to self-isolate for two weeks—and you should too. I'm so sorry."

Grace sat there with one shoe on, one shoe off, rewinding the conversation in her head. It was simple enough yet still didn't make sense. "Is this a dream?" she mumbled.

"No, sorry, you're not sleepwalking. I know it sucks—I called my doctor and she said that if I don't have any symptoms I should just stay home. I asked about getting tested, and she said I'm not an *Essential Worker*. How's that for a kick in the face?"

"We have to stay home for two weeks?" The reality was starting to sink in. No going out for groceries or wine or to get some fresh air away from her mother. She'd done this before, of course, a few months earlier, but life was just starting to get back to normal.

"We were outside most of the time, so you're probably fine. But if you get any symptoms, call your doctor. Sophia's really sick, I guess; we're waiting to hear about her immediate family. And I'm sorry Grace, but Miss Jacquelyn should stay in too. I didn't see that much of her, but you're—"

"Around her all the time," said Grace, finishing his sentence. "Fuck."

They gazed at each other on their small screens. It wasn't Miguel's fault, and she wasn't mad at him. Grace had been all too eager to have company and socialize. She winced, thinking about the call she'd have to make to Allison.

"Are you gonna be okay?" she asked him. Neither of them had the sturdiest of financial foundations, but at least Grace was sharing expenses with a roommate—though Coco was probably more companionable.

"Yeah. Might be able to go back on unemployment for a couple weeks."

"Yeah."

"You gonna be okay?" he asked.

"We'll manage." She gave him a tired smile. "Well, let's check in every day, okay?"

"Yes, absolutely. Self-isolation buddies."

"Keep me posted. Love you."

"Will do." He blew her a kiss.

She tossed the phone onto the bed. Now she was dressed up with nowhere to go. Slowly, she unbuckled the one sandal and dropped the pair back into her closet. She couldn't tell Miguel the doubt she was really feeling—not without guilt-tripping him—about being trapped in the house with her mother for two weeks. Jackie had been there less than three weeks. Grace wasn't sure she could handle a nearly equivalent period of confinement with her, especially while not being mentally or physically at her best.

In a flash of paranoia, she took an inventory of her symptoms . . . But on second thought, her ailment couldn't have come from Miguel because she'd seen him just hours before the headache and lethargy started. The incubation period was longer than that.

She trudged downstairs, cursed as too much milk sloshed into her bowl of cereal, and went outside to sit on the porch step and mope. While she ate, she brought up the grocery store app on her phone and started piling things into her virtual cart. The first delivery time she could get was early the next afternoon.

The street felt oddly deserted. She surveyed the motley group of shoulder-to-shoulder houses, contemplating what they revealed about the people within. The overstuffed flower box drooping from a window. The pastel Easter pendant, as resilient as a fake Christmas tree. Black-and-gold banners for one, or all, of the local sports teams. Political yard signs. A tiny overturned pink-and-purple bicycle in the middle of a lawn. Farther up the street, someone had half-assed a wheelchair ramp out of mismatched pieces of old plywood. It immediately reminded her of Hope.

There were more parked cars than cars on the road. Other people were staying home, too, she supposed. Some had probably lost their jobs. Grace hadn't experienced the neighborhood prior to the country shutting down. Had it been a happier place then? It was some comfort to recognize that everyone was in the same boat. Even as she saw the boat taking on water. It wasn't like the movies, where the world ended quickly in a maelstrom of explosions and special effects. This apocalypse was going to linger, tease them along with its slow-motion crises. Already she'd let boredom make her less vigilant. Did she have it in her to self-isolate better this time?

Grace snorted, laughing at herself, imagining her house filling up with a menagerie of deliveries as she and her mom made impulsive purchases, forever in search of the thing that would make them feel less empty.

24

"Did you get all of them? From upstairs too?" Mommy asked, as snappish as she'd been all evening.

"Yes." The laundry basket was heavy, full of towels that smelled like piss and puke. Grace headed for the basement.

"Are you blind as a bat?" Grace turned toward her mother's bitter voice. Watched her snatch a handful of dish towels off the kitchen counter and jam them into the laundry basket. "*Hot* water. Heavy duty."

"I know," Grace said, trying not to sound petulant.

"You know but you don't pay attention."

Grace descended the basement stairs, the gloom and spiders a reprieve from her mother's bad mood. She considered how much better it would be if she *were* a bat, able to fly and see the world through the pings and vibrations bouncing off her ears. She'd learned about sonar in school—SOund NAvigation and Ranging—and how it was first invented to detect icebergs. She and Hope had once watched a really good movie about a submarine that was trying to hide, while above it a ship lobbed bullets of sound through the deep water. The movie was so tense that she'd watched it while clutching her knees to her chest, her elbows to her ribs, amazed that a simple *sound* could pose such a threat. When it was over, her muscles ached and she understood for a moment what it was like to be her sister.

Before she'd even stuffed all the stinky towels into the washer, she heard her mother impatiently calling for her. Grace wasn't sure what to do: she couldn't abandon the load before starting the washer, but if she didn't reply, that would make Mommy mad too.

Mommy called again just as Grace let the lid fall shut. She leaped across a puddle on the basement's concrete floor and dashed up the steps two by two.

"Gray!" It was the third summons. *Three strikes, you're out.* The curtain to Hope's bedroom was tied back for easy access, and Grace skidded to a halt at the entryway, breathing hard. Mommy gave her a look. A look like a bad word that she couldn't be bothered to utter. She handed Grace a plastic cup with a straw in one hand, a wet washcloth in the other. "Cold water."

Hope had a fever. She'd choked while eating her supper and thrown up everywhere. Before heading to the kitchen Grace made a funny face at Hope, who grinned a reply. Grace knew she was lucky that she never got sick. In TV shows the TV mommies sat by their sick children and spoke sweet words or sang little songs while stroking their hair. When Hope was sick Mommy turned into a wolf and Grace felt like Little Red Riding Hood, about to be gobbled up; Hope probably didn't like it much either.

———

With the volume barely audible, Grace watched a sitcom as she folded socks, underpants, short-sleeve shirts. She hadn't finished her homework, but Mommy wasn't going to tell her to do it, and Grace had better things to do. The mommy-cat chair gave her a hug, and the truth was she liked folding laundry. It was warm and always smiled nice.

Mommy shuffled into the room and collapsed on the couch, eyes on the television. "Put those away when you're done?" Grace nodded. "And finish the towels?" Grace nodded again.

The show was ending and Mommy flipped to a different channel and raised the volume a bit. "Your sister's resting now. I think she'll be okay."

Grace had been through this enough times to decipher Mommy's code. *I think she'll be okay* was short for *I probably won't have to take Hope to the doctor*. Taking Hope to the doctor was expensive. And usually they just ran a bunch of pointless, overpriced tests. Going to the doctor was for *emergencies*, not a routine fever, flu, or cold. Grace had only been to a doctor when her school required it. She'd get a shot and a sticker and sit very still while someone listened to her heart.

The clothes folded, she glanced at Mommy just as a soft snore grumbled from her open mouth. She slept with her legs straight, arms at her side. Her head was slightly crooked on the cushion, like her neck was broken. The towels wouldn't be finished in the washer for a while yet, so Grace tiptoed to Hope's room.

Hope was asleep, too, propped up against three pillows so her upper body was at an angle. Grace crept onto the bed and kitten-walked on her hands and knees, as delicately as she could, until she was beside her sister. Very gently she laid her ear on Hope's chest and listened to her heart. It *thu-thumped* in a steady rhythm, as reassuring as a load tumbling in the dryer. Hope giggled.

"Your hair tickles."

Grace giggled too, and leaned against the wall, squished up in the corner of the bed.

"I'm bored," Hope said. "Tell me about your dreams."

"I don't remember them."

"Not that kind. The kind you dream up when you're awake."

Grace looked at the ceiling, searching for something she could say that wouldn't sound mean. Sometimes she fantasized about being adopted and having a new mommy, a daddy, and maybe a big brother. In her imagination she'd tried out all sorts of scenarios with various new families, and they were all better than the one she had.

"Well, I read this book," she said, finding something safe to share, "about this school for girls, a boarding school, and the dormitory was in a haunted mansion. The teachers didn't believe it, so the girls had to stay up until midnight and try to talk to the ghost to figure out what it wanted." Grace saw it in her head, the girls in their white nightgowns, tiptoeing through the darkened halls. "I'd like to go to boarding school."

Hope laughed. "That's your dream? To live in a haunted house?"

No, Grace's dream was to live somewhere *else*, and if it happened to be haunted, well . . .

She didn't care if Hope thought it was silly. Girls in stories like that always had lots of adventures.

"Your turn." She gave Hope a playful poke.

"I have big dreams. Don't laugh—promise you won't?"

"Like you didn't laugh at mine?"

Hope's face contorted, and Grace recognized the expression as remorse. "Sorry."

"I promise I won't laugh." Grace was more curious than ever to know what rolled around in her sister's head.

"Okay, so I like to imagine I'm in the Olympics. And sometimes I'm a swimmer, sometimes a skier, sometimes I'm riding a horse or a bicycle. I go very fast, like I'm flying."

That made sense to Grace. She liked to watch the Olympics too, and marveled at how strong and graceful the athletes were. They had abilities that neither Grace nor her sister would ever have, and she understood why Hope might fantasize about it.

"And I also imagine I'm a famous singer, with fabulous clothes— better than Mona and Rona. And I sing on a stage in front of thousands of people, and they clap and cheer. And everyone knows who I am wherever I go and asks for my autograph."

It took Hope a long time to get all the words out, and while Grace appreciated that the fantasies were important to Hope, Grace thought they were pretty boring. Her sister just wanted to be better than everyone else. She wanted people to worship her. Grace reached across her and plucked the washcloth from the bedside table. She wiped a stream of spittle from Hope's chin. For a minute neither of them spoke.

"You don't like my dreams?" Hope asked, wounded.

Grace shrugged. "They're okay. But everyone thinks about stuff like that. I thought you'd think about something more original."

Hope started coughing and Grace helped her lean forward, in case she choked or vomited. But it subsided, and she was fine.

"Well, there is another thing I dream about, but I didn't want to scare you."

Grace grinned. This was more like what she'd expected, something weird, like Hope.

"It's going to sound like a night dream, not a daydream," Hope warned. "But there's a very special reason why I think about it when I'm awake. Ready?" Grace nodded. "You ever have those dreams at night where you're floating, and you float up to the ceiling, or float around the house?"

Grace nodded. Those dreams always made her a little uneasy. They were fascinating because she really got the sensation of what it would feel like to drift through the air. But they were troubling, too, because she was never fully in control. Sometimes the dreams carried her to places she didn't want to go, where it was dreary and cold.

"When I think about the floating dreams," Hope shut her eyes, "really concentrate, I can feel it just like when I'm asleep."

As Grace watched, Hope floated up from the bed. Her limbs were limp and relaxed, and the sheet and blankets dropped away as she rose higher and higher. She hung suspended near the ceiling, her eyes shut in concentration, a pleased smile on her face.

Though Grace wasn't the one levitating, she felt as if she'd been transported to the chilly depths of a nightmare. She wanted to tell her sister to come down, to get back into bed, but her mouth wouldn't work and Hope kept drifting—like a balloon caught in a breeze—across the room and through the archway.

The words *Come back!* howled in Grace's head; she was too afraid to follow her sister.

"Grace!" Mommy sounded super angry, but Grace was less afraid of her than of Hope's new magical powers. Her muscles came back to life, and she sprang from the bed.

When Grace got to the living room Mommy was standing at the front door, which stood wide open. Grace scurried to her side, and together they watched Hope, giggling, sailing up, up, and away into the sky. She cleared the top of a mighty oak tree and kept floating farther away, her thin pajamas aglow against the black moonless sky.

"Hope!" her mother called. The night swallowed her cry, yet Hope's laughter wafted down to them.

It was sad watching her sister drift away, and a tiny bit scary, but Grace knew Hope was feeling happy and free.

"Bye!" Grace waved.

"What's wrong with you?" Mommy turned on her, snatching her shirt beneath her throat. Grace gagged, struggling to breathe. Her mother's snout curled in hate, revealing a wolf's sharp fangs. "I was counting on you! You promised me you were reliable! How could you let me down like this?"

Should Grace have done more? To keep her sister from slipping away?

25

"That one's just too easy," said Miguel, crunching a bowl of granola on the screen of Grace's laptop. "Isn't that exactly what Allison said to you?"

"Pretty much." Grace sipped her coffee. The words had actually hurt more coming from Allison than dream Mommy. When Grace called to tell her about needing to quarantine for two weeks she'd expected Allison to be understanding, even if disappointed, given the new world norm. Grace hadn't anticipated that Allison would go full mean boss and say, without apologizing, "This isn't working out." Now Grace didn't have a job to return to. Every time she thought this year couldn't get any worse, fate lumbered in like a tipsy Hold My Beer meme. It was getting old.

"I think your dreams are trying to do you a favor, processing all the shit you're going through."

"Maybe." Grace lifted her foot onto her desk chair. Her toenails looked gross. Uneven and dirty. "I need a pedicure."

"Don't we all." Coco meowed on screen, pushing her nose toward Miguel's yogurt. "What are you gonna do today?"

Grace shrugged. It wasn't like the first time when everyone had gone into lockdown at the same time. Then it had seemed okay—almost like a communal activity—to watch garbage TV all day and fret about the future. No one understood then what was happening or how long it would go on. There was a lot they still didn't know, but

Grace had already maxed out on isolation and boredom; she dreaded having a witness to her bad habits this time around. Jackie had taken the news of the loss of Grace's job and their need to stay home together with stoic resolve.

"Everyone restarted too soon," Jackie had said. "No one wants to follow the rules."

The rules were barbaric. Avoiding everyone who wasn't in your immediate household. Letting businesses die. The people who delivered all their stuff had to keep working so everyone else could stay home. And the medical staff still had to help the sick, even when their sicknesses could have been avoided with a little common sense. Meanwhile, people canceled their cancer treatments and stopped doing the things that had once kept them sane.

Grace knew she was in this predicament because she'd been too eager, too desperate to have some kind of normal fucking social life.

As if reading her thoughts, Miguel said, "I'll be more diligent this time, about wearing a mask."

"Me too. It's hard to know what to do when the thing you're afraid of is invisible. And you never saw it arrive, so how do you know when it's gone?"

Miguel nodded.

"So what are you up to, to pass the time?"

"I'm looking for some new hobbies." His demeanor brightened, and Grace realized her lassitude had been bringing him down. "They can't be expensive hobbies, as I have to watch my pennies. So no home redecorating or filling the apartment with houseplants—Coco would probably destroy them anyway. I'm thinking of maybe baking or cooking? At least those are semipractical and I can literally eat the expense."

Grace laughed. But she was reminded of the previous night's dream and her conversation with Hope, her assumptions that her sister would have less ordinary fantasies. In a similar way she expected Miguel to desire more exotic hobbies.

"Or maybe I'll get serious about my dating profile and really try to build a connection with someone," he said. "Maybe it's easier to start a relationship now, with fewer distractions. And don't say—"

Of course Grace thought online relationships were beneath the dignity of someone as good as Miguel, but she skirted the subject. "You could focus on your painting? Or . . . lots of places are putting classes online, cheap, available to everyone."

"You mean, follow through on one of those interests I bring up from time to time?"

"Exactly."

"Oh Grace, don't you know I only bring those up to sound like an engaging, well-rounded person? I really am a cat dad who just wants to eat cupcakes—I don't even want to *make* them, let's be real."

Grace burst out laughing. "I love you, lovey."

"I know you do." He blew her a kiss.

"You know, I'm thinking that after I've served my time I might look into being a delivery driver."

"Like DoorDash or something?"

"Exactly. That's where it's at now, everyone with money wants everything on their doorstep."

"That's a good thought." Finally he let Coco clean the bowl. She pushed it across the table with her nose as she licked it. "But just until you can find a salon worthy of your skill."

"Of course. Have you ever considered . . ." She hesitated to ask the question because she knew Miguel had never voiced wanting to start his own salon and bringing it up now would make it sound like she wanted him to help solve her future employment problem. Before she could find a tactful approach—merely inquisitive—Miguel started coughing.

At first Grace thought the audio on her laptop had gone wonky—a delay, an echo—because she heard the coughing in stereo. Then she realized that Jackie was coughing too, audible through Grace's closed bedroom door.

"Are you okay?" Grace's headache threatened to come back, a throbbing alarm against the inside of her skull.

Miguel took a sip of water. "Yeah, just feel a little tight in my chest."

"Shit Miguel, that's a symptom!"

"It's nothing—"

"It's not nothing."

"I'll keep an eye on it." They gazed at each other on their screens. Intense. Worried. "I feel fine."

Grace glanced toward her door. "I think I should check on my mom. Please call me if you feel even a little bit sick, okay? Call if you need *anything*, promise?"

"Promise."

They waved and exchanged air-kisses and closed their laptops.

———

She found Jackie on the sofa, snuggling a blanket and absorbed in a black-and-white sitcom. Grace had hurried down because she was concerned, but seeing her mother comfortable on the couch—exactly where Grace wanted to be, sulking over her horrible life—brought a sting of annoyance. The TV show was perky and ridiculous, about a housewife who could twitch her nose and alter the space-time continuum.

"I heard you coughing. Are you all right?" Grace hoped she sounded urgent and not short tempered.

"Fine, hon. Some water went down the wrong way."

Grace nodded and passed through the room. When she reached the kitchen she exhaled, a great gust that depleted her lungs and had her leaning on the counter for support. Stress was getting to her. What if Miguel was sick? What if Grace was infected, the virus readying its war on her body? And Jackie's too? She started pacing, frantic.

What if they were all going to get it eventually, even all the doctors and nurses? And delivery drivers! What if the hospitals filled up or there weren't enough supplies? What about the people all over the world, cogs in the supply chain? How many holes—absent workers—could the system take before it stopped running?

It wasn't a joking cliché anymore: she was going to lose her mind. She was spending less and less time with her damsels because her aliases were running out of reasonable advice—because Grace was running out of rational things to tell herself. Without the escape of cyberspace, she needed somewhere real to go, but where? As tempting as it was to hop in the car and start driving, it seemed wrong to abandon her mother. Grace marched back into the living room.

"Hey. I need to get out. Feeling a little claustrophobic. Do you want to go to the park? Take a little walk?"

Jackie grinned, putting the TV on mute. "It would be nice to get out for a while. Funny how it doesn't seem so necessary when you can do it whenever you want. But as soon as they say, 'Stay home!' then you think of all the things you can't do."

"Schenley Park is really close."

Jackie swung her feet off the sofa and bent down to massage her ankle. "That sounds lovely, but I'm not sure how much walking I can do. Still a little tender sometimes."

Some of the trails in the park were uneven or steep. It wouldn't be the safest place to take her mother—all the more so for how crowded it might be if everyone had the same idea. Another possibility came to mind: Allegheny Cemetery had lots of paved paths. It was pleasant there this time of year, green and lush, almost like a park—if one overlooked the headstones and mausoleums. It was also where Hope was buried.

Maybe she was overdue for a visit to her sister's grave. Perhaps it would put an end to the nightmares.

"We could go to the cemetery," Grace said softly.

Jackie's head jerked up, and she met Grace's eyes. "If you want to." She sounded cautious. "It would be nice."

"Okay, it's a plan. Let me just run upstairs and—"

"Grab my walking shoes from the closet?" Jackie asked as Grace headed for the stairs. "They're on the floor, on top of some boxes."

"Sure." Grace knew exactly where they were, having snooped in her mother's room. The prospect of an outing put a bounce in her step.

26

If Grace had been thinking of taking up walking as a new form of exercise, she soon realized she'd have to do it without her mother. She hadn't parked far from Hope's grave, so Jackie could enjoy at least a short stroll, but to stay at her side Grace had to move in slow motion. It wasn't at all obvious why Jackie needed special shoes to perambulate at their current pace, though the trip to her closet had reminded Grace that she hadn't solved the mystery of the little locked box.

"This really is a lovely place," said Jackie.

Grace heard the exertion in her mother's breath and wondered again about the illness that had killed Robert and sent Jackie to the hospital and then "home" to Pittsburgh. Robert had first fallen ill months before the pandemic. Grace didn't know what all his symptoms were, but Jackie's labored breathing, on such a gently rising slope, could be an indicator of lung damage. Could she have previously been exposed to the virus? In a parallel universe, Grace might suggest her mother get a chest x-ray. But with the surge in cases, the county had issued new precautions and Grace assumed every medical center was swamped—and probably the last place a reasonably healthy person should go.

"Do you want to take my arm?" Grace switched the blanket she was carrying to the other side and offered her mom her elbow.

"Thanks, hon. Not as fit as I used to be."

When it was time to leave, Grace might want to run ahead and get the car and come back to pick her up. For now, slowly guiding Jackie along, Grace took in the rolling hills and lofty trees, the stately grounds of the huge Victorian cemetery. The birds sang their merry songs, making the ambiance much more about life than death.

"It really is beautiful here," Grace said, almost as if she'd never noticed before.

Their pace slowed even more as they left the paved road and headed across the lawn.

"Almost there," said Grace.

"I remember. I probably should have come home more often, to visit Hope, and you. I'm sorry."

"Don't be sorry. You made a good life for yourself. You deserved that."

Jackie gave her arm a little squeeze. "Thank you, Grace."

The walk had aged Jackie—all the health she'd regained seeped out of her in the fifty yards since she left the car. If Grace had parked any farther away, her mother might have perished before reaching the grave site.

Hope was buried beneath the broad, shady canopy of a yellow buckeye. Grace spread the blanket on the small clearing beside the grave, silently speculating whether someday she or her mother might be buried there. She helped Jackie ease herself down, but Grace stayed on her feet. She took a moment to read her sister's headstone, though she knew exactly what it said. A smirk skated across her face as Grace thought how, if this were a dream, she'd find new words engraved in the granite, a cryptic message from her psyche.

———

Jackie closed her eyes and turned her face skyward, basking in the sunlight that filtered through the leafy boughs. Grace sat on the opposite corner of the blanket. She observed her mother, still unaccustomed to her more petite, more fragile form. When Grace was little, she hadn't thought that she or Hope resembled their mother at all. Daddy—Paul No-Last-Name—had been a blank canvas upon which she could create whoever she wanted. Sometimes Grace had attributed Mommy's anger to the fact that Grace looked so much like her dad—a thing she didn't know to be a fact at all. But she saw the unmistakable similarities now, the familiar averageness in her mother's features.

Perhaps it wasn't the time or the place, but her father was on her mind now: if Grace dug gently, perhaps she could excavate a little more info. The thing she'd always wanted to know was his last name. That would be enough for a Google search, and she trusted in her abilities to get the internet to deliver what she wanted.

"Why didn't you ever talk about our dad? At least tell us who he was?"

Jackie remained so still that Grace thought she'd dozed off. Then her mother sniffled and blinked her eyes a few times.

"He was such a disappointment, Grace." Grace waited for her to say more. Jackie awkwardly repositioned herself, switching from the one hip she'd been leaning on to the other. "Afraid I won't be able to sit like this for long, as lovely out as it is."

"We can go whenever you want." Grace knew she'd wrecked the peaceful mood. Her mother was somber now.

"Paul . . ." Jackie shook her head. "That motherfucker was the love of my life. That's the truth."

The force of her words startled Grace. She hadn't actually expected her mother to open up, but Grace saw Jackie surveying her past, assembling the bones of her story.

———

"We first met in high school. Just friends at first, but friends in the best way. Then there were years apart while we were exploring our options, figuring out how to make adulthood work. Sometimes Paul sent a postcard from wherever he was. California. New Mexico. Florida. We wrote letters and sent each other the occasional Christmas gift. My parents always thought he was a bum, lazy. But Paul just wanted to see everything.

"I didn't wait for him, exactly. I did my thing. Worked; took care of my parents. But maybe . . . maybe part of me did wait, put off getting married, having kids. I had this suspicion, this hunch, that Paul wouldn't come back until after both my parents were dead. They barely let him in the house when we were in high school. Every time I didn't hear from him for months they were sure he was in prison. But he wasn't like that."

A man started to materialize in Grace's mind, a hobo drawn in pencil. He had worn boots and strong hands, a weathered face. When he smiled it was genuine and wise.

"Want to know the worst thing I ever did?"

Grace held her breath and nodded, afraid to speak, afraid to do anything that would make her mother go back inside herself and shut the door.

"After my mother died—she lived for three years after my father's heart attack—I thanked Jesus. My parents were religious. And I actually got on my knees and clasped my hands and thanked Jesus for setting me free."

The implied sorrow of her mother's words—her mother's life—swirled in Grace's head. A tiny part of her thought Jackie had been on the verge of admitting to hastening her mother's death. But they were still revelations: Grace hadn't known that her grandparents had disapproved of her father or that they'd been religious. Or that Jackie had felt liberated once she was out from under them.

"I had to wait. To find out where Paul was. He didn't come back right away—but he came back. I thought that was going to be the beginning of . . ." Tears filmed her mother's eyes; she blinked them away. "We stayed in my parents' house—where you grew up. Paul had picked up various skills along the way. He found a good union job as a machinist. I got pregnant. I was in more of a hurry than he was, but I was going on thirty-three—my friends from high school practically had teenagers by then." Jackie licked her lips, swallowed, her eyes on something far away.

"I mean, things weren't effortless. But Paul seemed happy about becoming a father. I was a happy little homemaker—oh you should've seen me. The late months of my pregnancy was the only time in twenty years when I hadn't had a job. I cooked supper—not great suppers, some kind of meat with a side of potatoes. We ate a *lot* of potatoes. We laughed sometimes about how all of a sudden we were a nuclear family: working dad, stay-at-home mom, two kids—almost.

"We weren't married yet, but we kept talking about it. I guess I did most of the talking. Paul started to get restless. We'd take drives on the weekends. Long drives to nowhere. Through small towns. It was nice, seeing all those little places. Haven't thought about that in a long time. He tried. I give him credit for trying. But in the end . . ." Jackie slowly let out her breath. "I was so mad. I hated him, except that I still loved him. I fucking hated him and I fucking loved him."

Grace had always known her father had skipped out on the family, but it hadn't made her angry until now.

"He wasn't who you thought he was," she said. Hadn't she said that to a damsel or two? She could easily imagine how Young Jackie would've dismissed the warning signs. And idealized him in his years of absence. The damsels did it all the time—projected onto the men who they *wished* they were, blind to the true natures of the boyfriends and husbands they'd chosen. It was part of why Grace was still single; she didn't trust herself to see a man, a long-term partner, with true accuracy.

"No," Jackie insisted. "He was exactly who I thought he was. A man who couldn't set down roots. And maybe my parents were a little right: he didn't like having responsibilities."

One thing had always bothered Grace and still troubled her more than anything else—even with the knowledge of her mother's shattered heart. "Would he have stayed if . . . if Hope hadn't . . . Or if there'd only been one of us?"

A wry smile twisted the lines on Jackie's face. "That's what everyone thought. It was easy to let them think that." She sagged a little and shrugged. "I don't know, maybe that was the last straw. But I knew, I understood . . . it would've been hard to keep him around regardless. I'd hoped he'd take to being a dad, enjoy playing with you, and teaching you. He always said he loved new things and loved a challenge. He didn't even give himself the chance with you girls, not really. I think it scared him."

Grace didn't feel much sympathy for this faceless father who was afraid of his own children. Still, if she had any hope of finding out what he'd been up to over the past thirty-five years, she needed a crucial piece of information. "Are you ever going to tell me his name? I've considered doing one of those DNA tests, see if I have any relatives—"

"Please don't do that," Jackie said quickly. "I never told you his full name so you couldn't look him up."

"But why?"

"Because I would die if I learned he'd finally settled down somewhere, had a family that wasn't me. Take the DNA test when I'm gone, if you have to. But I couldn't live knowing he finally set down roots. With someone else."

All these years Grace had thought her mother hated Paul; now she knew it was actually Jackie's love for him that had kept her so reticent. Paul No-Last-Name wasn't a player or mean or drunk. It had never occurred to Grace that her mother had such a fairy-tale-gone-wrong past.

There was so much more Grace wanted to know, but this was beyond what she'd ever expected. Sometimes she'd fantasized about a tall, handsome daddy who knelt down with open arms to embrace children who weren't her or Hope. Now she understood this was her mother's worst fear.

"Thanks, Mom. I really needed this."

Jackie looked tired. "I thought we'd talk about Hope. But I guess this is part of it, isn't it? The most useless thing I've ever wondered is if . . . if Hope wouldn't have died if Paul . . ." She pulled her legs up and held out her arm, ready for Grace to help her to her feet. "Guess it's dumb to reimagine what couldn't happen."

Once on her feet, Jackie rubbed her lower back. Grace felt a little stiff too.

"We'll come back soon, if you want—and stop for flowers next time," said Grace.

"Find me a little stone? Doesn't need to be much more than a pebble."

Grace wasn't sure why her mother wanted a stone, but she searched in the dirt bed around the buckeye's exposed roots.

"Will this do?" She held it out for Jackie to see.

"Perfect. Set it on your sister's headstone. Doesn't matter where." Grace's face must have asked a question as she placed the little rock on the granite marker. "I learned that from Robert. That's what the Jewish people do. I like it—stones last longer than flowers."

Grace took her mom's arm and guided her back to the paved road. As Jackie waited in the shade, Grace went to retrieve the car.

27

The summer when they were nine and a half, Grace and Hope played outside every day with the neighborhood kids. They'd taken to playing various games in the alley—so Hope, in her motorized wheelchair, could join in. Many of the games were questionable inventions, and they'd prided themselves in not crying when they got poked in the eye with a stick or pelted too hard by whatever objects they were throwing.

Grace was friendly with the local kids, though she wouldn't have called any of them her friends. Hope bonded with Lizzy that summer—a girl Grace was wary of, her pale, freckled skin a thin disguise for the bully that lurked within. Lizzy spotted the mean thing in Hope, the thing that wanted to see what organs and bones really looked like. When Hope wanted to hurl a swear word at one of the Jablonski brothers and couldn't get it out fast enough, Lizzy swore at the boys for her. Sometimes Lizzy misinterpreted exactly what Hope was trying to say, but it was usually close enough.

Thinking back on it, Grace weighed the probability that she had been mean too—that all the neighborhood kids, struggling in their own ways to survive, had been one claw short of feral. That summer, for a few short weeks, they became a tribe. Their parents, glad they were out of the house, let them play until the streetlights went on. It felt like eternity. That summer was a dreamscape of endless days, of ruthless, magical victories. Grace mulled on it now, remembering how satisfying it had felt—how she'd come into the house at dusk feeling like a queen, a warrior, a survivor of a battle that crossed stormy seas. She'd crawl into bed with the contented exhaustion of someone immortal, simultaneously aware of her verdant youth.

Now that she knew something about her father, she felt like that again. Invincible. The afternoon with her mother had satisfied something, and as the long day slipped into twilight, Grace had the energy of a coyote emerging from its den to hunt. It had been a long time since she'd spoken to any of her damsels; she used to speak to each of them at least once a week. It was harder now, with her mother in the house—which had been a good thing when Grace was determined to be good. Now she craved the scratchy wrongness of donning an alter ego, the sustenance it gave her, like a vampire savoring a drop of blood.

It wasn't always about being a prince.

But where to make a call?

Jackie was in the shower. Grace's bedroom door was shut, and Jackie certainly couldn't hear her while the water was running. Only once since Jackie's arrival had Grace made such a call at home, and she'd waited until her mother was asleep and then went downstairs. Waiting would be the safer option, but Grace wasn't in the mood for safe.

She texted ShyShaina to see if she was up for a call and then huddled on the floor beside the fortress of her bed. If she angled herself toward the outside wall, and with the mattress as a sound buffer, her voice wouldn't carry. Or so she told herself. ShyShaina responded instantly.

Grace cleared her throat, ready to use her Deep Voice, and placed the call through Skype.

"Hey sweetheart . . ."

———

Immersed in Shaina's good news, "Preston" lost track of the time. Shaina had taken some rather miraculous steps toward getting her shit together: after threatening it for months, she changed the locks so her ex-boyfriend would stop dropping in, and she found a full-time job in customer service—an opportunity she hadn't had before the pandemic. ShyShaina would never have been able to function at a call center—with her nervousness around people and anxiety in busy environments—but now it was a good job that everyone was doing from home. (While Preston passed himself off as an app developer, Grace made a mental note about the possibility that she, too, could consider a customer-service position while she was stuck in quarantine.)

Preston was truly happy for Shaina, a sweet young woman who'd let herself get run over by family and friends alike. She sounded so upbeat and joyful and thanked Preston profusely for his encouragement, which made Grace feel triumphant.

The conversation restored Grace's faith that *anyone* could turn their situation around.

Her throat was sore by the time she got off the call. It was hard to talk in the Deep Voice for long periods of time, but Shaina deserved to revel in her successes. When Grace left her room, her mother's bedroom door was open and the television was on downstairs.

She sighed as she crossed through the living room, forced to accept that her mother had laid claim, by virtue of greater opportunity, to the spot on the couch Grace still considered to be hers. Jackie, oblivious, sat with her legs outstretched, eating a salad.

"There's lots more in the fridge," she said, her mouth full of lettuce, as Grace walked past.

"Thanks." But Grace wasn't heading to the kitchen for food; she needed something to drink. She filled a sports bottle with water—only slightly concerned that she couldn't remember when she'd last washed it—and glugged half of it down. Refreshed, she returned to the living room and plopped down on the other end of the couch.

They'd recently developed a mutual interest in true-crime shows, and Jackie was halfway through an episode of *Disappeared*. It was easy to catch the gist of what she'd missed, and Grace was immediately absorbed. She became aware of her mother staring at her but decided to ignore it.

"Grace?" Jackie stretched out her name, elongating it with a tone of inquisitive displeasure. Grace took a sip of water and flicked a glance at her. "Aren't you forgetting something?" her mother asked.

It had been a good day, but Grace sensed it was about to topple off its pedestal. She wasn't in the mood to play guessing games with her mother and had no idea what Jackie was alluding to. After a momentary stare-off, Grace gave in. "What?"

Jackie gave her the Are-you-daffy? look, blinking her eyes and pursing her lips. This time *she* lost the stare-off. "I realize you're an adult and you can make whatever careless decisions you want, break whatever rules don't fit in with your lifestyle, but . . . I don't think it's too much to expect you to be courteous and considerate."

What the fuck was she talking about? When Jackie proved unable to read her face, Grace had to actually say it. "What are you talking about?"

"The gentleman? In your room? While I think it's unwise to have someone over while we're self-isolating, you don't need to hide him. And I don't think it's very nice to just leave him alone while you watch TV."

Grace's mouth dropped open, but she quickly shut it when she realized she didn't know how to reply. *Fuck.* She'd been so sure she'd gotten away with it. Her heart pumped a little harder, and she hoped her blood vessels weren't turning her a guilty shade of red. Every ticking second would make it harder to lie convincingly. "I was FaceTiming with Miguel," she said, trying to add both amusement and annoyance to her voice.

Her mother had a disgruntled expression for every occasion. The one she put on now said, *Please, I'm not stupid.* "I know Miguel. That's not what Miguel sounds like."

It was too late for a better lie. She should've told her mother she was watching something online. Grace focused on the television, unsure what to say. Unsure what to do. *Disappeared* repeated its favorite image, custom made for each episode, a facsimile of the missing person walking away from the camera . . . and evaporating into thin air. Grace wished she had that option right now. Maybe if she didn't say anything, pretended the matter was settled, her mother would forget it and move on.

But Grace had forgotten that this version of her mother cared about things like manners and being a good hostess.

Jackie hauled herself off the sofa and marched over to the bottom of the stairs. "Young man, it's safe to come down!"

"Mom!" Grace jumped up but didn't bother to chase after her mother—it wasn't as if Jackie would find a man hiding in her room if she went upstairs to check.

"I have a nice big salad in the refrigerator, if you're hungry," her mother called.

"Mom, there's no one up there." The words were out before Grace realized the implication of what she was saying.

"Grace, what . . . what's wrong with you? I heard a man. My eyesight isn't as good as it was, but my hearing is just fine. I'm happy for you if you have a boyfriend. You don't have to keep secrets from me."

Torn between the crappy escape options of dashing outside or clenching her eyes shut like a toddler—*You can't see me!*—Grace collapsed onto the couch.

"It was me. You heard me."

She saw in her peripheral vision as her mother made her way back to the sofa, her footsteps cautious, her gaze baffled and a touch alarmed. The movements and expression of someone confronting the possibility that *Invasion of the Body Snatchers* wasn't just a horrifying movie but a horrifying and very present reality. Jackie sat very straight on the edge of the seat cushion; she aimed the remote at the television and *Disappeared* disappeared.

Grace had a decision to make: refuse and deny, or tell the truth. Jackie apparently intended to sit there, riveted, until Grace came up with an explanation.

28

"Sometimes . . ." Grace faltered. "I have another identity I use online."

Partial truth: a compromise. But Jackie looked more flummoxed than ever.

"Why? What does that even mean?"

"It's like . . ." Grace tried to think of something plausible, if untrue, that her mother would understand. "When I was little, and Hope and I had our paper dolls. We lived vicariously through them, and could make them whoever we wanted them to be."

"What does that have to do with what you sounded like? Who were you talking to?"

"I was talking to a woman who only knows me as a man. That's the identity I use online."

Jackie screwed up her face, really trying to figure it out. "So does that mean . . . Are you one of those transgendered people?"

Grace tried not to roll her eyes. This was already hard enough, and her mother's complete ignorance of the modern world was making it worse.

"It's okay if you are," Jackie quickly interjected. "I just didn't—"

"I'm not trans. I just use a male persona because . . . I understand the young women and the kinds of mistakes they make. I want to help them. In fact, I want them to *not* use dating apps to find a partner."

"Wait, they're interested in you? They think they have some kind of relationship with you? And they don't know . . . ?"

"Right." Grace watched as Jackie tried to piece it all together.

"But how . . . ? They don't know what you look like?"

Grace shook her head. "I use pictures I find online."

"You pretend to be someone else?"

"Yes."

"And you actually *talk* to people, like you're a man?"

"I kind of have to. No one will settle for just messaging anymore."

Jackie's confusion took a turn toward disgust. "Why?"

"As I said, I try to help them. They want to believe that some fantasy man is the solution to their problems, and it's not true, of course. So I try to help them be more confident, more realistic about their options."

The gruesome abortion dream flashed in her mind. Bethany and her mangled baby.

"*Them, they*," said Jackie. "*Anymore.* So you've been doing this for a while? How many women have you done this to?"

Grace felt like she'd explained enough. She'd told her mother the truth, and the interrogation was starting to make her skin feel like it was rippling and contracting. "As I said—"

"And you never tell them who you really are? Or why you're playing this game with them?" Jackie sounded combative now, and Grace didn't like it.

"It's personal. I don't think I have to tell you—"

"You lie? You just lie to people?" Jackie's lip contorted at such a sickening idea.

Grace had already admitted as much, though not in such specific terms. Once again, she didn't know how to get away from her mother's scrutiny. "There's a term for it, if you really want to know. Things are different—"

"The term is *liar*." Jackie shook her head, her message crystal clear: *No daughter of mine would do such a wicked thing*. Grace's blood was boiling, a combination of mortification and rage. She hated being under the spotlight of her mother's judgmental glare—all the more so for it happening so soon after ShyShaina's breakthrough.

"You don't understand." She sounded like a teenager—and felt like the teenager she had once been, full of omnidirectional frustration.

"I'm very disappointed in you, Grace." Jackie's ire morphed into something more forlorn. "I didn't think you could be so . . . intentional. So deliberately cruel."

"I'm not!" Grace protested. But before she could find the words to defend herself, she remembered thinking about that long ago summer, the collective savagery of her playmates.

"Maybe you're not who I thought you were." As if she couldn't bear to be in the same room with her any longer, Jackie headed upstairs.

All of Grace's fight melted away. Her circulatory system was on the fritz, and everything that had been too hot a moment ago was now turning to ice. Her whole body stiffened as she replayed her mother's words, overwhelmed by the probability that her mother was right. Grace had always found ways of justifying things, uncharitable thoughts, greedy actions. But what if she really wasn't the person she thought she was? What if the thing she called *helping* was actually *hurting*? Hadn't she suspected that very possibility? Otherwise, why keep hidden for so long the only hobby she was any good at?

———

Grace sat there in the doldrums of her conscience, unsure if she was a reasonably good person or a marginally bad one. She tried to summon a list of the good things she had done, so she could weigh them against the bad ones, but she was less sure than ever what constituted a Good Thing. Had she ever done anything out of pure kindness? Pure generosity? Weren't there, if she was being honest, tendrils of selfishness intertwined with every act?

But was that true or simply the flotsam of doubt left behind by her mother?

Another bit she'd nearly forgotten: how her mother could leave her questioning the value of her deeds or even aspects of her personality. It stung now, recalling how Jackie had never thought of her as "college material"—a verdict she would never have made about Hope. Grace came to believe in her own subpar intelligence, even while she was embittered by the lack of time she had for schoolwork. When she eventually did have more time, after Hope's death, she didn't care about her grades anymore. She'd found a comfortable place in being mediocre, where people didn't expect too much from her.

The longer Grace sat there and ruminated, the madder she became. She wasn't entirely sure of the source of all her anger, but she resented her mother for the effortless way she screwed with her emotions.

But as quickly as the fury came, the doubt was on its heels.

Should she have shown Jackie her vulnerable side—would that have elicited more sympathy? Grace wasn't blind to the reality that in spite of her plethora of cyberrelationships, she'd never been in love in real life. Catfishing wasn't simply her being *deliberately cruel*; it was her finding a way to feel good about herself. And if it was an inappropriate way, shouldn't a mother be a little more concerned about her daughter's self-esteem?

29

She knew it was a dream. Unlike some of the other nightmares she'd had, this one wasn't trying to fool her into believing it was real. But that didn't make it less unnerving.

Grace accepted that the setting was her bedroom, but in the manner of dreams, it didn't much resemble her room. Or rather, it did, but the dimensions were all off. It was hard for her to see exactly where the walls were, but the presence—the volume—of so many bodies gave the impression that they were very far away. Her bed was behind her, but as the human figures pulsed around her—jammed together shoulder to shoulder, pushing—she found herself drifting away from the safety of the one solid thing she recognized. Like a small boat carried off by the current. Soon she was amid them, lost in a crush of people.

They were meant to be her damsels. This her subconscious registered, even as the forms around her barely resembled human beings. They looked more like life-size dolls made of flesh-colored fabric. Featureless. Hairless. They ambled aimlessly in the crowded room.

Grace tried to worm her way through them, hoping to find the door and get out. But with each passing second, the physical pressure around her increased as more and more of the damsel dummies moved toward her. It was getting hotter and harder to breathe. If they all pressed against her, they would smother her like a mass of animated cushions. The very thought made Grace panic and start to push against them with more urgency. Sometimes one turned toward her, its blank face nonetheless *seeing* her—condemning her.

"Excuse me! I'm sorry!" Dream Grace could do nothing but apologize and try to force her way through. But it didn't matter how many she squeezed past. There were always more, their padded feet *swish-swishing* against the floor, blocking her exit.

She was ready for the dream to end. As she gasped for air she became aware of another sound in the room—a muffled murmuring. The sound of someone trying to speak while a pillow was pressed to their face. Multiplied by a hundred. The damsels were trying to tell her something, but they didn't have mouths.

A particularly determined one blocked her head on. In its desperation to speak, the fabric on the lower part of its face started to twist and strain. Hidden teeth were going to break through, and Grace didn't want to be there when it happened. Frantic, she scanned the others, attempting to look over their heads to find the door.

A phone rang.

Miraculously, the damsel dummies started backing away, opening a path so she could find the phone and answer the call. Halle-fucking-lujah.

Grace bolted into full consciousness. Her phone was alight, jangling against the darkness of the room and the hour. For the briefest moment she was relieved—to be out of the dream and awake. But then she saw who was calling and knew something was terribly wrong.

———

"Miguel?"

She heard gasping on the other end of the line. Then—"Sorry to wake you."

"What's wrong?" Grace threw off the bedclothes and turned on the light, getting ready for what was coming.

"I'm really sick, I don't think I can drive." Left unsaid was the emergency, the need for medical help.

"I'm coming to get you. I'll be there in ten minutes, okay?"

"Okay."

Grace disconnected the phone, and in her panic wasn't sure what to do next. Was there time to get dressed, or should she just grab the keys and go? Quickly, she pulled on yesterday's pants. And put a bra on under her sleep shirt. She grabbed her phone and ran.

At the front door, she hauled her purse over her shoulder as she stuffed her feet into a pair of shoes—she didn't even look to see which ones. The light came on at the top of the stairs.

"Grace? Where are you going?" Jackie held her arms against her body.

"I'm taking Miguel to the hospital." She unlocked the door, ready to flee into the night.

"Shouldn't he call an ambulance? You'll catch your death."

Grace didn't have time to argue with her. She plucked a mask from the hook where she kept her keys and raced out.

———

It was so quiet outside. Grace could barely remember what day—night—it was. She drove too fast, but the empty streets didn't care. She was hyper with adrenaline, close to weeping in despair.

As she screeched to a stop in front of Miguel's apartment building, she slipped the disposable mask around her ears, pressed it tight over the bridge of her nose. Miguel, in a matching mask, was waiting on the sidewalk, bundled in a fleece blanket.

"Oh lovey," Grace cried as he got in. His eyes were red and terrified. She waited until he buckled his seat belt before heading away. "Which hospital?"

"Presby," he wheezed. "Oh Grace, it's so fucked up. Carolina isn't feeling well. Her maid of honor is on a *ventilator*. So is our aunt."

"I'm so sorry." She couldn't tell if he was crying or struggling to catch his breath—or both.

"Thank you for doing this." As he began coughing he pressed the mask tight against his face and opened his window all the way. "I didn't want to call nine one one. I was afraid . . . just afraid, of everything. But I don't want to get you sick—I guess we're superspreaders."

"More like supergetters," she cracked, trying—and failing—to lighten the moment. The boorish part of her hoped she didn't have Miguel's unlucky genes. She rolled down her window, too, to let the deadly germs escape, and took a better stab at reassuring her friend. "It'll be okay, we have the best doctors."

At least for her, that was something of a comfort: knowing they lived in a city renowned for its medical centers. The University of Pittsburgh was one of many places around the world frantically searching for a vaccine. She zipped through Squirrel Hill, the streets deserted, and got onto Forbes Avenue—and pressed the gas pedal a little harder.

"I left Coco a couple days of food." He paused to catch his breath, sucking in the mask as he gasped for air. "If I'm in there longer will you check on her?"

"Of course."

"You still have the spare key?"

"On my key ring, always."

"And if . . . if I'm there for a long time, will you take her to your house?"

Grace shot him a glance, hating that the night—and their masks—hid much of his face. His question gave away his fear, his concern about . . . not coming home. Whatever emotion she'd once called Panic was nothing compared to how she felt now, a turbulent churning of dread and desperation. Months of pandemic news hadn't prepared her for this. She thought she'd been living it before, the #PandemicLife, but then it had only been *near* her, *around* her. And now it was gripping her heart, threatening to stop the muscle from beating.

"Of course, I'll bring her to my place tomorrow—no point in her being lonely and the last thing you need to worry about is Coco. I'll take good care of her and they'll take good care of you." Her voice broke.

Neither of them knew what else to say. A wraith traveled with them, leaning between the front seats like a reckless child. Grace reached out and gripped Miguel's trembling shoulder, but soon she retracted her hand, needing it to turn up the hill toward UPMC Presbyterian.

"Just drop me at Emergency."

"I was going to park."

"They might not even let you in."

She turned into the Emergency driveway, relieved that there wasn't a line of cars waiting to drop off sick passengers, as she half expected.

"Try to let me know what's going on, okay?" She pictured him in the near future with an oxygen mask over his face. "Text?"

"I will." He stepped out of the car. "Take care of yourself."

"Do you have your phone charger?"

"Yes." He bent toward the open car window. "I'll tell them you're my fiancée, so you can get updates."

She smiled behind her mask. Sometimes they pretended to be engaged, or related, in situations like this where it might be hard to get information.

"I love you, lovey," she said. "You're gonna be okay. You *got* this— but you can get over it."

His eyes crinkled as he smiled. "Love you too. Talk soon. Thank you for Coco."

Burying his face in his elbow as he coughed, he turned and walked through the hospital's automatic doors. Grace was so afraid this would be her last image of him—swaddled in his blanket, struggling to breathe, heading alone into isolation and uncertainty. She didn't want him to die surrounded by strangers. She didn't want him to *die*.

She cried all the way home. Her tears refracted the streetlights' glare, blinding her in starry bursts.

30

Grace tossed and turned for the rest of the night, and got up for good before her mother was awake. It wasn't rational, but all she could think about was Coco—home alone, confused by Miguel's sudden departure. She pictured Miguel talking to the cat—his usually high-pitched kitty voice racked with coughs—telling her he had to go but would be back soon. Grace had had a cat, many years ago. She'd loved that cat so much she thought she was *in* love with him, and it caused her some of the worst pain in her life when she couldn't make him understand the simple words that would soothe a person: *You're okay; don't be scared; I love you.* His death was the greatest loss of her life, and she swore she'd never have another pet.

She threw on the same not-quite-clean pants but this time put on a fresh top. The mission felt too urgent to take the time to brush her teeth, but she rinsed with mouthwash and whipped a comb through her hair. The cat wouldn't care about her appearance, but Grace might need to stop for gas.

The drive to his apartment took twice as long as it had in the middle of the night; people were on their way to work. It struck her as odd that anyone was still going to work. Shouldn't they all stay home? Barricade themselves behind their doors until the danger passed? Yet here she was—undeniably exposed, potentially spreading pathogens wherever she went. Out of guilt, she put on her mask as she parked in front of Miguel's, though no one was around. It had been a mansion once (by her standards), but now the building held seven apartments of varying sizes. Miguel had a spacious one-bedroom on the second floor.

Coco padded to the door, meowing as Grace let herself in. Good, the cat still recognized her; she rubbed against Grace's legs. The apartment smelled like Miguel—his aftershave and favorite magnolia candles—with an underscent of Cat. Fishy wet food and litter box.

"Hey fluffy girl, let's get your things together." She scratched the cat's head and then went to find all of the cat's paraphernalia.

It felt weird to be there without Miguel. She'd cat sat for him before, when he went on longer vacations and didn't want to overburden Kadin, his downstairs neighbor. But this time Grace knew he wasn't off somewhere drinking mojitos or spending lazy days on someone's deck. She envisioned him with an IV, getting blood work, a chest x-ray . . . what else? Hopefully he was in a regular hospital room and not intensive care. Or maybe he was still in the emergency department; she'd dropped him at the hospital barely four hours ago.

Coco followed her from room to closet to room, meowing the answers to Grace's questions: Where's your carrier? Do you have some favorite toys?

By the time she was ready to go it looked like she was taking everything Coco owned—her food bowls and food, litter and litter pan, bed and blankie, her brush. The carpeted cat tree was too cumbersome to put in the car, otherwise Grace might have brought that too. She carried the stuff out in batches, until all that was left was Coco in her carrier, mewling unhappily.

"You'll come back soon, Coco. I promise." This time she was glad the cat couldn't decipher English; Grace didn't like to promise things she had no control over.

She left Coco in her carrier on the dining room floor and went out to retrieve the rest of her things. When she came back, Jackie was leaning against the doorway to the kitchen, eyeballing the cat. Grace wanted to get everything ready first before letting Coco explore the house. She started with the litter box, setting it up in the corner farthest away from the kitchen.

"Shouldn't you put that in the basement?" Jackie asked, caustic with disapproval.

"Then we'd have to leave the basement door open." She brushed past her mother to fill Coco's water bowl. That went in an opposing corner of the dining room, next to her food bowl.

Grace had hoped her mother would wake up in a pleasant mood, refreshed by a good night's sleep, the previous evening's discoveries long forgotten. But maybe it wasn't realistic that Jackie would simply forget. *The term is* liar. Her demeanor expressed nothing but reproach.

"Why did you bring that here?" Jackie glared at the cat. And now Grace understood that her mother's previous question may have been directed at *Coco*, not just her litter box—as if Grace would ever consider exiling the poor creature to her damp basement.

"Because I don't know how long Miguel will be in the hospital. Her name is Coco. And the *one* thing I can do to help Miguel is make sure his fur baby is okay." She knelt down and unzipped the carrier. Coco poked her head out and looked around.

"Fur baby," Jackie snorted. "People want pets over children because they don't talk back. They don't grow up and embarrass you."

With her back turned, Grace rolled her eyes. She had no idea how she was going to make things okay with her mom again; engaging in her pissy mood certainly wouldn't help.

Jackie wasn't ready to let it go. "You're just bringing more germs in the house."

"We don't eat in the dining room anyway." The only thing that kept Grace from flinging sharp-edged jabs at her hard-hearted mother was her desire to stay calm and chipper for Coco. The cat deserved a warmer welcome. Grace petted and fussed over her to make up for it.

"All that fur." Jackie looked as repulsed as if Grace were caressing a pile of excrement.

Grace struggled to not raise her voice. "You don't have to like it, Mom. This is my house, and this is what I'm doing to help my friend. Who is sick, as if you give a shit."

"I give many shits, Grace. I like Miguel, quite a lot. But not enough to *die* for your misplaced guilt."

"What's that supposed to mean?"

"A *good* friend would have told him to call an ambulance. A *guilty* friend, who spends her life lying to people, has to prove that she's *worthy* of his friendship."

Grace left Coco to sniff out the litter box and faced off with her mother. "I love him. I'm worried about him. He's scared and I didn't want him to have to go alone. I should not have to explain that!"

Jackie, unimpressed, took a step back, deliberately increasing the space between them. "And I shouldn't have to explain that now we have to stay in quarantine even longer. Because you exposed us again. And God only knows what that cat has."

"She's an indoor cat! She doesn't have anything!"

"Miguel could've given it to her. It's not impossible. That happened to a tiger in the zoo." With the raised chin of haughty disdain, Jackie whipped around and retreated to the kitchen.

"If you're concerned," Grace said, hanging onto the doorjamb so her body invaded her mother's queendom, "about getting sick from me or the cat, you can stay in your room."

"Ha!" Jackie barked. "You'd leave me up there to starve to death."

"No I *wouldn't*." What a dumb thing to suggest. Grace wasn't sure if this hostility was coming from Jackie's umbrage over her catfishing, or a genuine fear of getting sick. The bickering would just get worse unless one or both of them cooled off.

Though Grace had suggested that Jackie should be the one to retreat to the second floor, Grace opted to remove herself. She scooped Coco into her arms and headed upstairs.

"You can check out my room," she whispered to the cat. "No nasty old women there."

31

Grace snapped a pic of Coco blissfully stretched out and asleep at the foot of her bed. She texted it to Miguel, hoping it would put a smile on his face. Every hour that he didn't text magnified her apprehension. It was too easy to imagine him incapacitated by medical gear—but maybe he was simply resting. Though Grace hadn't gotten much sleep the night before, she was bored of resting—and irked that she was holed up in her room like a naughty child while her mother watched TV and did whatever she wanted. After the previous day's debacle post-ShyShaina, Grace felt too guilty to pass the time with one of her damsels.

She ordered a cheeseburger and french fries through Grubhub—and an extra order of fries for Jackie, though she wasn't sure where her mother stood on delicious, greasy comfort food. When the driver messaged her that he was leaving the food by her door, Grace tiptoed out of her room (so as not to disturb the cat) and galloped downstairs. She opened the front door in time to see the driver returning to his car.

"Thank you!" She waved at him from behind the storm door, its barrier—and the no-contact transaction—a blunt reminder of her quarantine. Her mom was right: they had to restart their two weeks of self-isolation, but it was worth it to help Miguel. Especially if she never got to see him again. *Don't think like that!* The driver waved. Grace ducked onto the porch to grab her bag of food.

She went to the kitchen via the dining room and scrubbed her hands before putting her meal—and her mother's fries—on plates. The restaurant had included little packets of ketchup, but Grace got the squeeze bottle from the fridge. She tucked it under her arm with some napkins and carried the plates into the living room.

"A little snack," she said, setting the fries on the coffee table in front of Jackie. Grace took her new regular spot at the other end of the sofa and handed her mother some napkins.

"Thank you," Jackie said, with no emotion.

After squirting a fat glob of ketchup onto her plate, Grace handed the bottle to her mother. This felt like a pivotal moment: Would Jackie accept the peace offering?

She hesitated, but took the bottle of ketchup and squeezed a dainty dollop beside her fries. "Thank you," she said again.

Good. Better. Grace rested her plate on her lap and her feet on the coffee table and started on her cheeseburger. Big, messy mouthfuls. It tasted like charbroiled heaven. With a side of starchy nirvana.

"This is so good," she mumbled, sriracha mayo dribbling down her chin.

Jackie was back to watching one of her shopping networks, and while Grace really wanted to change the channel, for the sake of their fragile truce she let it be. Beside her, Jackie took ladylike nibbles on her fries, and it occurred to Grace that eating them at all might be her way of respecting the truce.

"I could've ordered you a salad," Grace said, "but I figured you already had some."

"It was nice of you to think of me. Thank you." Her mother's chilly politeness was off-putting. Grace knew it masked something more unforgiving.

The infomercial came to an end. Grace turned to her mom, trying to gauge if it was safe to find another show to watch. Jackie kept her gaze on the television, studiously ignoring Grace (or so she thought), though she was gobbling the fries with a little more enthusiasm.

"Mind if I turn on one of the true-crime shows?" It was meant to be an equitable compromise, something they both liked.

"Whatever you want," Jackie replied, feigning indifference.

Grace was getting annoyed. Her mother was being petulant. Since whatever Grace did was going to displease her, she went ahead and switched to *Disappeared*. They proceeded to eat in silence . . . until her mother started sniffing. *Sniff-sniff*, on repeat.

Reluctantly, Grace looked over to see what was going on. Jackie's nose was wrinkled, a sneer as exaggerated as her sniffing. Grace first assumed that Coco had sneaked down to have a poop, but when she tested the air herself, she didn't detect a foul odor.

"It's you," said Jackie, answering the unspoken question. "That disgusting mash of rotten meat. How can you eat that?"

The cheeseburger was two-thirds gone, but Grace glanced at it, so well conditioned by nightmares that she expected to find maggots squirming out from between the bread. But no, the sandwich was fine—a bit of a smooshed-up mess, but it was easier to eat that way. She crammed it in her mouth and took an unholy bite to stop herself from saying anything snarky.

"It's gonna ooze through your pores," Jackie said, eyes on the television. "While all the fat and flesh ferments in your intestines, the smell will start seeping through your pores."

Grace gave her mother a withering glare. But then a thought struck her—struck her hard enough to make her swallow wrong and start coughing: Hope would've said something like that. Her mother sounded like Hope, trying to convince her of some kind of crazy bullshit. There was a freaky image—grown-up Hope, Mommy's little clone.

"Why are you being such a jerk?" That's what Grace would've said to her sister, so why not her mom.

"Because there's nothing else I can do."

"What's that supposed to mean? And why do I keep having to say that to you? Christ . . ." Grace almost blurted out that they needed family therapy. But at the chance that Jackie might agree, she held her tongue. Her mother definitely needed to learn how to communicate like a normal person, without playing cryptic games. Grace wanted to walk away, refuse to humor her manipulative crap, but she was afraid that would simply prolong the inevitable. If Jackie needed to get something off her chest, better to not let it fester.

She gazed at her mother, waiting for her to speak. Now that she had center stage, Jackie crossed her arms. Closed off and defensive. Grace recognized the behavior. The show went to commercial, and Grace put it on mute. If Jackie didn't want to talk, she could stew there in silence.

———

"I just don't have a lot of choices," she finally blurted. "I tried to make the best of it—I'm trying. But I can't go anywhere. I can't do anything."

Grace wasn't sure how they got from rancid meat to here, but she empathized with her mother's frustration. "It's the pandemic. I'm sorry. It won't always be like this."

Jackie shook her head. "No. It's more than that. I don't have the energy I used to. You remember? I could go-go-go for hours. I fake it really well, but I don't . . . My body is failing me. My vision goes fuzzy. I miss driving. I miss being in control of my life. Richard and I didn't exactly have an action-packed social life, but we did everything together. He was so difficult at the end. I barely recognized him."

This was the mom Grace had anticipated when she'd first moved in—overwhelmed by loss. But Grace wasn't sure what to say or how to make it better. Preston or River or LuckyJamison would offer pithy advice in such a situation—*One day at a time.* Jackie would probably kill her if Grace spoke to her in platitudes. "It *will* get better," she said softly. "I think."

"Will it?" Jackie didn't sound bitter anymore, only sad. "I don't think my eyes or my energy is coming back. And this will always be your house. I know I can't stop you from doing anything, but . . . I don't have a choice about . . ." She shrugged.

"Are you really that unhappy here?" What was Grace hoping her mother would say? *Yes, you're too horrible to live with, I'm leaving.* Grace wouldn't feel good about that, but living together for the rest of Jackie's life didn't seem super realistic.

"I am disappointed with you, Grace, I'm not gonna lie."

The way Jackie said it, a matter-of-fact assessment, made it worse. If Jackie had sounded testy or crabby Grace could write it off as her mother's problem, not hers. Grace felt her organs shrinking, contracting into a knotted lump inside her.

"I'm sorry," she mumbled.

"I don't want to control your life. But you don't even consult me—about bringing home a cat, or running out in the middle of the night."

"You're right." Grace the hypocrite, shitty at communicating after all. "I've lived alone for a long time."

Jackie nodded. "I know. I haven't. I don't know what it's like. I know we're different. Are we too different to live together?"

It hurt Grace to hear her mother voice the contingency; coming from her it stung with rejection. As a teen, she'd been excited for her independence and had never considered the possibility that Jackie hadn't *liked* living with her. That Jackie had wanted something for herself was understandable; that Jackie had bided her time until Grace was a legal adult and then fled *from her* was a new and uncomfortable idea.

"I think . . . we have to get to know each other. As adults." She saw the truth in Miguel's advice more than ever. But now that her mother knew about the catfishing, Grace was afraid Jackie would overlook everything else about her.

"I want to reconnect with you, before it's too late," said Jackie. "I wouldn't have come back here otherwise. But I need you to do better. I'm sorry to have to say that. But you need to do better."

Jackie took the remote and turned the volume back up. Grace shrank into herself, wishing the sofa could give her a hug, as the mommy-cat chair from her childhood once had, and surreptitiously wiped a tear from her cheek.

32

The game was a sadistic mixture of spin the bottle and dodgeball. They played it in the alley and took turns being the Target. The Target got to spin the dirty Rolling Rock bottle, but they were selecting a Hitter, not someone to kiss. The Hitter's objective, naturally, was to hit the Target. Everyone used the same stick, but the Hitter got to choose three small rocks: round or flat ones might be easier to strike, but an angular one would do the most damage.

The Hitter would toss up the rocks, one at a time, and take a swing—like a batter sending practice balls to the outfield—aiming for the Target, twenty feet away. Each rock that struck the Target earned the Hitter one point. But the game deviated from dodgeball in that the Target couldn't dodge, not if they wanted to win. If the Target didn't duck or close their eyes or run away—if they stood there stoically through all three swings—they earned five points for that round.

Hope kept score; she wasn't coordinated enough to be a Hitter, and the neighborhood kids didn't want to be killed by her mom if they injured her—or her chair.

It was Grace's turn to spin. She felt smug and indestructible, having just had her turn as Hitter. Lizzy was still pressing a wadded paper towel to her busted lip; only one of Grace's rocks had met its mark—but it was a doozy. The sunflowers on Lizzy's shirt were dripping blood but she'd taken it well, afterward swatting away the tears so they wouldn't fall. The kids made a circle, and Grace crouched down to spin the bottle.

For a moment it looked like it was going to settle on Lizzy. Grace felt a crackle of fear at the enjoyment the girl would take in her revenge. But the bottle inched past her and stopped at Davy, the youngest of the Jablonski brothers. That he was short and scrawny did nothing to lessen the danger he posed. If anything, he was the most athletically coordinated of all of them, quick and strong. And vicious. Kids at school—who didn't know better—sometimes made the mistake of teasing him, calling him a hobbit or a shrimp. He didn't care if the name-caller was twice his size; Davy always attacked—an angered bull, his hard head a weapon even without horns. No one picked on him twice.

Grace stood on the designated spot, just behind a pothole, and watched as Davy sorted through the rubble at the edge of the concrete, looking for the perfect ammunition. She made the mistake of catching her sister's eye. Hope glimmered with mischief, looking altogether too gleeful about the impending likelihood of little Davy blasting Grace with shrapnel.

He took his position on the spray-painted *X*—a convenient street marking that they used for multiple activities. Grace clutched her fists at her sides, straightened her spine, and focused on a distant nothing just over Davy's head. On her first turn as Target that day, she'd flinched and turned aside—just once—but it had kept her from getting any points. She'd earned back a bit of the other kids' respect by firing that shot at Lizzy's mouth, but she had more to prove. In her peripheral vision they were smirking at her, transfixed by the prospect of seeing her fail or seeing her battered.

Fuck them. Grace wasn't here to entertain them; she wanted points. She wanted to show them she could give it and take it, and she'd be mad if she finished any lower than second place.

Davy took his first swing.

Crack! A solid hit—and it met its mark.

The jagged rock connected with Grace's thigh. She clenched her jaw tight and kept staring straight ahead, grateful that he'd struck her shorts and not her skin. It stung like mad, but she refused to even wince. On the sidelines, the kids were wide eyed with excitement, eager for Davy's second swing.

Grace held her breath. Stick

struck

stone.

She heard the kids gasp a nanosecond before she felt the pain.

The rock punctured the bony skin of her eyebrow. Her head wanted to recoil from the blow, but Grace was afraid of moving too much; she made herself rigid. She was on the verge of tears; her forehead felt like it had been whipped with a tail of barbed wire. It was almost soothing when the warm blood started cascading over her eye, down her cheek.

As Davy readied for his third swing, Keisha stepped forward, her hand raised.

"Hold up." Keisha, at twelve, was the oldest of the group. "I think that's enough."

"We get three swings!" Davy cried. "Everyone else got three!"

"You can have your three points, you got two solid hits."

The kids huddled around Keisha—all but Grace, who wouldn't risk sacrificing her score.

"Those aren't the rules," Joe said, getting in Keisha's face. Soon Davy's other brother, Dan, was yelling at her too.

"Come on, let's just finish this!" Grace shouted. She tasted the ripe, rusty blood on her lips. The whole left side of her face was wet. She couldn't do anything to stanch the blood until her turn was over, and their squabbling was just delaying it.

The kids accepted her verdict and moved back to the sidelines. Grace struggled to blink the blood out of her eye, unsure if it would be held against her if she closed even one. Secretly, she hoped Davy possessed a little mercy; he didn't have to swing for a home run if he didn't want to.

Apparently he wanted to.

All of a sudden there was nothing to see. Grace heard a squishy sort of smack as the rock connected with her face and an even louder gasp from the other kids. And then it was quiet.

She understood she'd been struck in her right eye. It hurt differently. More of a mellow burn than the sharp bite of torn skin. She could no longer see out of her left eye because of the cascade of blood, but she wasn't sure why she couldn't see anything out of her right eye, not even a blur.

"I get five!" she yelled, because she hadn't flinched. And then, quietly, "I can't see."

Why were the others so silent? No one was talking. She heard Hope's wheelchair, crunching over rubble. And then she felt someone's fingers on her arm.

"Come on," said Keisha, soft and scared, "I'll take you home."

The older girl led her away. Grace heard the others scuffling along behind them and the hum of Hope's power chair.

"Who won?" Grace asked, turning her head toward the general direction of her sister.

Still, none of the kids spoke. Grace's entire face felt wrong, inside out and upside down. But it was the silence that scared her most—even more than not being able to see. The savages were never quiet. They should be cheering or jeering, bickering or swearing. They never followed along obediently, even at school when a teacher yelled *Hush!* or *Stay in Line!*

Grace's feet knew when they had turned onto the walkway leading to her house.

"Keisha?" Mommy sounded stern and confused. Grace was a little confused, too—why was Mommy home? Shouldn't she be at work?

The other kids, probably fearing Mommy's temper, scampered away.

"Sorry," Keisha said. Grace couldn't tell if the apology was directed at her or Mommy. But then Keisha let go of her arm and took off running.

Hope maneuvered around her and up the ramp to the porch.

"Are you all right?" Mommy asked. Away from her playmates, Grace finally let herself cry. She expected to feel hands on her shoulders, to be guided into the house, into the kitchen, where Mommy would clean off the blood and patch her up.

"I'm okay," said Hope.

Grace stood there blind, shocked—realizing Mommy was fussing over her sister.

"Were you hit?" Mommy asked.

"Mommy—I can't see," Grace said. "What's wrong with me?"

"No, I just kept score," said Hope.

Couldn't Mommy tell that Hope was fine—and she was not? Grace tentatively felt for the ramp with her toe and took halting steps to make her way onto the porch.

The door opened. Hope drove her power chair inside.

"Mommy?" Grace cried.

The screen door slammed shut as they both went in without her.

———

Grace threw her arm over her eyes and groaned. Why did her dreams feel more intense than real life? Why could she *feel* everything like it was really happening? She kept her arm protectively across her face, stupidly wondering if the girl had lost her eye. *Not real, a dream. Right.* Right, their games had never been quite that brutal. Well, maybe they were—but no one had ever gotten so seriously injured.

She sighed, remembering she wouldn't be able to talk about this one with Miguel, at least not anytime soon. Was he sleeping well? Feeling any better? Were they giving him the fancy cocktail of drugs?

She sensed darkness around her, beyond her closed eyes and the sweaty crook of her elbow. Morning was a long way off. She got out of bed and stumbled toward the bathroom for a pee. Her feet knew the way, but it seemed darker than usual. No ambient light drifted through the windows; none of the usual digital devices emitted their red or green LED signals, miniature beacons in the blackness.

When she reached the bathroom and flipped on the overhead light, it didn't come on. Then she grasped the problem: the electricity was out. That explained it.

Except the electricity wasn't out—a fan was whirring behind her mother's closed door . . . and Grace's air conditioner was still running. So why couldn't she see?

Sounds drifted up from downstairs. A thumping. A swooshing. A body being dragged across the floor? No, not that heavy.

"Mom?" she called down.

More sounds. Fast running. Her mother couldn't run that fast. Another thump. What was going on?

Why can't I see?

"Gray?"

She shrieked and jumped at the voice, not expecting it to be so close. Her mother was nearby; her bedroom fan was louder now that the door was open.

"What's that cat doing down there?" Jackie asked.

Grace almost laughed at herself. She'd forgotten they had a furry houseguest. It was probably Crazy Cat Hour—the time in the middle of the night when cats freak out and run around. "Mom, I can't see."

If Jackie reacted, it wasn't audible.

"Mom?"

"What do you mean? The bathroom light's on."

"I mean I can't see . . . I'm blind."

"Can you see me?" Maybe Jackie waved a hand in front of her face.

"No—I can't see anything." She recalled the dream. Her pulse sped up, a frenzied drumroll. Her brain would burst like the crash of a cymbal. A body couldn't go on in such a state, but Grace was accelerating toward hysteria. "Mom, it's come true! I had a dream I was blind and it's come true!"

"Oh Grace, don't be ridiculous." Jackie sounded bored.

"I'm not . . . !" She blinked in fast succession, verifying the opening and closing of her lids. "There's nothing . . . I can't see a thing."

Jackie yawned. "That's because you refuse. I thought you'd buried it—I had some sympathy for that. But now I know you're just a liar. A liar living a lie."

Her mother's bedroom door closed, muffling the hum of the fan.

"Mom . . . ?" Why was her mother being so mean? So indifferent? *Just like the dream.*

An animal wailed at Grace's feet. She yelped, startled. *It's just the cat.* But the hysteria erupted. Her screams flew out in colors—red, purple, billowing ribbons of madness. With her eyes clamped tight she saw the cosmos, exploding stars, and still her howls painted the hallway. Her lunacy dripped off the ceiling, staining her hair.

33

Grace sat at the edge of her mattress, feet on the floor, head in her hands. She massaged her scalp. Pressed the sore spots around her eye sockets. The dreams had gone on forever. Hours. One nightmare tumbling into another. Every time she thought she'd finally awakened, she found herself in a new round of nocturnal quicksand. In all of them she was either blind or her mother was reminding her that she was a liar. She was only sure she was awake now because nothing was happening. She'd been sitting there for fifteen minutes. At least the nausea was finally gone.

She had to go downstairs and feed the cat, but she dreaded crossing paths with her mother. It didn't matter that Jackie had only been awful to her in her sleep; Grace was pissed at her anyway. Jackie had no right to treat her like an abomination, like she was defective, just because of the catfishing. Sure, it wasn't the most noble of avocations, even though Grace sincerely tried to create personas who were better than she was. And there were worse crimes. Probably everyone hid a secret or two; it was Grace's misfortune that her nebshit mother had overheard her. She imagined her mother with her ear pressed to Grace's bedroom door—and then tiptoeing away.

More and more she had the sense that Jackie was sneaky: incapacitated when it suited her, nimble and sly when no one was looking.

Her mother should be more understanding, that was the crux of Grace's resentment. Grace slipped into her version of a muumuu—a sleeveless, stretched-out jersey dress—with a sports bra underneath it to cover any side boob. The more she dwelled on everything, the more determined she became to excavate whatever skeletons her mother might be hiding in her metaphorical—or literal—closet. Did Jackie really think she was so perfect? It made Grace consider, again, the little locked box. Her mother had a secret, and Grace needed to know what it was. Perhaps it was something that would put them back on even ground, where they were *both* less than angelic.

The headache she'd awakened with was almost gone, thanks to the curative properties of Grace's desired revenge. Like little Davy from her dream, she needed good ammunition. Her mother was treating her unfairly and deserved a dose of her own judgmental medicine.

———

Grace would've preferred to go out to the backyard and sit in the sun. She wasn't enjoying being in the same room with her mother, and the house smelled weird—beyond her mother's embedded perfume, which Grace had acclimated to and could barely detect anymore. But if she went outside she might miss an opportunity to hunt for the box's missing key. Maybe Jackie would take a nap on the sofa. Or a long bath. (And if that meant Grace would have to help her naked, slippery mother out of the tub, as she'd done on previous occasions, so be it.)

As they folded the towels that Grace had just laundered, Jackie sat mesmerized by the sales pitch on her favorite channel. A pair of identical twins were peddling a "stylish yet versatile" luggage set, which Grace thought was an especially cruel thing to hawk during a global pandemic when no one could travel; Jackie seemed unaware of the irony. The twins were of an indeterminate age thanks to Botox, and they had the irritating habit of finishing the ends of their sentences in unison. *At least Hope and I are never that annoying.*

She caught herself the instant she thought it—the instant she put her sister in the present tense.

That hadn't happened in almost twenty-five years. It was the dreams, she told herself. Hope was on her mind more than she'd ever been. Grace tuned out the television and opened her laptop. If she was going to apply for a job, she'd need to make a résumé—which would be short, given that she'd worked at Barbara's for most of her adult life—but for now she investigated her various employment options. She was leaning toward a delivery job, as it would get her out of the house, but a customer-service position might pay better or at least more reliably without its reliance on tips. No part of her wanted to stop being a hairstylist, but the pandemic's resolution kept moving farther away. Steady work might help preserve her sanity.

Jackie stacked the towels neatly in the mesh tote. She covered her mouth with her hand as she yawned.

"You didn't sleep well?" Grace asked, for the sake of politeness. Jackie wasn't the one with eggplant-colored bags under her eyes from constant fitful nights.

"That cat was making a racket."

Grace suppressed her grin but was pleased to see Coco so comfortable on the floor beneath the big window, comatose in a diamond of sunshine.

"I don't have to work down here, if you want to nap with the TV," Grace offered.

"No, better not. Best to get through the day and go to bed tired." Jackie sat up a little, gazing toward the front window. "I wouldn't mind sitting on the porch though, if you can take a chair out."

Grace had to restrain herself from throwing aside her laptop and jumping up to haul whatever Jackie wanted out of the house.

"I have the folding chairs that go with the card table. Or I have a camp chair. It's a little raggedy, but comfortable." Coco lifted her head when Grace flitted past on her way to the basement.

"The camp chair's probably better."

———

Ninety seconds later Grace was on the front porch, placing the camp chair in a shady corner.

"You only have the one?" Jackie asked.

"I'll have to get some outdoor furniture one of these days. Is this good?"

Jackie eased herself down. Smiled. "Nice. I can watch the cars go by. The people. It's not too muggy today. Sure you won't join me?"

"I have to work on my résumé." Grace opened the screen door.

"Gray? Bring me a glass of iced tea, please?"

Sure, if it made her mom happy enough to stay outside for a while. Grace hurried to the kitchen and filled a sports bottle with ice and Jackie's sun-brewed tea.

"Thanks, hon," Jackie said as Grace handed it to her. At least she'd earned a *hon*.

"I'm gonna go work at my desk—it's better for my back. Do you have your phone on you, in case you need anything?"

"And call you from the porch? I think I can just yell really loud." Jackie smirked. "I'm fine Grace, you don't need to hover."

"Okay . . ." Grace knew she was failing some sort of subtlety test, overcompensating to hide her motive. She slipped inside, pondering her options if Jackie caught her in the act.

The solution came with a snap of her fingers: she could claim she was doing some housekeeping. Before heading upstairs, she went down to the basement landing and grabbed the bucket of cleaning supplies—paper towels, all-purpose spray cleaner, a dust rag, the bottle of Febreze.

Coco meowed a question at her as she crossed back through the dining room—likely having to do with the inadequate amount of food in her bowl.

"I'm going upstairs? Want to come?" Without waiting for the cat to answer, Grace scooped her up and, with one glance back at her mother on the porch, headed upstairs.

34

Guilt plucked a sour note in Grace's resolve as she stood in her mother's doorway. She wouldn't want anyone snooping through her own crap . . . But then again, it was Grace's house—the room was technically hers. She left the door wide open intentionally—the better to pass off her ruse—and set the bucket and the cat on the floor. Coco uttered a disgruntled yowl and fled back downstairs.

"I know. It really does stink in here." Grace squirted Febreze over the bed. And for good measure, spritzed the air around the room.

The entire mission would be pointless without the little wooden box. Grace checked the dresser drawer where she'd first found it, and there it was between the folds of a soft cable-knit sweater. For now, she left it atop the dresser. She surveyed the room. Where would her mother put the tiny key? It might depend in part on the magnitude of the secret held within the box. For easy access, the jewelry box would be a logical place to store it.

Compared to her own jewelry chest—an antique-store monstrosity that overflowed with every style of bauble Grace had ever liked, from the classy to the garish—Jackie's collection was prim and proper. Grace could barely remember if "Mommy" had worn jewelry when she was little. *Hope would know. (Not helpful.)* Petite faceted gems glittered from their tidy rows: gold chains with sparkly but subtle pendants; a tennis bracelet with *X*s and *O*s; gold stud earrings with modest diamonds or emeralds; hoop earrings in different sizes. It was all so sedate and refined. Was Jackie sedate and refined? Most of the pieces, Grace imagined, were gifts from Glen and Robert—for her birthday or their anniversary. Perhaps Valentine's Day?

Grace felt like an archaeologist, discovering an unknown person from her mother's belongings. Here was a woman who had turned her back on her hardworking, low-paying younger life. This woman wasn't broken by loss and didn't have to spend her days and nights mucking up bodily waste. The jewelry box revealed what Jackie would wear to show her Florida friends that she was comfortable financially, without ever being ostentatious. The pieces might have served as periodic reminders that the men she married had honored her and provided for her better than Paul No-Last-Name ever could have. Jackie's treasures were fine pieces, items with true value. They had durability in a way Grace's things did not.

She glanced around the room, appreciating her mother's furnishings differently than she had before. The headboard, nightstands, dresser. They were wood, solid, made to last. As were the hodgepodge of frames on the wall. In contrast, Grace bought cheap things at IKEA or trendy things online. And now that she looked closer, the pictures that she'd called "reproductions" were numbered prints.

Was her mother's evolution a product of age? Or of marrying and changing her lifestyle? Grace rejected the likelihood that this more genteel version of Jackie had always lurked within her; neither Jackie nor Grace had grown up in a home with artwork or heirlooms. Perhaps this explained why her mother felt okay about judging her, having acquired the solidity of enduring things.

I have artwork. Did Miguel's paintings count? Or wasn't he famous enough?

Grace hadn't meant to get so distracted. The missing key wasn't in the jewelry box, and that was good: Jackie hadn't intended for the box's contents to be accessible to everyone. A *secret* needed better precautions.

Coco meowed from the doorway but wouldn't come into the room. Guilt plucked another bitter note as Grace heard an accusation in the cat's sharp tone: *Shouldn't you be checking on my daddy?* That's what a good friend would do—it's what Grace intended to do, right after she found what she was looking for. The cat sprawled on her side just beyond the door, her tail flicking, her eyes on Grace. Judgmental eyes— and tail. Or so it felt.

Back to the task at hand. Grace was overwhelmed by her options and couldn't figure out where to start. In a movie, a key might be taped beneath a drawer. Or it could be in a more random place that Grace would never find: rolled in with a pair of socks, hidden in a medication bottle, pinned to the inner lining of a coat. That line of thinking was only going to frustrate her, so she started with the nightstands.

Each had one shallow drawer. The nightstand on the far side of the bed must have been Robert's, its contents untouched since he died. A man's reading glasses, flecked with dandruff. A couple of paperback books. A key ring—with full-size keys. A little tub of Vicks VapoRub. One hearing aid. A black comb. The drawer pulled out easily, and Grace raised it over her head to examine the bottom without disturbing the contents. Nope, nothing there.

Her mother's drawer was even less interesting. A datebook from the previous year. A travel pack of Kleenex. A wristwatch. Several ancient tubes of lip gloss. A few pens. An old phone charger. Once again, Grace lifted the drawer to check the underside. Once again, nothing but a panel of grainy wood.

The dresser was the obvious place to try next, though Grace was pretty sure she couldn't hoist the drawers without emptying them, and that seemed too risky. Instead of rummaging through them (having done that the first time she poked around her mother's room), she pulled each drawer out one at a time and crouched to examine it. Nothing, nothing, and nothing. But the lowest drawer was a problem; even if she lay on her back, she wouldn't be able to see the entire bottom. A flashlight might help, but she didn't have one handy. *That would be a good thing to keep in a bedside table.*

Upon further thought, Grace ruled out the last drawer as a viable spot for the key on the grounds that if she couldn't easily reach underneath it, then her mother couldn't either.

Where to look next . . .

The cat snapped her head forward, alert.

A second later, the front door opened. Grace acted on instinct: she snatched the little wooden box and her bucket of cleaning products and slipped across the hall to her room. Her mother, as it happened, wasn't on her way upstairs, so Grace crept out to spray more Febreze—toward the bathroom, toward the stairs—so the scent of it in Jackie's room wouldn't seem odd. Softly, she pulled her mother's door closed and retreated to her own room.

Grace sat on the porch step, a plate of salad on her lap.

"It's a lovely evening to eat outside," Jackie said from the camp chair, eating from a bowl.

"Mm-hmm." Grace had too much on her mind to engage in conversation, though her mother wasn't wrong.

Miguel had texted, confirming he was on the infectious floor, not intensive care, but otherwise was too exhausted to chat. He sent her the phone number for the nurse's station so she could find out what was going on. When Grace called the nurse had gushed about how nice Miguel was, "such a friendly soul," but was less effusive with actual facts. All Grace knew was that he was stable and on oxygen—not intubated, which was her greatest fear, but via a face mask. When Grace had asked about a prognosis, the nurse said the doctor would try to call her tomorrow and maybe he would know more.

Most of Grace's questions had been answered with a faux-cheery "He's stable." The nurse hadn't said any of the things Grace really wanted to hear, reassurances like "He's young and healthy—he'll have no problem beating this" or "His pulse ox is going up every hour."

Grace didn't like uncertainty, and somehow it had become the ruling force in her life. She picked the vegetables out of her salad until there was nothing left but lettuce. Stable was better than declining. But Grace didn't think it a good sign that Miguel was thirty-four and on oxygen.

After they were done eating, Jackie said it was getting too dark for her to see. Grace helped her inside and then washed their dirty dishes. She didn't think it was her imagination that her mother was preoccupied too. While their mostly silent supper hadn't been uncomfortable, Grace sensed a heaviness. She didn't really put a lot of effort into wondering what was on her mother's mind, consumed as she was by her own issues. But she was startled out of her rumination when Jackie yelled from the living room.

"Stop it! Get away from there!"

Grace ran in to see what was going on. Coco slunk past her, retreating in fear.

"Were you yelling at the cat?"

"She was scratching the sofa," said Jackie, eating a dessert of popcorn as she watched TV.

"I don't care about the sofa—please don't yell at the cat."

"If you say so. But she'll rip it to shreds."

"But yelling at her won't help. All you'll do is scare her. Cats don't connect words with actions."

"Cats are dumb."

"Cats don't speak English."

"Okay. It's your sofa. Just trying to help."

Grace doubted that her mother was trying to help. Jackie and Coco seemed mutually disapproving of each other, and Jackie's mercurial moods left Grace with infinitely more sympathy for the cat. It wasn't rational, but she felt superstitious about taking care of Coco, as if it were a test: If Coco did well in her care, Miguel would fully recover. If she did less than well, then Miguel might die. Coco was already flustered enough without Jackie adding to her stress.

As had become her strategy for defusing things with her mother, Grace headed for her room.

"Still working on that résumé?"

The snide question made Grace stop on the third step. It sounded almost (*exactly*) like Jackie was doubting her—doubting Grace's excuse for spending much of the day upstairs. In fact, Grace was returning to her room to try picking the lock on the little box (*bobby pins might work*), but her mother couldn't possibly know that.

"Looking for a job, yes."

"Good luck with that."

Was she really that surprised that her mother was such a master of casual scorn and sarcasm? Instead of asking Jackie why she was being such a bitch, Grace left, taking the remaining stairs two at a time. *Fuck her.*

God, how she hoped something truly scandalous was in that box. A stash of heroin. Some sort of priceless gem—stolen!—that Jackie could never have afforded. An outrageous receipt, an incriminating clue, a naked photo. Grace would stop feeling remorse for burglarizing her mother's room if she had something to thrust in Jackie's face. Knock her mother off her high horse. Force her to acknowledge that they weren't so different after all.

35

Grace lounged on her bed, listening to Spotify as she fiddled with the bobby pins. The evening was lusciously cool and she didn't need the air conditioner. Her other window was open, letting in the verdant aroma of things in bloom. It all felt so decadent and luxurious, lolling around in her perfumed room, accompanied by the sad, dulcet tones of Billie Eilish, girl genius, as she tried to pick open her mother's treasure box.

What would River say? *Only a bully feels better about themself by taking someone else down a notch.*

What would SunSoakedSergei say? *Don't lower yourself to other people's standards.*

What would Preston say? *If you don't want it done to you, don't do it to someone else.*

Yeah, the princes talked the talk, but they were paper dolls, and Grace, the voice behind the curtain, didn't live by the rules of the high road.

What would Miguel say? *You're so bad!* But then he'd help her.

What would her damsels say if they knew this was the person they'd trusted with their secrets?

She wasn't an expert on locks, but it didn't feel like there was anything inside the little keyhole for the pin to catch. If the consequences didn't matter, she'd hurl the box against the wall or go downstairs and get the hammer. But she still hoped to solve the mystery and return the box without being discovered. The music was a balm for her vexation, even as it morphed into something more rebellious.

Later, she wondered why she hadn't heard anything (the music wasn't *that* loud). She questioned that before she wondered how Jackie *knew*.

Grace's door opened. Her mother loomed in her peripheral vision.

She didn't knock. She should've knocked. But it happened so quickly that Grace didn't have time to get mad—or stuff the little box under her pillow. For an endless moment there was only their immobile gaze: Grace's with a busted hue; Jackie's flat and determined.

"This'll help." Jackie tossed something.

A tiny key landed on the soft bedspread beside Grace.

It's a dream. But as soon as she thought it, a different internal voice negated it.

No it's not.

Grace jerked into a sitting position, unnerved by that second voice: it wasn't hers. And it sounded more confident than Grace ever did (even when she playacted a prince).

Now that the key was beside her, Grace was reluctant to take it.

"Go on, Grace. It's time." As had happened so often in her nightmares, her mother's countenance lost its edge. Its menace. And with that loss, Jackie became a different person: smaller and less intimidating, sorrowful and old.

Now that Grace was being commanded to open the box, it was the last thing she wanted to do. But her mother stood there patiently waiting. Why did Jackie want her to see what was inside? Or perhaps she was merely granting permission, accepting the inevitable, seeing how Grace had already claimed her right to know.

A skein of snakes slithered inside her as she grasped the key, warm in her sweaty hand. She was certain now, with the dread alive in her bowels, that she absolutely did *not* want to see what was inside the little wooden box. *Too late.* She wouldn't be able to *unknow* whatever she was about to see, and it was going to change her; she knew that to her core.

And she was mistaken in thinking earlier that Miguel would've helped her—Miguel would've told her to leave Miss Jacquelyn's things alone and mind her own damn business.

Jackie waited, a somber but resolute statue.

Grace wished it was a dream, an unreal thing that she could leave behind. How had this become her life, where nightmares were preferable to the itchy, crawling reality that was threatening to tear open her skin, rip out her eyes?

She put the key in its tiny keyhole and turned. The box opened without resistance. Her mother stepped closer.

"What . . . ?" Grace didn't understand what she was seeing beneath the open lid. The box felt light—and hadn't rattled—because it was filled with white feathers.

Her mother reached forward and took a handful of the feathers. She blew them from her hand so they floated through the air.

"What are these? Why do you have them?" Grace asked, struggling to form a coherent question. She was missing something, but what? If her mother expected her to know the answer to this riddle, she was mistaken.

Jackie inhaled and exhaled the slowest breath of her life, as if this response took everything she had.

"These are from the pillow you used to smother your sister."

36

Wake up. Wake up! WAKE UP!

But no matter how many times Grace screamed it in her head, she still held the box in her hand. Her mother still stood beside her. A dusting of white feathers fluttered at their feet . . . the ones that weren't nestled in the box like ravaged wings.

"What did you say?" Grace whispered, hoping she'd heard it wrong.

"These are from the pillow you used. To smother your sister." The words were barely audible this time, as if Jackie had run out of energy.

Grace's mind ricocheted from past to present, dizzying memories like broken puzzle pieces. And then she considered the more recent past, desperate to recall every interaction she'd had with her mother since she moved in—good and bad, ordinary and strange. Jackie was nothing if not earnest: she clearly believed in what she was saying. But now Grace wondered if there was something deeper to her mother's erratic behavior—some kind of dementia that Grace hadn't been warned about.

"Mom . . ." Grace's confusion gave way to cautious worry. "That's not what happened. You know that's not what happened."

Jackie lumbered over to Grace's desk chair and collapsed with a sigh. "You think I saved a box of feathers, all these years, without a good reason?"

Her mother sounded so appropriately doleful; it was unnerving. Grace inspected the feathers. They could've been from any pillow, from any time.

"These could be from anything." A shiver convulsed her spine. The feathers were creepy. The conversation was creepy. Her mother was creepy. *I'm living with a crazy woman.* "Hope died from *pneumonia*."

"Hope *had* pneumonia. That wasn't how she died."

"Mom." The pity she'd felt was curdling. Even if her mom was senile or had some sort of brain tumor, that didn't excuse what she was saying. "I didn't . . . You have no right to say—to accuse me of something like that. I loved my sister!"

"I know you did. I know you loved her. When you were younger, I thought it was good that you locked it away. That you had no memory of it. I considered myself at fault too. You should never have been her caretaker. I was glad you could grow up, have a life, free of the trauma of what happened."

"Mom—this is insane! I couldn't *forget* that! You're suffering some sort of—"

"You didn't forget," Jackie said, so certain of herself. "You repressed it. I don't know what I expected when I came here, who I thought you would be after all this time. But I've learned . . . I see how unsettled your conscience is. Between the sleepwalking and the lying—"

"I don't sleepwalk!" Grace wasn't sure that was true. But she didn't have the option of denying her fabricated personas.

"When it happened, I thought it might have been an accident—a fit of anger. Something made you snap and you didn't mean to do—"

"I didn't!"

"But I've been wondering more and more, as I'm getting to know you better, if you meant it. And I'm not without sympathy—I know I bear some responsibility for what happened. There were things I couldn't deal with then—financially, emotionally—but I'm a different person now. You're torturing yourself and you don't even realize why. You've locked it all away so tight."

"This is absolute bullshit." Grace scooped up the fallen feathers. As agitated as she was, she still handled them delicately. Reverently. She secured them back in their box.

"Grace, I want to help you."

"Help me?" Bile roiled in her throat like she was going to vomit. She thrust the box at her mother. Jackie accepted it and held it tenderly on her lap—bringing to mind the unwelcome image of a funeral, of a mourner cradling an urn of cremains.

"Help you face the truth," said Jackie. "Set you free. So you can truly live the life you want. I shouldn't have let it go this long."

With every passing moment, tandem in this whirling delirium, Grace became more convinced that the pouty, petty, nasty version of her mother was the real one and the composed, sympathetic, reasonable-sounding Jackie was artificial—a persona, as well developed as Grace's, that existed for a more malignant sort of manipulation.

"Mother. This cannot possibly be the truth. Someone would've known. Someone would've been arrested. Probably *you*."

Jackie shook her head, unflappable in the face of Grace's denials. "I saw the signs. The petechial hemorrhaging. Her bloody nose. Blood on the pillow. And when the EMTs arrived, they knew me, from the nursing home. Ambulances came to the nursing home practically every day. And I explained about Hope's cerebral palsy. And the pneumonia was real—she'd just been to the doctor. But I told them she'd gotten stuck against her pillow, after a spasm or a seizure."

Now it was Grace's turn to shake her head. Her mother's story rolled effortlessly off her tongue. But so could the lie of a demented person. Yet there was something so simple and logical about her mother's claim: Hope very easily could've died that way.

"Is that what happened then?" Grace demanded. "She suffocated herself?"

"Oh Grace."

"Do not *oh Grace* me! You just provided a perfectly realistic explanation!"

"What I provided for the EMTs was a lie. To protect you."

"You're just fucking with my head. Get out. Get the fuck out." Though Grace pointed across the hall, she really wanted her mother out of her brain, out of her conscience. Out of her house.

Jackie tucked the chair back under Grace's desk before wearily heading for the door. She stopped there, not quite ready to leave.

"Out!" Grace bellowed.

"Don't you even want to ask? How I knew it wasn't an accident?"

"No."

"Her bloody pillow. You set it above her head, not under it. Before the EMTs came, I put it back and rolled Hope onto her side."

"Get. Your lunatic ass. Out of my room."

"I was protecting you."

A murderous rage swept over Grace. It wouldn't help her claims of innocence if she started hurling things at her mother or flung her down the stairs. She felt the flame licking its way along the fuse. Jackie must have seen it too—a bomb about to explode. Her eyes widened, and she nimbly backed out of the room, closing the door behind her.

"You're making me insane!" Grace's skin was on fire. She pulled at her hair, screaming in frustration, hoping the slaughtering noise of her own despair would extinguish her boiling emotions.

Like a child, she threw herself on the bed and wailed. How could her mother do this to her? Grace had never, ever been as vile a person as her mother wanted her to believe. There was something wrong with Jackie. She'd permeated Grace's house with her foul, festering sickness. Grace just wanted her life back—her job at Barbara's, her coworkers and clients, the restaurants she loved, the easy reliability of her old routine, her days filled with people. And Miguel—at work, after work, his near-daily presence in her life. She was falling apart, and instead of helping her, her mother had swept in to pummel the broken pieces, reduce her to something too small to repair.

Except the bad luck had started before her mother's arrival. The downward spiral began right before Grace moved into the house, with the start of the pandemic. Had she made a mistake, buying her own home? Had she set some curse in motion? She would sell it in an instant if it meant her life would rewind, go back to how it had been before the slow apocalypse started unraveling the world.

Little claws scratched at her door. Grace wiped her nose on the back of her hand and got up to open it a crack—just enough for Coco, half-boneless as cats were, to slip inside. Jackie's door was closed; Grace hoped she was packing. She would enthusiastically help her mother get resettled at a senior-living place—in fact, Grace would make that a priority. Jackie's internet skills probably weren't good enough to do a thorough search, so it would be up to Grace to find something suitable. She'd set her job hunt aside until she found somewhere else for Jackie to live.

Coco leaped onto the bed, and Grace flopped down beside her. As she petted her, the cat closed her eyes and purred.

"You're a good girl," she whispered in the cat's ear. "We're both good girls, right?"

It wasn't the same as having Miguel to talk to, but she was grateful for the cat's indulgent presence. Stroking her soft fur had a tranquilizing effect. When this was all over, when Coco was home with Miguel and Grace had her life back, she'd find a cat to adopt. It was time. She wanted to share her love with someone. She drifted to sleep on images of living with Miguel, in a bigger house with a bigger yard, and a menagerie of rescued cats. They were so easy to love. And so easy to care for.

37

Grace stayed in her room the next morning. She let Coco in and out, per the cat's desire, and made phone calls. Miguel's oxygen mask had been replaced with a nasal cannula and he was up for a short chat. Grace tried to get Coco to meow for him, but the cat only stared at her or sniffed the phone. Had Miguel simply been on vacation Grace might have cracked a joke about kidnapping his baby and keeping Coco for herself. Instead she reassured him that the cat was a sweetheart and doing well but missed him. Miguel insisted he was "hanging in there," but the wheezing as he breathed was worse than ever.

"I can try to come see you, after my two weeks are up," she offered.

"Are you feeling okay? And your mom?"

She wanted to tell him about Evil Jackie and her terrible accusation. But that conversation needed more than a couple of minutes. And in truth, she was a little afraid to discuss it with him. Miguel didn't yet have an opinion of her as a liar—and maybe someday she'd have to confess her shameful sins to him—but her mother made her feel like utter crap about herself. She couldn't handle it if Miguel wondered, even for a second, if Jackie's claim could possibly be true.

"We're fine," she told him. Miguel's words started to slur as he drifted toward sleep and they said their goodbyes.

For the next few hours she called nursing homes and senior communities. Grace wasn't sure if Jackie had enough money to afford assisted living, which was the ideal option, but it wasn't covered by Medicare in Pennsylvania. It was probably a moot point for the time being anyway, as every place she called relayed the same information: all the apartment buildings were in lockdown and not currently accepting new residents. And no one thought her mother sounded ready for a nursing home. *Grace* was ready.

A couple of the places unhelpfully informed her that Pennsylvania was moving toward an age-in-place policy, where eldercare agencies visited "your loved one's home" so they could live out the rest of their lives in the comfort of familiar surroundings. In their current situation, that sounded like the very definition of hell. There was no way Jackie was going to age in place in Grace's home. The best she could do was put Jackie on a couple of waiting lists.

It wasn't the quick resolution she had been hoping for, but the pandemic was taking a terrible toll on the elderly. Perhaps the buildings might reopen to new tenants sooner than anticipated if they found themselves with too many vacancies. *You're a bad, bad girl, Grace.* Whatever. Empty apartments weren't profitable. Capitalism didn't work without people continually handing over their money.

Her stomach rumbled, a grouchy messenger that told her to stop acting like a spiteful teenager, starving in her room all day so she could avoid her mother. But she really didn't want to see her. How could Grace look her in the face, or be civil to her, after Jackie had accused her of suffocating her sister?

Grace pressed her ear against her bedroom door, hoping to discern Jackie's whereabouts. There were no sounds of her—no clattering noises from the kitchen, no mumbling voices from the television. She poked her head into the hallway. Jackie's door was closed, but that was normal now, since she didn't want Coco getting fur all over her bed.

This was stupid. Just because Jackie was a fruitcake didn't mean Grace had to humor her insanity or hide herself away. Grace threw open her door and jogged down the stairs, ready to reclaim her domain. Yet, halfway down, she was relieved when she saw her mother sitting on the front porch. Grace was tempted to turn the dead bolt and lock her out . . . But she resisted, refusing to become the unethical monster Jackie believed her to be.

———

In the kitchen she did a quick inventory, checking the cabinets, refrigerator, freezer. Nothing had been further rearranged, but Grace needed to stock up on her own food. Let her mother eat like a rabbit if that's what she wanted; Grace added meatballs, bacon, and frozen chicken strips to her shopping list. For now she had the last burrito. It was fuzzed with freezer burn, but it only needed ninety seconds in the microwave. She excavated a single-portion cup of applesauce from her canned goods and carried her meal to the living room.

For the first time in forever, she got to sit in her preferred spot on the couch. As she ate, she watched a true-crime show about murderous families. Periodically she glanced toward the porch, where she could see the back of her mother's head. For a fleeting moment she felt sorry for her mom, who seemingly didn't have any friends to call, anyone she stayed in touch with.

Grace was almost done with the burrito before she wondered why Coco wasn't beside her, nosing in on her food. Perhaps the cat didn't like spicy Tex-Mex, though Grace was pretty sure she'd taste anything if given the chance.

"Coco . . ." She made the kissy sound that was most likely to draw the cat's attention.

Her meal finished, she flicked off the TV and carried her dirty plate to the kitchen sink.

"Coco . . ." Kissy-kissy call. Though she didn't bother to wash her own plate, she quickly rinsed out Coco's water bowl and gave her a fresh refill—something Grace should've done before breakfast, but she'd been in too much of a hurry when she fed the cat, determined not to cross paths with Jackie. She got the half-full garbage from the cabinet beneath the sink and scooped clumps of pee and poop out of the kitty litter. That didn't draw the cat's attention either, like it usually did. Grace knotted the garbage bag and left it by the back door, for now; later she'd take it out to her trash can.

The cat was probably asleep somewhere, ignoring her. But where? Her house wasn't that big, and if Coco wasn't in Grace's room or on the main floor, there were only two places left: the basement and her mother's room. She tried the basement first. It was nice and cool in the cellar, but it smelled like moldy weeds, a stagnant pond.

"Are you down here? Come here, baby." She checked behind the washer and dryer but was glad when the cat wasn't wedged in the crack with the spiderwebs. If one of the cardboard moving boxes had still been in box shape, that would've made a good cubby for a cat, but the cardboard was flat, stacked in the driest corner. There weren't any other places for Coco to hide; Grace could see everything else—her folding table set, a few plastic bins of mementos and decorations and miscellaneous junk, a rickety bookcase that had come with the house and held the laundry products and backup cleaning supplies.

Crap. That meant she had to search her mother's room.

On the way back through the first floor she considered popping onto the porch to let Jackie know she needed to go into her room. Her mother had unpredictable strategies for revenge—Grace considered it possible that the whole shit show with the feathers was retribution for meddling with Jackie's things. But Grace was getting antsier by the second about the cat's whereabouts. Didn't cats go off to hide when they were sick? As a compromise, she'd tell her mother after the fact—after she'd found Coco.

———

She dreaded opening the door to her mother's room almost as much as she'd dreaded, in the end, opening that damn box. It didn't matter how innocent the room looked, how well put together; it was boo-by-trapped. Grace made the kissy sounds and turned the knob, praying the cat would burst out, happy to escape from her fetid prison. But alas.

On her knees, Grace checked under the bed. She checked under the dresser, though the fluffy beast would barely fit under there. Grace's pulse was part bass drum, part ticking clock. If Coco wasn't in Jackie's closet, Grace wasn't sure what she would do.

The cat wasn't in the closet.

"Shit. Shit." Her heart drummed faster, clacking against her ribs. Desperate, Grace strode across the hall and checked her own closet, well aware that Coco couldn't have sneaked in—couldn't have pried the door open—while Grace had been just feet away, making calls and googling.

She recalled Miguel saying that Coco liked to stretch out in the bathtub when it was really hot out, and sometimes he'd let the water drip for her. It wasn't that hot, but it was possible the water was dripping.

But no, the cat wasn't in the tub or behind the toilet or in the cabinet under the sink.

"Fuck. Fuck. Coco, come here Coco . . ." Oh God, Grace was going to flunk the test. Coco wasn't going to be okay, and then it would be Grace's fault if Miguel didn't recover.

Should she check the lower cabinets in the kitchen? Or under the sofa? She descended the stairs so quickly her feet practically slid. "Coco!"

Frantically, she looked in places the cat couldn't possibly be, unless Coco possessed an invisibility cloak or had reduced herself to the size of a beetle. But Grace scanned behind the couch, under the couch, behind the television and its stand.

"What are you doing?"

Jackie's presence startled her, but Grace didn't have time to deal with her; this was starting to feel like a crisis.

"I can't find the cat." She strode past her mother through to the dining room. Coco wasn't under the table, but she could be on one of the dining chairs. She leaned under the table: the chair seats were empty.

"I let her out," said Jackie.

Grace bolted upright. "What . . ."

"She was nosing at the door."

"You let her outside?" She gripped the tabletop, overwhelmed by a cacophony of emotions.

Jackie stood there with her arms crossed, indifferent to Grace's distress. "Animals like fresh air, Grace. Don't look at me like that."

Grace felt like a teakettle about to boil with screams. "What the fuck is wrong with you?" She raced for the entryway and slipped into a pair of shoes. "When? How long has she been out?"

"She's a cat, an animal, with natural animal instincts. You're overreacting."

"She's an indoor cat! Someone *else's* indoor cat!"

"You need to learn to manage your anger."

"I have! I was!" But as Grace heard herself losing control, she realized she hadn't been furious with anyone during the years when she and Jackie had lived apart. Without Jackie's presence, Grace hadn't had a temper to manage. "Where did she go?"

"I let her out the front. So she could sit with me on the porch."

Grace dashed out the front door, unsure which way to look, which direction to start. Jackie came out after her, returning to her chair.

"She's probably exploring. She'll come back when she's hungry."

Rabid with exasperation, Grace uttered a short scream, then leaped off the porch.

"You're being dramatic," Jackie spat. "But last time I saw her she was heading that way."

Grace turned around long enough to see her mother pointing around toward the backyard. She took off sprinting down the strip of grass that separated her house from her neighbor's, but then slowed to a speed walk, afraid she might startle Coco.

She was half-aware of herself muttering like a crazy person, whispers invoking various gods and profanity and fluttery prayers. Coco was not going to come back when she was hungry. Coco would only smell strange and foreign things in this wild, stupefying landscape; she'd have no idea which way to go. Grace imagined her skulking through people's yards, terrified. She imagined her crossing a street—and freezing midstride as a car hurtled toward her.

"Coco . . ." She had made the kissy noise so many times her lips were about to cramp. Grace stood in the middle of her little backyard and did a three-hundred-sixty-degree scan. Would Coco climb up a tree? Would she hide in someone's garage? It wasn't until Grace was facing her own back door that she saw the furry orange ball, pressed in the corner where her steps met the house.

"Coco!" She almost wept in relief. The cat uttered a pitiful mewl. Grace hunched down and made herself small as she tiptoed toward the cat, hoping Coco wouldn't run off. "Good girl, good girl, it's okay baby."

As soon as she was close enough, Grace scooped the cat onto her shoulder and gratefully accepted that Coco dug her claws in, hanging on for dear life.

Seconds later, they were both inside. Coco jumped away, using Grace's shoulder as a springboard, not quite ready to forgive or be consoled. The scratches she left were deep and painful, and Grace went right for the alcohol—not the rubbing alcohol, but the bottle of rosé that was chilling in the fridge. She quickly thanked all the gods and goddesses for keeping Coco safe—and for the wine's easy screw-off top.

After a much-needed glug-and-swallow of the crisp, sweet rosé, Grace marched through the house and poked her head out the front door.

"I found the cat. If you ever let her out again I'll kill you." She didn't wait for her mother to reply. Bottle of wine in hand, Grace made a purposeful retreat to her room, where she planned to drink until drunk.

38

Even her dreams were drunk. They caromed from one giddy scenario to the next, entertaining in their efforts to scare her. There was the one with the UFO enthusiasts, waiting in an orderly queue to get beamed up onto a hovering spaceship. Miguel was in the dream, laughing beside Grace as they watched from their picnic table, eating fried chicken. Somehow they were the only two to notice that the spaceship's elevating "beam" was actually a straw. The UFO enthusiasts weren't boarding a ship but were being sucked into a giant alien's mouth.

The night was like a carnival of mind-numbing rides. Later she recalled the dizzying colors, a fun house of horrors with few specifics. One snippet lodged in her memory: she was in her house getting ready to go to a party, but she couldn't find a pair of shoes. Or rather, every pair she found—in her closet, by the front door—had legs attached to them. Some were only short stumps of leg, ending midcalf, wearing her sandals or flip-flops. Others had knees and thighs, their feet stuffed into her favorite autumn boots. She had no memory of the dream resolving—of finding a pair of unoccupied shoes, of donning them and heading out.

The semiconscious part of her wondered if there was a parallel universe in which another Grace endlessly ran around the house looking for shoes. Endlessly finding only disembodied legs.

———

Grace strolled through the Rite Aid, killing time before meeting Talia at the library. If she and Talia had really been friends, Grace would've asked her to meet at the drugstore, and they could've judged the merits of the shimmery eye shadows and bold nail polishes together. But Talia was her assigned project partner for their world-history class—a pairing that had made the serious, curly-haired girl roll her eyes. The other Allderdice eleventh graders regarded Grace's social standing as something between White Trash and Pothead. That made Grace roll *her* eyes. She wasn't that trashy, and she'd only tried pot a few times. For Talia's benefit more than her own, Grace had made a real effort with her research; she hoped her partner would be pleasantly surprised.

In the meanwhile, she took in the amazing array of junk and necessities that filled the store's shelves. Vitamins and first aid gear. Shampoo and shavers. A half-dozen different brands of cosmetics, all competing for the same eyelashes and lips. Pantyhose. Tampons. Adult diapers. School supplies, light bulbs, a random selection of electronics. Grace meandered around the store, preoccupied by her inability to decide if she should buy snacks before meeting Talia. Was Talia more a Doritos girl or a KitKat girl? If Grace aimed to be extra considerate—buying both salty and sweet snacks—would her partner just gossip to everyone that Grace the Pothead hadn't been able to get through a simple project session without succumbing to the munchies? Perhaps instead of food she should get a couple of Diet Cokes.

None of this would have mattered if she hadn't liked Talia. But the truth was Grace liked a number of the girls in her classes who never gave her the time of day. Her most recent best friend had moved to Cleveland over the summer, and Grace refused on principle to continue associating with the kids on her street (most of whom really were glassy-eyed potheads). Eleventh grade was pretty lonely.

When Grace turned into the greeting card aisle her awareness snapped into sharp focus as she realized where she'd wandered. The birthday cards were so bright and festive. And familiar. She stopped to admire them, unable to keep from smiling as she remembered being in this store—in this very spot—with Hope. Stealing baubles for their paper dolls. Jewels for Mona and Rona.

A tsunami of grief threatened to pummel her. Grace was usually good at keeping Hope out of her thoughts. But now she craved her, yearned in that impossible way for Hope to be there beside her. Grace wanted it so badly she saw ghost glimpses of Hope's power chair, heard her yapping about how dumb high school was. The dumb teachers and dumb rules and dumb after-school clubs. How dumb it was to have to get up so early and eat lunch so early and have daily homework that was only stupid busywork. *No smart person would waste their time on that crap!* But with Grace as her assistant, Hope would've gotten straight As—even if Grace got B minuses for turning in the same work. They could've griped about that too.

Grace needed someone to gripe with. Her mom had no interest in her teenage world. When Grace allowed herself to think about it, she wasn't sure how she'd managed to survive these years without her sister.

A tear slipped down her cheek. She stopped it with her tongue; it tasted delicious. Salty. Cataclysmic.

Fuck this. Refusing to fall deeper into her maudlin mood, she grabbed four snack-size bags of potato chips in different flavors. If Talia gave her shit about it, Grace would eat them all herself.

She awakened feeling melancholy. The dream had been as accurate as her memory of that day. Talia had thanked her for the chips. They'd huddled on the floor in a far corner of the library, crunching greedily as they worked, giggling when they feared they were being too loud.

They'd gotten an A on the project, and while Talia never rolled her eyes at Grace again, they also never became friends. She had come into the salon once, during Grace's early years at Barbara's. Talia's appointment was with another stylist, and she and Grace had pretended they didn't see each other.

That's not what Grace was sad for, though. She'd been young enough when Hope died that she hadn't yet started imagining the *future*, the unknown land of her older life. Young Grace hadn't projected herself into scenarios where there was an empty space where her sister would've been. For many years Hope was simply *gone*. It wasn't until Grace was a few years older that she started thinking things like *Hope would be in college now*, or *I bet Hope would've auditioned for* Project Runway, or *Would she have gotten married?*

It was cruel that Jackie wanted to revive her loss, compel Grace to think about these things. And perhaps her mother recognized that and was trying to make up for it: she was in one of her perky, best-mom-on-the-block moods when Grace came downstairs. Apparently she'd ordered a grocery delivery; bags were scattered around the kitchen floor. As soon as Grace came in, Jackie's face lit up. She stopped putting the food away and slipped her bony hands into a new pair of silicone hot mitts.

"I made you some breakfast." Jackie opened the oven and pulled out a cookie sheet neatly stacked with buttermilk pancakes.

"You did?" Grace couldn't fathom why her mother was being so congenial, but her mouth watered at the sight of the perfectly golden-brown pancakes.

"I'm in a cooking mood. If you want sliced strawberries on top, I just had a couple pounds delivered—they should be in one of these bags. Or, I got real maple syrup." Jackie set the cookie sheet on the stove and picked up the syrup bottle from the counter, displaying it like a game show hostess.

Grace stood there in a state of semishock. Though in many ways this was the preferable form of Jackie, it was also the more confusing. But Grace could roll with it for the moment, especially since she never spent money on real maple syrup.

"Thank you, syrup would be perfect."

"And I started the coffee pot. It should be ready in a minute."

"Thank you." As Grace stood there somewhat stupefied, Jackie forked three pancakes onto a plate and then carried it—and the syrup bottle—into the dining room. Grace sheepishly followed her and sat at the table, disconcerted by her mother's obsequious behavior. Jackie, performing like a waitress in a fine restaurant, uncapped the syrup for her.

"Thank you," Grace mumbled again. As she drizzled the dark-amber goo over her pancakes, her mother spun back to the kitchen. "You aren't eating?"

"I already had my fruit shake." Jackie resumed unpacking the groceries.

Grace didn't feel right about consuming her mother's thoughtfully prepared breakfast while Jackie kept on working. Of course, it could still turn out that this show of rapprochement had hidden strings attached and the meal might come with a dessert of emotional whiplash. But it could also be a genuine olive branch, an actions-speak-louder-than-words attempt to heal their rift. It was Grace's turn to make a move. She craned her head toward the kitchen.

"You can sit with me? Keep me company. I'll put the rest of the groceries away after I eat."

Jackie smiled. Closed the refrigerator. "I did wake up a bit manic. Okay, I'll get my tea."

She returned a moment later with a mug in each hand, coffee for Grace—which she set beside her plate—and her steaming concoction of slightly noxious herbs. As Jackie settled in across the table, there was an awkward hole in their conversation.

"These are really delicious." While Grace had the impression they were playing a game, acting out versions of themselves that had no past, the pancakes were legit top notch.

"Glad you like them, hon." Jackie held her mug between the fingertips of both hands and took tiny sips. She was very good in her role—a savvy opponent.

Grace heard the deep voices of her alter egos in her head, reminding her that the best strategy was to take the high road. It was rarely a difficult pathway to spot, even when she crossed it grudgingly. "I'm sorry about what I said yesterday. After finding Coco."

"I'm sorry too. I really wasn't trying to hurt the cat."

"I know. I'm just extra sensitive right now. Because of Miguel."

"I know."

It got easier after that. It didn't feel as much like a performance. A more natural conversation tiptoed in, and when Grace was done eating, she washed the dishes—and took out the garbage that had been sitting there since the previous day. She let Jackie boss her around as they put away the groceries, not really caring anymore that her mother had very specific ideas about where things should be.

"You know what might be fun?" The kitchen was immaculate now as Jackie leaned against the counter. Fortunately she didn't wait for Grace to guess an answer, as she had no idea where her mother was going with the question. "I got all the ingredients to make a lasagna—ricotta cheese, mozzarella, spinach. Tomatoes, fresh basil. I even planned to make the pasta from scratch."

"That sounds amazing."

"Would you like to do it together? I know I wasn't much of a cook when you were young, and I didn't have anything worth teaching. But . . . I've learned some better tricks since then."

Jackie's smile seemed warm and genuine. The last few weeks had been so rough, and Grace desperately needed these moments to recuperate.

"I'd like that."

They took their time, unencumbered by a schedule. Jackie got them started with the marinara sauce. Next they made the sheets of pasta. Grace enjoyed that step the most: it was like working with adult Play-Doh. She liked the challenge of rolling out the sheets, trying to make them even and thin.

"I'll have to get a pasta maker," Jackie said brightly. "Then we can make fettuccine and linguine."

Grace wasn't sure what the difference was, but starchy pasta dishes were a million times better than salads and shakes. "I could get you one for your birthday?"

"That's a sweet offer . . . but now I'm not sure I want to wait that long."

"How about an early birthday present?"

"Deal!" Jackie laughed.

They got their fillings ready, and soon it was time to layer everything in the big stoneware pan—something Grace wasn't aware her mother had purchased.

The house filled with tantalizing aromas as the casserole slowly baked. There was a movie in Grace's Netflix queue that she'd been wanting to see, and while she'd once hoped to watch it with Miguel, Jackie sounded eager to watch it too. Halfway through the movie, the lasagna was finally ready to eat.

"Dining room, or in front of the TV?" Grace asked, getting the forks and napkins.

"TV." Jackie handed her a plate of steaming, gooey, cheesy-tomatoey pasta—and flashed a girlish grin.

They were having fun—genuine, effortless fun.

When they were back in their places on the couch, Grace hit play and took the first bite of their masterpiece.

"Mm. Scrumptious!"

"It is, isn't it," Jackie agreed, again with that innocent, delighted grin. "And there's enough for days."

Grace hadn't had many Girls' Nights (unless Miguel counted), and maybe her mother hadn't either. *Is this what I would've had with Hope?* But as soon as she thought it she knew the answer was no. She and Hope had never been equals. Grace had been at her beck and call; Adult Hope would have dominated Adult Grace, just as it had been in their youth. Jackie was bossy back then, too, but hadn't she also been in Hope's service? Grace looked at her mother's profile. There she was—Grace—in the contours of her mother's nose, chin.

Growing up, Grace had felt invisible, overshadowed by Hope's unique charisma. Now she understood how invisible Jackie had probably felt too. Their problem, after all, might not be one of too many differences but too many similarities.

Could they work with that? Use their common ground to navigate toward an enduring peace? When she'd awakened that morning, Grace would've insisted the answer was no. But now she felt the embryonic stirrings of hope.

39

For the first time in months, she started the day without the feeling of being at war with something. Well, except for a slight headache. Coco greeted her with a chirpy meow and followed her to the bathroom. When Grace got out of the shower, the cat was sitting on the closed toilet lid, a feline ballerina licking one extended leg. It made Grace laugh, thinking how the girls in the house were getting in sync.

The morning was heating up fast, and as Grace went downstairs she was grateful that Jackie had thought to turn on the dining room air conditioner early enough that it was already cool. Grace paused in front of it for a second, letting the cold air billow the long fabric of her maxi dress.

"Good morning," she said to Jackie, en route to starting a pot of coffee.

"Someone's in a merry mood." Her mother sounded surly. Jackie chopped fruit next to the sink, seemingly intent on keeping her back to Grace.

"Didn't you sleep well?" Grace poured water into the coffee maker.

Jackie shot her a scowl. "Why are you all dressed up? It's not like we can go anywhere."

"I like to wear flowy dresses when it's hot out." She fanned the material against her legs. "Keeps me cool."

For the sake of the previous day's progress, Grace opted to overlook her mother's sour, skeptical expression. She empathized with how a bad night's sleep could tarnish a person's ability to function. While the coffee maker did its magic, Grace got out a microwaveable plate. They'd gotten lucky that it hadn't been a scorcher the previous day, or they might not have wanted the oven on for hours. Grace faintly remembered a dream about eating more lasagna, and it had been a driving factor in getting her promptly out of bed, showered, and dressed.

"I'll just have a little piece for breakfast," she said, half to herself, as she opened the refrigerator. "And lunch. And dinner."

She'd expected to see the big stoneware dish hogging up the middle shelf, but it wasn't there. Just as she'd searched for the cat in impossible places, she pushed aside the containers of berries, checked the top shelf and the bottom shelf, looked in and around the leafy greens as if the lasagna were merely lost in a refrigerated forest. It wasn't visible through the produce drawer. It couldn't fit on the door.

Grace snapped her fingers, reasonably sure that her mother had already cut the casserole into meal-size portions and stored them in the freezer. The fog of icy air felt lovely . . . but there were no Pyrex containers of lasagna in the freezer, just partial loaves of old bread and the less-desirable remnants of her too-lazy-to-cook eating habits.

"Where's the lasagna?" she asked her mother.

Jackie spun around from the dishes she was washing. "The what?"

"The lasagna—big cheesy masterpiece, meals-for-days . . ." Jackie gazed at her, uncomprehending. "The amazing sauce you taught me to make? The pasta?"

Oh fuck. A new war was underway—a scrimmage of staring, a battle to see who would crumble in doubt.

"Mom, please don't fuck around. Yesterday was such a good day, we made so much progress—"

"Yesterday you threatened to kill me."

"What?"

"Over that damn cat."

"That wasn't yesterday. Mom, we spent the day cooking, and watching a movie, and we apologized for all of that."

Her mother stared at her long and hard. Finally, she dried her hands and turned to Grace, her body stripped of its taut combat readiness. Jackie sort of melted against the counter, like she needed something to hold her up.

"What's wrong with you?" Jackie asked with solemn wonder.

Grace knew what was happening: her mother was trying to convince her, by exaggerating her maternal concern, that the previous day hadn't happened—and that Grace was nuts. Wow, Jackie was a sublime actor, but the attempted manipulation was unforgivable. This was what Grace had been expecting, in some form, when her mother first presented those pancakes.

"Are you a sociopath?" Grace asked, deadpan.

"Are you?"

"Did you put it in the garbage?" Grace whipped open the cabinet door beneath the sink, forcing her mother to scoot out of the way.

"What are you doing?"

Banana peels. Melon rinds. The sticky innards of a cantaloupe.

"So you already took the garbage outside." Grace strode for the back door, intent on going out to inspect the trash can. But she stopped. There was a grocery bag by the door. By all appearances—and rank smells—it was the bag with the kitty-litter scoopings from the day *before* yesterday.

"It's not my job to clean up after you," Jackie said, watching Grace wrinkle her nose at the trash. "Even if it is stinking up my—our—kitchen."

Grace tried, tried, tried to remember more of the previous day. She remembered cleaning up the kitchen and taking the garbage outside—Good Girl! And she recollected all the things she'd done with Jackie during the day—rolling out the pasta, seasoning the sauce. It had smelled so savory and delicious while it was in the oven . . . though she couldn't recall much of the movie.

It bothered her that even with concerted effort she couldn't remember any of the little things, like taking care of the cat or texting Miguel or performing her bedtime routine. And surely those things had been part of her day. Those were things she did every day. Unless . . .

Her vision went fuzzy and the bones in her legs started to liquify. She grabbed the counter so she wouldn't collapse.

"Grace!" Jackie hurried to her side, trying to help her stay upright.

"Was it a dream? Was it all a dream?" The headache surged, slamming into the front of her skull. Grace winced. The night had started with weird dreams, about UFOs and finding feet in her shoes. But after that . . . What happened after that? Grace thought she'd awakened and lived out an ordinary, unexpectedly pleasant day. "Was I asleep?"

"Let's go sit down. Can you walk?"

Jackie gripped her waist, guiding her, as Grace held a hand across her forehead like a visor, pressing her temples. They shuffled into the living room, and Grace dropped onto the couch.

"I don't understand what's happening with you," Jackie said as she sat beside her.

"That makes two of us." Grace kept her eyes shut.

"Maybe you should see a doctor."

"Maybe." She stopped massaging her head and looked at her mother. "It really didn't happen? None of it? The pancakes? The lasagna? The movie?"

"I'm sorry, Grace." She sounded wounded, full of remorse. "Is that what put you in such a good mood? The dream?"

Grace nodded. "We cooked together. And apologized about—yesterday. We had a nice time. It felt so *real*. It was a whole *day*!"

"Hon, you're not well. And I'm sorry if I contributed to your stresses, I know there's a lot going on. And I know you'd be so much happier if you were at the salon every day, and if Miguel was fine, and if you could do all the things you were used to. But you need to take care of yourself."

Tears spilled down Grace's cheeks as she nodded. Her voice squeaked as she tried not to sob. "I just want to feel normal again."

"I know, honey." Jackie took her hand, urging Grace to her feet. "Come on, let's see if you can get some real rest. Catch up on some sleep."

Grace remembered this side-by-side walk up the stairs, only last time she was helping her mother, not the other way around. "I wish we'd had that nice day together. Mom, it was so nice."

"We will, we'll have another chance."

40

Jackie led her to the bed, but sleep was the last thing Grace wanted. More likely what she needed to do was never fall asleep again and see if reality sorted itself out while she kept a watchful eye on it. She still couldn't shake the feeling that her mother was involved with this somehow, the Widow Sandwoman with her bag of toxic dust.

"I don't need more sleep." But Grace sat on her bed, leaned against her headboard. "Maybe just a lot of coffee."

"Coffee won't fix anything, but I'll bring it up. Do you want something to eat? Some fruit?"

Was Grace really sure that her mother wasn't poisoning her in some subtle, devious way?

"Do we have any oatmeal?"

"I'm not sure—I'll see."

While her mother was downstairs, Grace texted Miguel:

How you doing?

She didn't think he was going to reply, but two minutes later she got a response:

Ok. No-go new. Tires.

Grace assumed this was autocorrect's attempt at "nothing new" and understood he was tired. Nothing about the butchered words on her screen made her happy. She saw two Miguels in her mind: gregarious and colorful, with a beaming smile and a quick comeback; listless and pale, the cell phone slipping from his hand onto the hospital sheets. He might have already fallen back to sleep, but Grace sent him one of the pics she'd taken of Coco and a string of rainbow-heart emoji.

Jackie returned with Grace's travel mug of coffee and a plate of toast.

"No oatmeal, sorry. I'll put it on the shopping list. I made you some peanut butter toast with sliced bananas."

"Thank you." The good dream flickered in her mind, Jackie's capacity for kindness.

Grace pictured herself as a child with a cup of hot cocoa and peanut butter–banana toast—though she was pretty sure she'd prepared them herself. The memory became sharper, and she saw an ugly, rainy weekend when she and Hope were around ten. Grace had made them the yummy snack, which she had to help her sister eat, and they'd watched a science fiction movie on TV.

"I know you're disinclined, but try to get some decent sleep," said Jackie. "Everything's hard right now, but you're gonna get through it."

"Okay. Thank you." She sipped her coffee and listened to her mother go back downstairs. Jackie started coughing, the sound diminishing as she headed for the kitchen. *We're a mess.*

She appreciated that her mother was helping her, especially as their living arrangement had been made under the pretext that Grace would do the caregiving. It was fortunate that Jackie was well enough, but Grace was worried about her mother's cough. And her wily brain. And her own discombobulated brain. And Miguel's lungs. And her mother's lungs.

Was there any part of her current existence that Grace *wasn't* worried about?

She found herself in a self-reflective mood as she ate her breakfast. There was no way to make sense of the dream that felt like an entire lived day, or her disappointment that it hadn't been real. It was too fresh, too raw, so she shoved it aside and focused on something that had been claiming more territory in her thoughts: Had she really, *really* been as burdened in her childhood as her memory wanted her to believe? Had she really spent *that* many hours tending to her sister, or did it just seem that way because of a child's uneven sense of time? Looking back on it, it didn't seem realistic that she and Hope had been on their own, unsupervised, as often as it may have seemed.

Jackie had worked full time, but Grace remembered her being there in the mornings and getting Hope ready for school. And giving them breakfast. If she and Hope had been on their own every day, wouldn't it have been for a *short* time—the window between when the babysitter left and their mom got home from work? Yes, there had been the occasional evening when Mommy had to stay late or run errands before coming home. As a child, had it all felt like always and forever?

Did it matter?

It mattered because it bothered Grace now to think of how burdened she'd felt—that was a real memory—when perhaps it had only been her selfish impression of the responsibilities their life situation had demanded. *It's so unfair.* That had been a frequent motto—*it* being every chore that Grace had undertaken when Hope had none; *it* being every minute of her own life that she'd given to helping Hope or Mommy that she'd wanted all to herself.

She might have been selfish. Probably was. But weren't most children?

The coffee eased her headache, and the toast was filling, and she told herself she should go take a long walk and clear her head with a little exercise. But her eyelids were noncompliant, naughty theater curtains dropping over her field of vision even though the show wasn't over yet. She didn't want to sleep her life away—

Her eyelids sprang open as she wondered if this was what Miguel was feeling. Was Grace sick? Was her mother? Did they both have milder forms of the virus? It was almost reassuring, as being sick was better than going mad. Or maybe it was a sickness of madness—a new variant. A mutation.

Grace felt herself mutating as she dropped into sleep. Her body folded itself into something weightless as her consciousness detonated into the fragmented infinity of the unknown.

41

The stained-glass windows were beautiful in spite of the dreary day. Hope's funeral was held in a church Grace had never been in, and the pews were filled with people of all ages. Mommy's coworkers came (and a few of the elderly residents). And kids from school (with their parents). And families from the neighborhood. Everyone said nice things to Mommy as they gripped her hand or leaned in for a feeble hug. They whispered to Mommy that Hope was in heaven or that she was an angel. Even if Hope were in heaven, Grace considered it very unlikely that her sister was an angel; Hope just didn't have the temperament for that, though she would probably enjoy having wings and flying around.

It was creepy to imagine a ghostly Hope watching her from above, hovering near the ceiling, spying on everything she did.

Nobody said very nice things to Grace. They just looked at her and frowned and maybe patted her cheek like she was five, not almost twelve. From Grace's perspective, Mommy still had one more daughter but Grace didn't have any more sisters. She'd heard people say, long before Hope died, that parents never got over losing a child, that it was the worst possible thing that could happen. Grace didn't understand why people didn't say the same thing for someone who'd lost a twin. For all their differences, they were as bonded and alike (at least genetically) as any two people could be. For as many times as Hope had driven her bonkers, she'd also been a best friend. And Hope was always the fearless one, the one unafraid to be alone in the house when it looked like a horror movie outside. Hope had been the one with all the ideas for things to do and games to play.

As Grace sat in the front-row pew, she felt very small, apprehensive of what it would be like to go home to an empty house, truly alone. Time would tick more slowly without Hope there, hours and hours of solitary uncertainty. Grace remembered all her cranky wishes: praying for more time to herself, more time to do her homework, more time to make her own decisions. But now her wishes had come true, and this wasn't what she wanted. She didn't want to do her homework if she couldn't help Hope with hers first. She didn't want to decide how to spend her afternoons if it meant Hope didn't exist.

On the ride to the cemetery, Grace sat in the limousine with Mommy. They gazed in opposite directions, watching hard flakes of snow skate across the windows. Grace wasn't dressed warmly enough, her tights and dress shoes no match for the biting wind. When Hope's casket started sinking into the hole, Grace thought it was going to descend forever, like the elevator in the coal mine she'd visited on a field trip. An endless plunge into the darkness. When she tried to grip her mother's hand, she found a statue of ice beside her. Her mother didn't move, didn't cry; Grace wasn't even sure she was breathing.

Their home, which had once been a hubbub of activity—a thousand things to do and not enough hours or hands to do them—fell into an uncomfortable stillness. Mommy stopped rushing around impatiently and didn't bark at Grace to do even the most basic chores. After work her mother didn't collapse on the couch for a quick nap; she'd just sit there, staring at whatever Grace was watching on TV. Wherever Mommy ambled through the house, Grace found wet footsteps: the temperature inside was too warm for someone made of ice.

That went on for a while. Neither of them spoke much, especially to each other. They went about their business—Grace to school, Mommy to the nursing home—and lived like roommates. When her mother worked later shifts, Grace cooked supper. When her mother worked earlier shifts, Grace got herself up and ready for school. Eventually they emptied Hope's bedroom and turned it back into a dining room.

Her mother started talking about selling the house when Grace was a junior in high school.

"I don't want it anymore. Do you?"

Grace shrugged and shook her head, knowing her mother had grown up there too. A horror grew inside Grace, the awful possibility of never being able to get away from one's childhood home. Such a failure might curse a person's chances of ever reaching adulthood.

"When you're done with high school, I'll sell it."

"Okay." The house was full of ghosts; leaving the house forever became the beguiling reward for getting through high school.

"And maybe move away," Mommy added.

"Okay."

"You'll want your own place, won't you?"

Yes, Grace wanted her own apartment, even if it was a tiny room in a sweltering attic.

In those last couple of years together, she remembered her mother always being on the far side of whatever room they were in, a distance between them greater than was possible given the square footage of their house. If Grace came in and her mother was already home, she'd see her dollhouse figure a hundred yards away in the kitchen. Or if Grace came downstairs and her mother was on the sofa, it was a raft bobbing away on a CinemaScope ocean.

Her mother got Grace settled in her tiny attic apartment and paid for her training at the Pittsburgh Beauty Academy, and then completed her disappearing act. Watching Mommy drive away wasn't so different from how it had been when they'd lived together in the house; her mother had long been a hazy silhouette, always receding. Finally they were in different homes, in different states, and perhaps as Grace was free to claim her adulthood, her mother could finally thaw and become a person again. They did well without each other, a fact Grace wouldn't deny.

She dreamed of emptiness, of falling, of drifting through outer space. It was a troubling dream, cognizant of the cosmic void, of the improbability of any sort of rescue or reprieve. She feared it would go on forever. Until suddenly it became difficult to breathe.

I'm out of oxygen.

But that was silly—she didn't even have a space suit.

Her lungs heaved, desperate to draw in air. But when she opened her mouth, the only thing she sucked in was cloth. Something was pressing down on Grace's face so hard she couldn't even open her eyes.

42

Her heart jolted, strong and arrhythmic, like a lifeless patient under shock paddles. Grace had an awareness of impending death—and even if it was a dream, she no longer trusted that to keep her safe.

Her thrashing hands connected with another pair of hands—the ones pressing the pillow to her face. Grace started kicking and writhing. She pulled at her attacker's wrists, praying her bitten-down nails were long enough to gouge skin. Finally she got her legs untangled from the sheets—and pulled her knees up and kicked with both feet. Her attacker took a stumbling step backward, and it was enough for Grace to push the pillow off and roll away.

She nearly tumbled off the other side of the bed, gasping and heaving, blinking against the brightness of the overhead light.

During the brief duel she'd had a single impulse: to fight for her life. Now, one leg on the bed, one leg off, she sucked in air and identified her assailant.

Jackie. Her mother. Winded, hair disheveled, gripping the pillow in both hands.

"What the fuck are you doing?" It came out raspy. Grace's throat was sore—had she been screaming? Paralyzed by shock, she tried to process what was happening. The why of it. The what-the-fuck of it. The lingering possibility that she was still asleep.

Her mother tossed the pillow aside, smoothed back her hair, rubbed her wrists where Grace had grabbed them. She sat with one hip on the edge of the mattress, as if she might tell a short bedtime story.

"Did you just try to kill me?" Grace got to her feet on the far side of the bed, ready to flee. She kept her eyes on Jackie, unsure how fast her mother could move.

"No hon, I was just smothering you." She said it in her nice, good-mother voice.

"What the fuck's the difference?" Grace was tempted to call nine one one. But as she ran the scenario through her head—insisting to a dispatcher (then a police officer and maybe a doctor) that her nearly seventy-year-old mother had tried to suffocate her, and maybe poison her, after infecting her with night terrors—she knew it was a lost cause. Jackie would be the composed one, the rational-sounding one, as she paraded out Grace's known defects: a liar, a catfisher, a sleepwalker. And her pièce de résistance, her claim that Grace was a murderer of disabled sisters.

"The difference, hon, is I don't want you to die. I just want to jar your memory, so you remember what you did."

"Because you're trying to *help* me." The sarcasm she oozed was thick as an oil spill, but none of it touched Jackie.

"Exactly."

"We're not having this conversation again." Grace dropped onto the bed, weary, cautious to maintain a safe distance as she considered her options. It was the middle of the night, and she was possibly infected by the virus, but could she run out to a twenty-four-hour store? At the top of her shopping list was a lock to keep Jackie out of her room (especially while she was sleeping) and maybe a weapon (if not an actual gun). Where was the nearest twenty-four-hour Walmart? It probably wasn't crowded this time of night, and she could wear two masks to ensure she didn't breathe on anyone.

Then what? Maybe Grace could go stay in Miguel's empty apartment. But that was only a short-term solution—this was *Grace's* house. It was obvious they couldn't continue living together, and she couldn't afford to wait however many weeks or months it would take for the senior communities to open up to new tenants.

"Do you have enough money for a hotel?" Grace asked.

"Why?" Jackie sounded suspicious.

"I think you should stay somewhere else. I was looking for senior apartments, but they're all in lockdown. There are several hotels at the Waterfront—it's ten minutes from here."

Jackie rolled her eyes and snorted. "You're overreacting. I wasn't going to hurt you—"

"You scared the shit out of me!"

"Grace, *please*. Please just do this *one* thing for me: *think* about that evening."

"I haven't forgotten it."

"But do you ever let yourself think about it?"

If only her mother were a ranting lunatic, a disheveled parody of someone who was severely senile or mentally ill. As much as Grace wanted to, it was hard to simply dismiss her—and Jackie wasn't wrong: Grace never let herself dwell on Hope's last hours on earth.

"Don't you think I feel guilty enough? Do you think I never tormented myself? Never wondered how things might've been different if I'd just gone in to *check* on her more often?"

"Oh . . ." Jackie nodded, gaining understanding. "That's what it became. In your head. That nonguilty kind of guilt. So it wasn't what you *did* but what you *didn't* do."

Grace abruptly stood, snatched up one of her pillows and stuffed it under her arm. She started tugging on the comforter, determined to collect her bedding and go downstairs, but Jackie was sitting on it. Grace kept yanking until Jackie got up. It was ridiculous to think it was safer to sleep downstairs. Her mother could still put a pillow over her face, but at least Grace would be closer to the front door—could run out into the night calling to the neighbors for help if it came to that. She gathered the comforter into a messy, bulging ball and headed for the open door.

Jackie stepped in front of her, beseeching. "Just *think* about it. That evening. The details. What you were doing. What Hope was doing. There's no reason not to think about it if you did nothing wrong. You know I *never* blamed you for not checking on Hope more often, *never*."

After making her plea, her mother stepped aside and Grace trundled past, arms loaded with bedding. But she stopped at the head of the stairs.

"If I do what you ask—think about . . . Hope—will you get the fuck out of my house?"

"I'll pack up and go. To a hotel, wherever you want. But you have to really try. Dig deep, and if the memory's really gone . . . I'll leave you alone."

Fucking Jackie sounded completely sincere.

"Fine." At least the end of their cohabitation was within sight.

43

Grace deliberated over keeping a weapon with her—a kitchen knife, a pair of scissors. It was a bit too easy to picture accidentally stabbing herself as she rolled over in her sleep. In the movies everyone liked to grab a heavy iron poker for self-defense, but they were all rich people with mansions and fireplaces. She didn't even have a tennis racket with which to whack away at an intruder (or homicidal mother).

Did Jackie *really* believe that Grace had suffocated her sister—and that the memory could be joggled loose by experiencing *just the right amount* of smothering?

Good lord, they were a fucked-up pair. It wasn't out of the question that the "therapeutic asphyxiation" was revenge for Grace threatening to "kill" her over the cat. Any reasonable person would know that "I'll kill you" is a figure of speech, an empty warning produced by exasperation. But Jackie often preferred to react emotionally rather than logically. Like mother, like daughter?

With the comforter mostly tucked under her knees, Grace lay awake on the couch gazing toward the front window, beckoning the dawn. The porch obliterated the sky, and everything that wasn't directly under a streetlamp disappeared in shadow. It was Crazy Cat Hour, and periodically Coco zoomed through in pursuit of an invisible gremlin. Grace tried to entice her over with a toy, dangling the stuffed mouse by its tail, but the cat preferred the gremlin.

The sofa was comfortable enough, but Grace was reluctant to close her eyes. What did people take to stay awake? Cocaine? Speed? She was too acclimated to caffeine and had no clue how to procure anything but pot.

She wished she could call Miguel. He was so behind on the cork-screw twists of her daily life. Before everything blew up, if one of them had been busy and they were out of touch for a week, it was easy to get caught up; once upon a time her days (and nights) had been wonderfully mundane. Now, how would Grace even begin to explain any of this? Miguel sent her short texts when he was up for it—he'd thanked her earlier for the flowers she'd sent the previous day—and those few seconds of communication felt like a lifeline to the outside world. He was the one in the hospital, but Grace was a captive in a disorienting purgatory.

She toyed with the idea of going to the hospital—not to visit Miguel but to get tested. Check herself in. With the way things were at home, it was probably safer there, in spite of the pandemic. It was hard to tell anymore what was cause and what was effect, but she really didn't feel well. Intermittently the back of her neck was sweaty, wet enough to make her hair soggy as she finger combed it off her skin. But as soon as she was ready to crank up the air conditioner, a chill would scuttle across her body, nullifying the need. So she lay there. Hot, then cold. Clammy, then shivery.

Determined not to sleep, but too lethargic to actually get up, she thought about the deal she'd made with her mother. It would be easiest to just lie and tell her she'd thought about it and nope, no recovered memories of killing her sister. She couldn't wait to help Jackie pack up her things, ferry her to the Waterfront. But her mother would know she was lying. She'd squint at her, trying to drill into her conscience, and Grace would confess under the scrutiny. Better to just spend a minute thinking about that evening—and then she could tell the truth. And haul Jackie's ass to a hotel in the morning.

Coco finally stopped running around and made a nest for herself in the sofa corner near Grace's feet. Gently, she stroked the cat's silky fur with her toe. Perhaps Jackie wasn't asking for a lot—five minutes of reminiscing—but it felt all sorts of ways malapropos. Grace had mourned and dealt with her shit in her own way, and she resented her mother's demand that she now invest a little more effort. And then there was the simple cruelness of it, like a diabolical child who delighted in ripping off other people's scabs.

44

Hope was back in her room, the curtains drawn. Mommy had been very specific about where Grace should and shouldn't spend the evening: not upstairs in her bedroom (because she might not hear if Hope needed anything); not in Hope's room (because her sister's immune system was fragile and the last thing she needed was Grace's cooties—not her mother's exact words). That left the living room and the kitchen.

Grace washed their supper dishes, one eye on the blackness beyond the small window. She hated how early it got dark in the winter. It looked like midnight, but it was just after six. Everything about being alone in the house was worse when the sun wasn't shining. The gloom settled around her like something stiff and scratchy, and Grace privately acknowledged that the problem wasn't that Mommy wasn't home; Grace was afraid of the dark. It didn't help that their stupid old house had high ceilings with stupid little light fixtures that barely illuminated the rooms. In winter, the rooms shrank into shadows, leaving only glowing islands of safety.

Her birthday wasn't for another six weeks, but she decided then and there that she was going to ask for a lamp as her gift. And not a desk lamp (she didn't have a desk), but something with a big fancy lampshade that could handle a high-wattage bulb. She snorted and laughed, imagining herself carrying it from room to room, plugging it in, switching it on. Her mother might scoff, call it a daft request, but

Grace would remind her that she was going to be twelve and a lamp was practical (*mature*) and a better use of money than the name-brand makeup Hope would beg for. She saw a vision of them, six weeks in the future—

Hope leaning into the glow of the birthday lamp as Grace applied her sister's makeup, per Hope's exact instructions. And then her sister would say, "Just try on some eye shadow," and Grace would look at herself in the mirror and dab a little on each eye. So in the end, both of the gifts would be for both of them.

With the dishes neatly stacked by the sink to dry, Grace scanned the rest of the room, looking for anything out of order. She winced, spotting the splotches of tomato soup on the floor and table. On the one hand, Grace understood why Hope wanted to try and do more things on her own—like feeding herself—but Hope was never the one to clean up the mess. Grace got on her knees with some wet paper towels. She couldn't leave a single speck of evidence that Hope had left her bed and come into the kitchen for supper. Mommy didn't need to know how they bent the rules, and Grace would be the one to get in trouble even though her only crime was caving to Hope's demands.

"Grace!"

Before responding to her sister, Grace double-checked that the kitchen was as it should be—as Mommy would want to find it when she got home.

Grace slipped past the decorative curtain and sighed. This was the exact kind of night—cold and dark—when all she wanted was to make a fort of Hope's room and stay in there with her all night. Not only did Hope have a lamp on the card table beside her bed, but she also had a space heater. The lamp was ugly with a body like a lump of painted lava, but it was bright, and her room was by far the warmest. Hope needed these things, the extra light and warmth, so she could manage better when using her commode chair and be more comfortable when having a sponge bath (when they didn't feel like carrying her upstairs to the bathroom). The card table had enough room for the medical stuff Hope needed when she was sick and the books and fashion magazines she liked to keep near at hand.

"I'm really thirsty. My mouth's gummy." Hope made a face, emphasizing how gross it felt.

Grace plucked the sports bottle from beside her bed. "I'll get you more water."

"Could you put a lemon wedge in it?"

Grace stopped at the archway and gave her a smirk. "Where did you learn to be such a diva?"

"Lemon helps."

"We don't have any. Do you want some tea?"

"Okay."

Hope started coughing as Grace headed back to the kitchen. It was a phlegmy, deep cough, and Grace wondered if she was contagious. Maybe it was better, after all, if Grace didn't spend too much time in there.

When the water in the saucepan was near to boiling, Grace turned off the flame. She poured the steaming water into a travel mug, only filling it halfway, and dropped in a peppermint tea bag. While she waited for the tea to steep, she filled her sister's sports bottle with fresh cold water and then stood there leaning against the counter. With her back to the midnight window, she pondered the rest of her No-Mommy evening.

There was a show Grace wanted to watch at seven. She was supposed to finish her homework first. And if the television noise bothered Hope in any way, Grace was supposed to turn it off. *As if Hope would be sleeping.* Grace rolled her eyes at Mommy's rules. The do-your-home-work thing was kind of a joke. And Mommy was clueless if she really thought Hope would *sleep* or *stay in bed* through any mildly interesting activity. Regardless of a fever or a cough, Hope was not one to let life pass her by.

If Grace turned on her show, Hope would want to join her in the living room. If (*when*) they heard Mommy at the door, it would take a lot longer than a few seconds to transfer Hope from her wheelchair back into bed, so Grace's real dilemma—if she chose to turn on the TV—was accepting that they (*she*) would get in trouble when their mother came home. Was the show worth hearing Mommy yell at her about how irresponsible she was?

Mommy believed her list of rules qualified as Parenting, and thus she expected Grace to fully follow those rules, making Mommy in charge by proxy. But Hope wasn't that easy to boss around, and it wasn't fair that Mommy pretended otherwise. Even while sick, Hope wouldn't die from eating supper in the kitchen or watching a little TV—but she absolutely would be a royal bitch if Grace didn't help her get out of bed. One way or the other, someone was going to be mad at Grace; she had to decide if tonight it would be her sister or her mother.

Maybe the soothing tea would put Hope to sleep, then Grace would be off the hook. When the tea was a shade too dark, she took out the tea bag and filled the rest of the mug with cold water: *sipping* wasn't exactly something Hope had a lot of control over. Grace made sure the lids were tight on both containers, and with one in each hand, she left the kitchen. She moved the curtain to Hope's room aside with her elbow—and almost dropped the beverages.

Her sister was covered in blood.

———

Grace lurched to the table to deposit the mugs and grab a towel. "Why didn't you call for me!"

Blood dripped down Hope's chin, yet she was smiling. Blood dribbled down the front of her nightshirt and pooled in the blanket across her lap.

"We need to call nine one one!" Grace frantically mopped at the blood, and Hope laughed.

"Scared?"

Yes, Grace was scared. She pivoted toward the kitchen, where they always kept one of the cordless handsets plugged in.

"It's not blood, you wimp," Hope called after her, laughing.

Grace stopped, spun back around. "What?"

"I coughed up my tomato soup." Hope tossed her head and laughed.

"Why is that funny?"

"The look on your face."

Grace's panic morphed into something else. She imagined herself a pissed-off bull with a pike in her back, huffing out fire-hot breath. This was why she could never feel sorry for her sister. Grace spent the next fifteen minutes washing the reddish goo off Hope's face and neck and helping her change into a clean nightshirt.

"You're a fucking diva bitch," Grace mumbled.

"It's good practice."

"For what?"

"For when I'm a famous designer."

"You don't *have* to act like a bitch," Grace said.

"No. But if my assistants are too impatient for my words, at least they'll get my tone."

On another day Grace might have burst out laughing at her sister's moxie. But it was an exceptionally trying night, and Grace was tired. After covering Hope with a spare blanket, Grace took the soiled one into the cellar and stuffed it in the washer. The basement was the worst part of the house—darker, colder, diseased with shadows—and as soon as the load was underway, she fled upstairs to watch her show.

———

"Grace!"

Grace sat cuddled in the ever more ragged mommy-cat chair, leaning toward the glow of the remaining lamp—a twin to the painted-lava blob in Hope's room. She studiously watched the television and ignored her sister.

"Grace!"

Just in case Mommy asked when she got home, Grace kept her schoolbooks half on the wobbly end table beside her, half on her lap and did a couple of minutes of homework during the commercials.

"Grace!"

It wasn't like she didn't know what Hope wanted. Having decided to let her sister be the angry one, Grace hiked up the volume with the remote, trying to blot her out.

"Come on! I'm sorry!"

Ten seconds later: "I'm bored! Come on, Grace!"

"You know Mommy will get mad at me!" Grace yelled over her shoulder. "If you shut up you'll at least be able to hear it."

Hope shut up for twenty seconds. Then, "I'll take the blame! I'll tell Mommy I made you! Please?"

"It won't matter." She clicked the volume up another notch.

Just as Grace was getting into the show, finally able to concentrate, Hope let out a piercing shriek—the kind of sound Grace might make if she found a tarantula crawling up her leg. She leaped out of the chair and dashed to her sister's bedside, expecting to see . . . something.

Another vomity mess. A many-legged creature advancing toward Hope's pillow. Instead, Hope offered her version of a guilty smile.

"What?" Grace demanded.

"Sorry. Just thought I saw a face at the window."

It was a creepy enough thought that Grace went to the window and peered out. With the bright room reflected on the glass, she couldn't see much of anything. The miniblind was a bit mangled, but Grace lowered it and tried to force the crooked slats to do a better job of blocking out the night.

Hope reached for her, her arm and fingers hyperextended.

"There's nothing there," Grace said, returning to the bedside. Hope's finger snagged her shirtsleeve.

"Okay. I'm *sorry* sorry and you have to accept my apology."

"I do. But Mommy wanted you to stay in bed and rest, and you've been up and about all day."

"Just a little TV," Hope begged.

"No. Read a magazine. Take a nap."

"I'm too snuffly to sleep. I'm all stuffed up."

"Mommy will give you some medicine when she gets home." Grace disentangled her sister's finger.

Hope flopped against her pillows, defeated or mock dead, Grace wasn't sure. She escaped back to the living room, growling a little in her throat when the show went to commercials just as she was getting comfortable again. During the break she finished a couple of math problems, proud of herself for multitasking—*don't forget to put the laundry in the dryer!*—and for finally getting her sister to accept she'd lost the battle. When the show came back on, Grace shoved her math book aside.

From the other room, Hope started singing—loudly. She'd advanced past humming, and while she didn't actually say all the words, she vocalized the melody. Loudly. The song was more or less in tune, but that hardly mattered.

"Shut up!" Grace yelled. Hope continued singing.

Grace raised the television volume to a near-deafening level. She gritted her teeth, hoping a little patience would win this new stage of the war. If Hope's mouth was so dry, if she was really so stuffed up, surely she couldn't go on singing for very long. But her warbling became more like screeching, and it was making Grace crazy.

Once again, Grace leaped from her chair and raced to her sister's room. She flung back the curtain just long enough to scream, "Shut! Up!"

Back in front of the TV, Grace lowered the volume because that had become an annoyance, too, almost as bad as her sister's caterwauling. She thought Hope was finally out of breath, but a moment later—perhaps after gulping some water or tea—Hope launched into a new song.

Grace pressed herself into the mommy-cat cushion, hands mashing her ears. She wanted to outscream her sister or burst into tears or throw on her coat and run out into the night and leave Hope to fend for herself.

With every passing second, the noise and her sister's obstinate will were shredding her composure. She felt like the sound was stripping off her skin in thin pieces—the same way she peeled off random strips from the ancient wallpaper in the upstairs hallway. But she didn't have a plaster wall hiding beneath her facade but raw, oozing flesh.

"Shut! Up!"

If only their mother could witness this and understand the degree to which Hope was *not* the frail girl she imagined. If only this was what her mother, instead of Grace, had to deal with every day.

Hope's voice was a nail pounding through Grace's skull. "Stop it! Please!"

Her eardrums exploded. Her skull shattered. The bony plates joined the piled strips of bloody skin. Hope had reduced her to this fireball of pain, nerves exposed, her lacerated body nothing but a fragile, searing cluster of overloaded senses. Grace's voice joined her sister's in a howling duet as she charged into Hope's room.

From afar, Grace saw herself yank the pillow from beneath her sister's head.

From afar, she saw herself press the pillow against Hope's face.

———

Grace transferred the blanket from the washer to the dryer. As she curled up in her favorite chair, she was quite pleased with herself. The house was clean, the laundry nearly done. Grace's homework was well underway, and for once she hadn't let Hope break all the rules. Mommy would come home soon and find Hope sound asleep in her bed, and Grace would finally earn her mother's praise.

45

Grace tumbled off the sofa, the dream branded into her consciousness. She paced the length of the living room, back and forth, oblivious to the dawning light that was slowly returning color to everything in the room. The nightmare was not a surprise—she'd expected to dream about her sister's last night. Even the story line wasn't a shocker: it was the scenario her mother had fed her; it was exactly what Jackie wanted her to see. What bothered Grace was how she'd *felt* while seeing the images unspool.

It felt right.

Right in the sense that while inside the dream she'd had no confusion. The scene had moved forward with confidence, like a windup toy that marched perpetually onward when given a wide-open space. And Grace had had the sensation of knowing what was going to happen next. She remembered wanting a lamp for her birthday. The tomato-soup vomit. Her decision to let Hope be mad at her. And then the annoying power of Hope belting out her favorite songs.

What bothered Grace now, what kept her pacing, was her appalling inability to answer a single question: If everything else in the dream rang true, did that make the murder true as well?

She had no memory of that part.

In her memory, Hope finally shut up. And while Grace happily—obliviously—went about finishing her chores and watching

TV, her sister struggled to catch her breath. And when Mommy came through the front door, Grace had one moment of perfect satisfaction, seeing her mother's serenity that everything on the home front was as it should be. The moment was shattered when Mommy went to check on Hope. First Grace heard her bellowing Hope's name. Then Mommy made a mad dash for the kitchen phone and called nine one one.

"My daughter's not breathing!"

Grace remembered sinking into her chair, wishing she could disappear, wishing the mommy cat could come to life and carry her away. She should have known that Hope couldn't go on with all that singing and yelling, not with the state her lungs were in. She should have gone in to check on her instead of being smug and thrilled that her sister had finally shut the fuck up.

The paramedics came. While they were in the dining room, Mommy sent her upstairs, told her to go to bed. Mommy didn't say "Your sister died," but Grace knew: Hope just wasn't one to stay quiet during a dramatic turn of events. Her feet were almost too heavy to carry her up the steps. Grace wanted to go outside and lie in the snow. And freeze to death in the scary dark. Why had she thought Hope's silence was okay? Why had she felt victorious when she never heard another peep from her sister's room?

The days after that were a blur. Until the funeral.

Grace was sure, so sure, of *most* of those memories. But . . . but a splinter of her imagination could see herself screaming at her sister—it wouldn't have been the first time. Was it possible? Could it have happened just as she'd seen it in the dream?

She almost punched the television screen when she passed it but retracted her fist at the last second. *This is bullshit!* So many of the nightmares she'd had were a confounding mixture of reality and horror. None of them had been completely true, so why should this one be the exception? Her mother was fucking with her, trying to convince Grace that she was the crazy one. Jackie wanted her to torment herself, to question everything that had happened in the past, and Grace didn't want to play along.

Her phone rang.

Just as in the dream, Grace knew what was about to happen—which only made her question, yet again, if she was trapped in a nightmare.

"Hello?"

It was the nurse's station on Miguel's floor. Grace wanted to hang up or, better yet, hurl the phone across the room. She pulled it away from her ear but still heard most of what the woman on the other end was saying.

". . . sorry but Miguel took a turn during the night . . . moved to intensive care . . . breathing tube . . . doctor will call later . . . the phone number where you can reach his nurse . . ."

She should've been running for a piece of paper and a pen, scribbling down the precious phone number. But Grace just stood there in a stupor. She heard herself say "thank you" before tossing the phone onto the sofa.

So this was how it was going to be. Previously her life had been merely a thousand ways upside down. Now it was a million. Now Miguel might really die. And a crack had formed in her certainty that she couldn't possibly have put a pillow over her sister's face.

Could I have put a pillow over my sister's face?

In the anemic morning light, she saw a mirage of herself in her sister's room, holding the pillow down. And Grace knew, from recent experience, exactly what that felt like—the physical pressure on the nose and lips, the emotional mayhem as the heart and brain fought to survive. But as the illusion sharpened, Young Grace pulled the pillow away before it was too late.

"That's what I'll do if you don't shut up!"

Such a threat could've been uttered. It wasn't beyond the realm of plausibility.

A sound made her look toward the stairwell, a nasally rumble that cut off with a sharp inhale and then started again. Jackie was snoring, loudly.

Was her mother congested? Struggling to breathe in her sleep?

"Okay." Grace had fulfilled her end of the bargain. She would dutifully check on her mother, and start packing Jackie's things.

46

Grace didn't linger at her mother's bedside. Though Jackie continued to breathe loudly through her open mouth, she was obviously sound asleep and not in any distress. Grace opened the closet door and reached for the high shelf where the empty suitcases were stacked. They were light but bulky, and she tried to balance them on her head before backing out of the closet. Slowly, she turned around, readying to transfer the luggage to the ground.

Her hands stopped working. Her vision betrayed her and she lost her grasp on the material world. There were ghosts in the room—in the space between the bed and the open door to the hallway.

They looked real, even as Grace saw through them to the walls, the furniture. A sandy-haired man was on his knees, dressed in rugged work pants and boots. He had a sparkling smile, which he bestowed on the little girl and little boy who ran into his open arms. Beside him stood a woman in a simple dress and heels. A housewife from another era, she dried her hands on an apron as she admired her wonderful, handsome man.

The suitcases slipped from Grace's hands and clattered to the floor.

Her mother jerked awake with a snort. The ghosts winked out of existence.

Grace gasped, certain of what she'd seen: something impossible. Could that have been Paul No-Last-Name and the woman he married, at least as feared by Jackie? The children he went on to have—the family he went home to every day? It was her mother's worst nightmare, that the love of her life would finally settle down. With someone other than Jackie.

"What's going on?" she mumbled, struggling to sit up, her eyes only half open.

"Were you dreaming?" Grace asked in a state of shock. "Were you having a nightmare?"

She was tempted to flee the room, run straight out of the house and never come back. How could she have just seen her mother's dream? What was wrong with her—*them*? But the magnitude of the vision kept her rooted where she was. Paul No-Last-Name might, for Jackie, feel like something that could never be adequately resolved. But Grace felt the closing of a drafty door that she hadn't realized she'd left ajar. Had she just seen her father's face?

Jackie, not awake enough to communicate, rolled herself off the bed and stumbled to the bathroom. Grace felt an urgency, a desperate need to make a decision *right now*. In that instant, she decided her mother had to go. The ghosts and everything else would leave the house *with her*.

Grace hauled her mother's largest suitcase onto the bed and unzipped it. A whiff emerged, masculine, and she imagined Robert packing his toiletries, his aftershave. Her mother's things didn't have to travel far, so Grace didn't worry about being tidy. She picked a dresser drawer at random and gathered up half its contents.

"What are you doing?" Jackie shuffled back in.

"Time to go." Grace packed like a robot—lift, swivel, dump, lift, swivel, dump.

"Grace—"

"I did what you asked. Thought about it. Now it's time for you—"

Jackie crawled onto the bed. She collapsed across it sideways, as the suitcase took up the lower half of the mattress.

"No no no," Grace whispered, freezing in place, clutching a pile of Jackie's wrinkle-proof casual shirts. Now that she was forced to focus on her mother, she didn't need to ask what was wrong; it was obvious. Her mother looked like she'd been visited in the night by a vampire. Weak. Pale. The life drained right out of her. She lay on her side, eyes closed.

With waning zeal, Grace dropped the shirts into the suitcase. "Mom?"

When Jackie didn't answer, Grace hoisted the suitcase onto the floor. She got on her knees beside her mother. "Do you need me to call an ambulance? Do you need to go to the hospital?"

"No. Just tired."

She felt her mother's forehead with the back of her hand but couldn't tell if she had a fever. "Are you breathing okay."

Jackie gave a little nod. "Just tired."

Grace got off the bed and helped her slither into a more comfortable position, head on the pillow. In spite of having barely slept, Grace felt wide awake. She stood there staring at her mother, unsure what to do. Obviously, in this condition, Grace couldn't drop her off at a hotel. In normal times it might have been prudent to seek a medical assessment, but now she really wasn't sure. The news made it sound like every hospital was understaffed and overwhelmed. If her mother didn't have the virus, they probably wouldn't even keep her there.

"Fuck."

Jackie was fast asleep, and her breathing sounded rhythmic and normal. Lots of people rode out the virus—and everything else, these days—at home. Grace wasn't sure of her mother's symptoms, so she couldn't even call a doctor and ask for advice. She decided to wait and see. When Jackie woke up, Grace could ask her more questions and then determine what to do.

At least, in such a weakened state, her mother no longer posed a physical threat.

Before leaving the room, Grace considered the suitcase, now shoved against the closet door. If she put everything away, Jackie might not even remember that Grace had barged in and started packing her things. *But she's not staying.* At least not for long. Hospital or hotel. One way or the other, Jackie would soon be spending her nights elsewhere. Grace left the suitcase where it was.

She went downstairs and got some ice water to leave by her mother's bedside. How familiar it felt, bringing the water, leaving the bedroom door open so she could hear if the bedridden occupant called out in need.

From the doorway, Grace looked at her mother's sleeping form. Spiders skittered across Grace's shoulders and down her spine, and she pulled at her shirt, scratched her back as if they were real. If she watched her mother long enough, would another diorama appear? Phantoms from her mother's slumber? Grace shuddered again and scurried downstairs, half hoping she'd never have to step foot in Jackie's room again.

47

It had been a good idea to take her own temperature—she still didn't feel well—but the battery in her thermometer was dead. Grace sat on the couch with her laptop and a strong sense of déjà vu; it seemed like all she did anymore was get online and order stuff from Amazon. Vile, money-grubbing corporation or not, the bastards had everything. She selected one of those trendy thermometers that you held in front of your forehead and added backup batteries to her cart just in case. While she was at it, she scrolled through her options for reasonably priced disposable masks. And after finding the right cat litter, she indulged in a sixty-four-ounce jar of Jelly Bellies, never mind the expense.

She almost deleted her entire cart when she saw how long it would take for everything to arrive—even Amazon's prioritized deliveries were still taking days to weeks longer than their regular deliveries once had—but in the end, she clicked "Place Order." If she was out of quarantine before everything shipped, she'd go out and buy what she needed and cancel the rest.

With necessities on her mind, she went to the kitchen to engage in her new hobby: assessing their food supply. She never used to stock up, but now she felt uncomfortable if the fridge wasn't jam-packed. She was craving chilled, easy-to-eat things like yogurt and ice cream. They had neither. It was hot out, but would her mother want soup? It was an expensive, impulsive way to shop, but Grace quickly put together a

Giant Eagle order of Foods for the Unwell; it was early enough in the morning that she could schedule delivery for later that day.

Coco rubbed her ankles, eager for breakfast. Grace wasn't usually up and around at this time, but it was easier to acquiesce to the cat's demands than to listen to her beg for an hour. She prepared a half can of wet food, which Coco greedily snarfed, and then put out some kibbles for her to munch on during the day. After scooping out the kitty litter and taking out the trash, the lack of sleep started to creep in. Grace felt a tightness around her eyes, but she didn't want to sacrifice this quiet time to herself for the sake of what would surely be a troubled nap. Sleeping was hardly worth the bother anymore. She brewed a pot of coffee.

It was nice having the first floor to herself, not having to worry that Jackie might come down and commandeer the TV or the kitchen (or put a pillow over her face). Soon she'd have the whole house to herself again. And then, when she'd physically and mentally recovered from the havoc her mother had caused, she'd figure out her finances. Surely she wasn't alone in her pandemic struggle; maybe the bank was offering some sort of grace period for mortgage payments. And she was ready to start driving for Shipt and/or Lyft as soon as she was done self-isolating, assuming she felt well enough. Grace carried her coffee into the living room, comforted by the sight of the nest she'd left on the couch. She curled her legs under her and turned on the TV, keeping the volume low.

She remembered Hope belting out her songs, drowning out the television.

All the shows seemed more insipid than they had, even the ones she'd always liked. They were pointless or derivative or exploitative or just plain idiotic. How had this garbage once entertained her? Grace needed distraction more than ever, but every channel she tried only reminded her of how futile her existence had become. In light of a global economic collapse, a dangerous virus, and the ineptitude of everyone's response, the TV comedies were insufficient and the dramas were trivial.

Her left hand started scrolling through phone apps before Grace consciously decided to check on her damsels. She hadn't interacted with any of them since Jackie made her feel like such shit about being a *liar*. But most of them were still calling out from the ether, begging for a response. *Where r u?* Worse, some of them were concerned that their charming princes were sick. *R U OK? I'm so worried bout u baby.*

Grace wished she had a friend out there—a real friend, someone who knew the details of her actual life. She toyed with the idea of calling Barbara. When Barbara emailed her staff regarding her decision to permanently close the salon, she'd gushed her apologies and vowed to hold a "retirement" party once they could all socialize again in person. For a few days, the emails had flown back and forth as everyone promised to stay in touch. They all agreed to keep each other apprised of what they ended up doing; they followed each other on Facebook or Instagram if they didn't already. Several of the stylists signed their final missives with variations of "Let me know if you need anything!" And then they were gone. No longer a motley crew attached to the same workplace and schedule.

Now her former colleagues, the family she had seen every day for years on end, existed in a new category: People I Used to Work With. Except for Miguel, of course. Grace decided she would fall apart if she attempted to talk to Barbara, and she didn't have the energy to fall apart.

The coffee was helping her feel a bit more like herself (whoever that was), but it was also increasing her awareness of being hot. She tugged on the neckline of her nightshirt, fanning herself with the material. It wasn't necessarily the coffee's fault—the humid day might be to blame or an undiagnosed fever or the fact that she sat encircled by her comforter—but it was becoming unbearable. Grace switched off the television and went upstairs.

She peeked in at Jackie from the hallway: she was just as she'd left her, sleeping on her side, snoring softly. Her mother looked so frail and harmless.

Instead of heading for her air-conditioned bedroom, Grace locked herself in the bathroom. She left her nightshirt atop the closed toilet lid and stepped into the shower without waiting for the water to heat up. The cool spray rained down on her. It was just what she wanted, what she needed, and she shut her eyes, luxuriating. But that proved to be a mistake—she saw bad things when she closed her eyes. Miguel on a ventilator. Hope in her bed, lifeless.

Could I have killed my sister?

As she soaked her hair, she recalled what her mother had said about finding the pillow. The blood droplets. And according to Jackie the pillow had been above Hope's head, not beneath it. But Hope really could've had a seizure. And the pillow really could've been dislodged if she were thrashing on the bed. Just because Jackie believed a certain scenario didn't mean she was right. It was hard to fathom that her mother had been carrying this twisted knowledge around for twenty-five years.

No wonder she didn't want to be part of my life.

Grace mashed her fingers against the tiled wall, needing its support. Suddenly she had to consider her past through a different lens. Had Jackie been more than a mother in mourning? Had she also been a mother with a terrible secret about her surviving daughter? Could Jackie have felt uncomfortable around her because of what she knew—*thought* she knew?

It was like watching *The Sixth Sense* for the second time, seeing all the earlier scenes with a new understanding. Grace reminded herself that Jackie could believe something that *wasn't* true. Yet it fascinated her to contemplate the possibility that for all these years, Jackie might have been protecting her by never admitting her suspicion.

48

Grace wouldn't let herself nap. Once upon a time, her mother had suggested such a strategy, staying awake during the day so she could go to bed in a state of utter exhaustion. She busied herself with tasks: cleaning, doing laundry, brushing Coco's fur, putting away the groceries when they arrived. When she felt composed enough to handle it, she tracked down Miguel's ICU nurse. It took some doing, and she was put on hold multiple times and transferred around the hospital. She apologized to the nurse for "misplacing" the number (and chastised herself for not having made more of an effort during the morning's call).

Miguel's nurse, Kerry, put Grace at ease almost immediately. She sounded so assured and competent. When Kerry told her that Miguel was stable, it didn't annoy Grace like it had when he was in a regular room; now it meant something crucial. Kerry explained that it was important for Miguel's blood oxygen level not to drop below a certain number. His numbers had gone up and down when he'd only had a nasal cannula, but now that he was intubated, his level was steady.

"How long will he have to be intubated?" Grace asked.

"That's the million-dollar question. Everything about his recovery will be easier the less time he has the breathing tube, and the less time he's sedated and in the ICU. Dr. Bihariya will assess him at least once a day to see if he might have improved enough to be extubated."

"Is that . . ." Grace wasn't sure how to ask her question. She'd heard too many recent news stories of someone's mother or husband who got a breathing tube and never recovered. For so many, the breathing tube was the start of an irreversible decline. "It's not just . . ." Her voice cracked. "The beginning of the end?"

"No no, it doesn't mean that. For older patients it can be harder to stop the downward spiral, especially if they already have chronic issues. But Miguel doesn't have any other health problems, and he's otherwise young and strong. While the machine is helping him breathe, the rest of his system can focus on beating the virus. Don't lose hope."

"Okay." She hadn't thought of it that way—the machine as a helper, giving his body a break. It was a better image to focus on. Coco crawled onto her lap. Maybe she knew they were talking about her daddy. Grace stroked her, and the cat's soft fur helped her stay calm.

"You're designated as Miguel's only visitor. His family isn't in town, and it sounds like they're dealing with a lot right now. We are permitting ICU visits with full protective gear—gown, gloves, mask, and goggles."

"I'd like to, I will, but I was exposed. I'm still in self-isolation."

"Oh okay. How are you feeling?"

"Not great. My mother's pretty sick, she lives with me, but I don't know if it's the virus."

"You can both come in and get tested, if you're concerned."

"We'll see. We're both breathing okay, so."

"That's good. You know we're here. We have iPads and we can FaceTime with you—that's another option."

Grace was glad Miguel was in Kerry's hands; Kerry had solutions. For days Grace had had only the sense of encroaching doom, but maybe the nurse was right: Grace couldn't lose hope.

Kerry explained how the nursing shifts worked in the ICU and encouraged Grace to call the direct number whenever she wanted an update. "There's always someone here."

"Thank you. Maybe next time we could use the iPad, just in case Miguel can hear me? I could just tell him I love him."

"Of course!"

Even though it had been a productive call, concluding with more thank-yous, Grace burst into tears after they disconnected. It seemed even more real than it had before. Now it was a waiting game, and there were only two ways his oxygen levels would ultimately go—up or down.

———

Jackie was ready to eat late in the afternoon. Grace brought her more water and single-serve containers of applesauce and yogurt. She stood by her mother's bed and watched her spoon the easy-to-eat foods, gauging her overall health to the degree that Grace's observation allowed. Jackie's hair was plastered against the sides of her head; sleep had given her a mohawk. There was a tremor in her hand. Her skin had that translucent quality again, the bruise-like softness she'd arrived with.

"Do you feel like you have a fever?" Grace asked. Jackie shook her head. "My thermometer is dead, but I ordered a new one. I can call a doctor and see if they think you should go in to be tested."

"I don't have the virus."

"You don't know that."

Jackie licked her spoon, nodding. "I can't deny it anymore. I wanted to, because I was afraid, but . . . I have what Robert had."

"Which was?"

Her mother gazed at something far away and shrugged. "Something no one understands, unless you see it, and feel it. It was hard watching him decline. And his behavior—I resented it at first, I thought he was being brutish. But then I came to see that what he'd lost in physical vigor he gained in mental clarity. And he wasn't just being mean—he was as hard on himself as he was on me. I gradually started to understand . . . the power of the truth."

Grace realized she couldn't wait a week for the thermometer to arrive; she'd have to get one, even if it didn't have all the bells and whistles, in her next grocery order. Jackie might claim she didn't have a fever, but there was something loopy about the look in her eye. A jittery kind of excitement. She didn't act or appear like she was completely present, which made Grace wonder if she herself looked like that in the minutes or hour after one of her confusing dreams.

"Are you feeling better? Did it help to sleep?" She half expected her mother to start describing endless hours of nightmares. *Did I see my father?*

"I'm feeling better because I finally accept my fate. It's a gift to finally see everything and everyone for what they are."

Grace wished she could turn to Miguel and swap grins, nervous and amused, while sharing the telepathic understanding that they were witnessing someone in an altered state. Jackie sounded like she was in a feverish or religious delirium, but Grace suppressed the urge to crack a sarcastic comment.

"Do you want something else to eat?" Grace nested the empty cups together, ready to head back downstairs. The room was less creepy when Jackie was awake, but still.

Her mother ignored her question and continued with her urgent train of thought. "Before Robert died he admitted many mistakes. Mistakes he made with his first wife—he'd cheated on her, and hid things from her. And while he was a good father in his later years, he'd come to understand how he'd been neglectful. He hadn't felt, as a younger man, that anything he might say or do would impact his sons, so he let Clara do the child-rearing. It was only when they became young men and he saw the directions they'd gone in—selfish, wayward—that he started imparting fatherly advice. His relationship with them improved tremendously, though he had to accept that he couldn't change them; his job was to accept them."

Grace quirked an eyebrow. Was this heading toward an apology or an admission that her mother had judged her too harshly?

Jackie still had that faraway gaze; she barely seemed aware that Grace was standing there, anxiously waiting to leave. "Robert had never really understood how you and I came to live such separate lives. He accepted it, and never pressed me on it . . . until he got really sick. Then he accused me of so many hurtful things. Abandoning you. He wondered if I was more hard hearted—selfish—than he'd ever understood. Had I been one of those *cold* parents who resented all the responsibilities that came with raising children? And then I finally started to tell him. About waiting for Paul. And wanting to get married and be a housewife. I told him more about Hope."

Her mother's head swiveled and she finally met Grace's eyes. Jackie's contemplative spaciness was abruptly gone. In its place was something cold and impenetrable; Grace retreated a step. "He was the first person I ever told. About what you did."

Grace shut her eyes, shaking her head. "I didn't—"

But Jackie didn't care what she had to say. "He helped me understand what my responsibility was—I had to stop avoiding the past, and acknowledge it head on. I'd been ignoring it, and ignoring the consequences of keeping that secret. And he said that after he died I should go to you, and help you."

"I don't need your help."

"I told him I didn't think you'd ever admit it, that you'd blocked it all out. And he reminded me that my mission wasn't to *change* you if that's not what you wanted. But I had to try and bridge the gap— between us, and give you the missing piece of your life. It's up to you if you put it all together now. I wasn't distant from you for all the reasons you probably imagined—maybe you think these reasons are worse. But I lied for you, to protect you. I wasn't going to lose another daughter, but for so long you were just the reminder of all the mistakes I made.

All the things I couldn't undo. But Robert made me see I wasn't helpless. He gave me . . . the power of truth."

Her mother shut her eyes and lay back on the pillow, a beatific smile on her haggard face. "Now it's yours. Do with it what you will."

Grace rolled her eyes and left the room. She was tempted to close Jackie's door behind her—let her mother make a little more effort if she needed Grace's help—but Good Daughter that she was, she left it open.

49

What the hell had gotten into her mother? Did she think she was some sort of avenging angel? Grace hadn't known Robert well enough to guess if he would've planted such shit in Jackie's head as he lay on his deathbed. Perhaps her mother had gone mad with grief, and for all these weeks she'd been battling to hold it together. People said that sickness brought out a person's true character—a sense of humor, a bitchy despair, a serene acceptance. Maybe Jackie had a savior complex, however misguided it might be.

Grace tossed the spoon in the sink and threw away the plastic cups. She wasn't hungry, but she got out the ice cream and scooped some into a bowl. Thunder rumbled behind her, and she opened the back door to see the sky. It was getting darker. She watched through the screen door as she licked at the cold, creamy treat. A tendril of lightning rippled over the neighborhood, quickly followed by an explosive clap of thunder.

Her mission continued to be finding ways to distract herself. Watching a storm wouldn't have been her first choice, but at least it was something a little different. While the ice cream felt good going down her throat, she was barely aware of its flavor. Her mother's accusation had become a sickness of its own, a parasite that was working its way through Grace's bloodstream, attaching its offspring to her organs. It was one thing when she'd consoled herself with the possibility that Jackie could *mistakenly believe* something. But now Grace knew that her mother had discussed the matter with Robert, which meant it wasn't a newly conceived invention, designed to rattle her. Unless the bit about Robert was part of an ever more elaborate deceit.

No one in their right mind would create such a histrionic lie. But that left Grace where she'd started, unsure if Jackie had gone around the bend or . . . Grace had once been 100 percent sure that her mother's version of Hope's death couldn't be true. Now she was only 70 percent sure. Sometimes less.

Rain started pelting the screen, and Grace quickly shut the back door and locked it. She returned to her nest in the living room, all too aware of her *Groundhog Day* existence. Hadn't she been living this day for a week already? Laughing at herself as she did it, she turned on the television to check the weather, as if she didn't already know it might rain. She flipped to a local channel and a red banner streamed along the bottom, warning of flash flooding and severe thunderstorms. After another shattering peal of thunder, Coco scampered in and crouched at Grace's feet.

"It's okay, Coco." She rubbed the nervous cat's head. Grace and the cat both bolted upright at an unfamiliar sound, the *rat-a-tat-tat* of BBs bouncing off the windows. But the windows weren't being shot at—it was hail, growing louder by the second.

Coco darted upstairs to find somewhere better to hide (probably under Grace's bed), while Grace hurried to the big back window to watch the spectacle. It wasn't her brightest idea to stand at a window in such a storm—there'd been a few tornadoes in Pittsburgh over the years—but the novelty of it gave her a little thrill. The hail, fat as gumballs—the big ones that cost twenty-five cents when she was a kid—pummeled the windows. And then the wind shifted and the hail beat against the side of her house.

The electricity blinked off, taking with it the illuminating brightness of the television and lamps.

I was blind—and blinded—in a dream.

It looked as if it had snowed in the backyard. Hail clustered in the low spots. Grace had never seen a hailstorm that lasted more than a minute. She grinned, absorbed in Mother Nature's show. A branch splintered off her back neighbor's tallest tree, and she gasped as it crashed down. Then it occurred to her that the electricity was still off, and given the force of the wind, the relentless rain and destructive weight of the hail, power lines could be down. The longest she'd ever been without electricity was a couple of hours, at most. Even that had been too long, and she had a sinking feeling that this storm, which had earned a red alert banner, was worse than anything she'd experienced before.

———

Her excitement fizzled in tandem with the downpour. The thunder and hail moved on to batter another neighborhood, leaving Greenfield soggy and stunned. The storm had been a coveted diversion, and Grace was almost sad to see it go. She stayed at the window for another minute, watching the balls of ice melt into the summer mud.

Now what?

The sun was setting. It was eerily quiet in the house without the constant rumble of the air conditioner and the refrigerator. *Oh shit.* She stepped into the kitchen and stared at the silent appliance, full of brand-new perishable food. Surely the electricity would come back on before all the food spoiled, right? She flirted with the idea of eating the rest of the ice cream. It wouldn't matter if the old loaves of bread thawed—they would still be edible; the same couldn't be said for a tub of melted sugary milk.

As she was about to rescue the ice cream, it occurred to her that everything in the refrigerator would last longer if she didn't open the doors. She retracted her hand but was hungry now that she didn't have access to the food she'd just purchased. In quick succession she ruled out all the things she couldn't eat: a bowl of cereal (not without jeopardizing the milk in the fridge); popcorn (not without the microwave); frozen ravioli with jarred sauce (nope and nope). *Fuck.* The electric stove was, without power, a fancy dead box.

She rummaged through her utility drawer in search of a flashlight.

"Oh." She'd forgotten about the old clunky thing she now gripped in her hand. It was probably twenty-five years old and ran on hefty cylindrical batteries. She pressed the switch and was pleasantly surprised when a weak yellow light came on. She clicked it off to preserve the batteries and dived back into the drawer, feeling with her fingers for the item she hoped to find. It took a minute to locate it among the mess, but she finally retrieved the tiny LED flashlight–key chain. A more practical person would have such a key chain attached to their keys; Grace preferred useless, kitschy key fobs.

The miniature flashlight was incredibly bright but sharp and narrow like a laser beam. It was better than nothing. Grace had a couple of plump decorative candles in her living room, but she wasn't sure about lighting them. She clearly remembered Miguel's tale of horror, recalling how Coco had once gotten on his table and sauntered past his romantic candles—and set her tail on fire. Hopefully the flashlights would be enough for now; hopefully she wouldn't be in the dark for much longer.

Good Daughter that she was, she made her way upstairs—dismayed by how much of her house was already in shadows. Only the living room benefited from a large picture window, and even that advantage was dwindling with the overcast sky and encroaching night. In another thirty minutes it would be too dark to see.

"Mom?" Grace stood at her mother's bedside. Without the fan, the air felt dense and warm. Jackie stirred. "Mom? The power's out. I'm leaving a flashlight here."

Grace flicked on the light to show her and then set it on end where her mother could reach it.

"The storm?" Jackie sounded as groggy as she looked.

"Yup. Really big one. Be careful if you have to get up. Do you need anything? Do you want me to open your window?"

"No. 'Tsokay." Her mother rolled over and went back to sleep.

As Grace headed downstairs, Coco followed her. The cat was fine now that the thunder and lightning were over, and unlike Grace she could see perfectly well in the dark. Grace stood in her living room, unsure what to do with herself. Couldn't watch TV. Couldn't do anything online. What else was there? She heard Miguel scoff at her and suggest she read a book. But even if she had something she wanted to read, it wouldn't be easy to do under the harsh glare of the tiny LED flashlight.

She checked her phone, wishing she'd thought to charge it earlier in the day. It was at 58 percent power. As tempted as she was to use it as an entertainment source, she knew she should save the charge in case of emergency. But she made one phone call, to Duquesne Light to report her power outage.

The recorded voice informed her that they were aware of an outage in Oakland, Squirrel Hill, Greenfield, and Hazelwood. That was bad; that was a big chunk of the east-end neighborhoods. The voice estimated the power would be back on by eleven thirty p.m. It was almost eight thirty. As Grace sat there in the darkening gloom, she imagined other people in their houses and apartments, at a loss for what to do, sitting there in the lifeless husks of their technology-driven homes.

She lay down on the sofa. For now, with the doors and windows closed, the rooms were preserving their air-conditioned chill. *Like the refrigerator.* Boredom had a soporific effect—one that Grace couldn't fight. The room grew darker, until finally it wasn't worth keeping her eyes open anymore.

50

Grace set the dining room table, meticulously placing the flatware and folding the cloth napkins, nervous about her dinner guest. She'd cleaned the entire house top to bottom, and though she'd offered to order in something special, she was glad now that her mom was doing the cooking. Tantalizing, savory aromas filled the air.

There was a knock on the front door.

"She's here!" Grace called toward the kitchen and then hurried to the door and opened it. "Hi! Welcome!"

There she was, all grown up. Hope. Dressed in all her finery. Grace couldn't afford to buy the garments her sister designed, and by comparison she felt like a paper doll wearing a child's approximation of dress clothes. Hope rolled in past her, and Grace didn't notice how her sister navigated the step: one moment she was outside, and the next she was inside. Jackie bustled in from the kitchen and threw her arms around Hope.

"Oh darling, you look wonderful!" Jackie kissed both of her cheeks.

Grace stood against the wall, out of the way, and got a more thorough look at her sister. Hope wore palazzo pants in the same bright pattern as her blouse. Grace had never been able to create such intricate, sophisticated attire for Mona and Rona, primarily because she couldn't draw well enough. Only rich people could pull off garish fabrics, she thought. When poor people did it, they looked tacky and cheap. Her sister's hair was long and blonde, twisted into a chignon. Her nails were perfectly manicured and polished, and her ears were adorned with emeralds set in gold.

Hope maneuvered her wheelchair into the dining room, bypassing Grace as if she weren't even there. She stayed hidden in the entryway for a moment, listening as Jackie and Hope babbled in the other room. (Hope's speech was somewhat improved from the chaotic articulation of her youth.) Grace looked at herself. Her nails were uneven, and the polish was chipping. Her shoes looked dumpy and worn, and the clearance outfit she'd gotten in Shadyside was a little too tight. Oh well. It wasn't a surprise that she couldn't compete with her sister—though it had been a surprise that Hope had deigned to come back to Pittsburgh to see her new house.

"Your little cottage is adorable," Hope said as Grace joined them in the dining room.

How long had Grace been standing by the front door? Jackie had already served the two of them the first course of their dinner. The candles were lit, and they were drinking wine. Grace ducked into the kitchen to fix herself a plate of food.

Jackie was at the head of the table, so Grace sat across from her sister. Hope's movements, though still stiff and sometimes jerky, were better than they'd once been. She was able to feed herself without spilling *too* much on her beautiful clothes. *Maybe that's why she wears such busy patterns.*

"I framed the *Vogue* layout, every page—I'm so proud of you!" Jackie beamed at Hope.

"Thank you. You'll have to come to New York for fashion week. You can come to the Paris show too, if you want."

"That sounds so exciting, but I don't even have a passport."

Grace watched them interact. Here were her only known relatives, and they seemed like complete strangers.

"And what have you been up to, Grace?" her sister asked. "Still at the same salon?"

Was that a subtle dig at her lack of ambition? "Yes."

"You must be doing well." Hope directed the comment at the four narrow walls of Grace's *cottage*.

Instead of replying, Grace poured herself a full glass of the dark red wine. And drank.

Hope's hand took a sudden wrong turn and smacked her goblet, sending it crashing to the floor. "Oops. I'm sorry."

It was unlikely that Hope was sorry; a smile tugged at her lips. But Grace came around the table to clean her sister's spill. She collected the broken pieces of glass into her cupped hand.

"Just need a few paper towels," she mumbled, getting to her feet, head down, unable to stop herself from acting like a dutiful servant.

As she passed Jackie's chair on her way to the kitchen, her mother abruptly stood. With two hands she grabbed Grace's blouse—and ripped it off her body. "Just use this."

Grace stood there in shock, shards of glass in her hands, elbows pressed against her stomach to cover her exposed bra. Jackie flung the torn shirt in her face and sat back down.

"You're going to cut yourself. Dump it here." Her mother held out Grace's wineglass, intending it as a place to deposit the shattered remnants of Hope's goblet.

Confused and unsure what to do, Grace emptied her hands over the glass. Wine splashed as the fragments dropped in. And then Jackie returned the glass to Grace's place setting, as if she might yet drink the rest once she sat back down at the table. Her ripped blouse dangled from her arm. Her mother and sister resumed eating their meal as if nothing had happened, while Grace stood there half-undressed. She was too humiliated to protest, and the shirt was already destroyed, so she got on her knees beside her sister's wheelchair and sopped up the bloody wine.

"Ready for the next course?" The question was directed at Hope.

"Yes please! You've become a wonderful cook!"

With the aplomb of a world-class waiter, Jackie picked up Hope's plate and then her own and whisked them off to the kitchen.

Grace felt a drop of cold water land on the skin of her back. She looked up and saw Hope's face looming over her. Hope gulped from her water glass; Grace thought she intended to throw it to the floor or dump it on her head. Another icy droplet struck her skin and Grace realized it was the condensation dribbling off the glass. Hope set her water down but continued gazing at Grace, still on her knees.

"Are you mad I didn't invite *you* to New York? Or Paris?"

Grace shrugged. She really wasn't a traveler, so she didn't care about going to fashion week. But her sister's intentional omission stung a bit, as surely Hope knew.

"Well, if you didn't want to feel left out, you shouldn't have killed me."

———

Grace awakened thirsty. The house was pitch black and eerily quiet. Her hands fumbled around the surface of the coffee table until she found the miniature flashlight. She turned it on and went to the kitchen. The dream had left her craving ice-cold water, but the best she could do, without opening the freezer, was let the tap water run. She guzzled it, wishing it were colder, and refilled the glass before returning to the living room.

When she checked her phone, it was after midnight. She called Duquesne Light again and this time the recorded message said they hoped to have the power back on by four a.m., but due to "widespread outages," it could be later. With the flashlight's narrow beam pointed at the floor, she made her way upstairs to use the bathroom. She didn't bother to shut the door. And when she was finished using the toilet, though nothing was wrong with the plumbing, she didn't bother to flush. The world was ending—outside, inside. She had every right to abandon the niceties of civilization.

Alone in the dark, with no other means of escape, she lay back down on the sofa and hoped sleep would return quickly. Not so long ago she'd wanted to avoid sleeping so she could avoid dreaming. But now it was worse to be awake, worse to be left with her thoughts. She could tell herself the nightmares weren't real, and there was some comfort in that. But in their absence, in the light of day, came the dawning prospect of something she couldn't face.

———

Barbara went all out for her retirement party and held it at LeMont, the schmancy five-star restaurant atop Mount Washington. Grace had always wanted to go there, and while her coworkers flocked together with their cocktails, gossiping, she gazed at the incredible twilight views of the city and its rivers.

Miguel sidled up to her, taking in the panorama. "It almost makes it worth losing our jobs."

She gave him a smirk. "Not quite."

"Get drinking, Barbara got us an open bar."

Grace walked across the lounge to the bar and ordered an artisan martini. It wasn't the kind of drink she usually had, or could afford, but it was a special occasion—and she didn't have to pay for it. She felt a bit like Cinderella in her sparkly dress and strappy heels; if she was lucky and the night went well, she wouldn't turn back into a pumpkin (or was that a bumpkin?) until *way* past midnight.

She joined her merry band of coworkers.

"Your dress is fabulous," said Allison, knocking back the last of her drink.

"It really is," Barbara agreed. "Where did you get it?"

"It's one of my sister's designs."

The group murmured appreciation and praise, though Grace—looking down at the shimmering fabric—was suddenly uncertain if she should give Hope all the credit. Hadn't Grace originally drawn this dress for Mona?

Her colleagues erupted in a chorus of laughter, casting glances at her. Grace smiled uncertainly; she hadn't heard the joke.

"What did I miss?" she whispered to Miguel. When she turned she saw it wasn't a cocktail he was withdrawing from his lips but an oxygen mask.

"I'm sorry, Grace," he said. "You got the short straw."

"What straw? We didn't pick straws."

The stylists threw back their heads and laughed again. Grace didn't know why it had happened, but somehow she had become the buffoon, the party's involuntary entertainment. She looked to Miguel, wanting his support, his reassurance, but he was busy with his oxygen mask, sucking in air.

"Who's going first?" Barbara asked.

Allison waved a floppy, drunken hand. "Me me me!"

Going first for what? Allison came toward her, wielding her favorite pair of scissors. Did she intend to cut Grace's hair?

She backed away from Allison. "What are you—"

Before the question was fully out of her mouth, Allison leaned forward and snipped through one of her dress straps. Grace uttered a noise as if she'd been injured, but she wasn't in physical pain. She clutched the ruined fabric against her chest to keep her dress in place. A thousand accusations cycloned through her head—*You bitch! You ruined Hope's dress! What the fuck is wrong with you!* Before she could protest, Demetri stepped forward, scissors gleaming, and snipped off her hand.

What?

Grace opened her mouth to scream, but no sound emerged. Her head wouldn't turn, her neck wouldn't bend, but she could see her other arm in her peripheral vision and . . . It was made of card stock. She was two dimensional. Her severed card-stock hand floated to the floor.

One by one the stylists stepped forward, hair shears at the ready. They made a quick cut here, a little snip there. *Snick-snick-snick-snick.* When they stood back to assess their work, Grace saw her beautiful paper dress on the floor, slashed to pieces. The entirety of her other arm was on the floor too, so she couldn't even cover her naked paper self. Her coworkers grinned and nodded, pleased with their butchery.

No sound would come from Grace's throat, and she discovered her mouth was stuck in an O shape. She tried to swing her body toward Miguel, needing his refuge, but the movement made her lose her balance. She felt herself toppling backward, but she fell softly, gliding on her back toward her huddled tormentors. They resumed talking and drinking, unaware of Grace, a paper carpet, at their feet. The maître d' came to show the party to their table. Without another thought they walked over Grace, her gaze fixed on the ceiling, and left her behind.

51

Grace could tell without getting off the sofa that the electricity was still off. The refrigerator was silent. None of the lamps had come back on. She was grateful for the morning light, a reprieve from the stifling darkness. Coco was spread out on the coffee table beside her, sleeping peacefully. It really didn't matter what time it was (6:49 a.m.), nor did it matter when Duquesne Light now believed the power would be restored—but she called anyway. One o'clock p.m. After they'd missed their previous estimates, Grace wasn't holding her breath.

The night had lasted forever, a decade longer than usual. She got up and shuffled to the kitchen. For additional light, she opened the back door. What she really wanted was coffee, but of course the coffee maker wasn't operational. Nor could she heat water up on the stove. Could she let the tap water run until it was scalding hot and jury-rig a cup of java? She had the water running, her finger under it to monitor the temperature, before her brain kicked in. She turned the faucet off: she had an electric water heater; there was no hot water.

She stood there, hungry and thirsty, overwhelmed by the sensation that her entire house was a broken toy. Lacking other options, she filled a glass with tap water and got a box of crackers out of the cupboard. Before she headed outside, she dashed off a quick note—DO NOT OPEN!—and taped it to the refrigerator's handle, just in case her mother had recovered enough to come downstairs wanting her morning fruit shake.

Barefoot and still in her nightshirt, Grace sat on her back stoop and ate crackers. The neighborhood was quiet, the air cool and dewy, and the daylight a notch underdeveloped. It was lovelier than she'd expected. Refreshing in its nascent emptiness.

It felt like the world was shifting backward in time—not by days or months but centuries. *We're becoming primitive.* She imagined having a firepit in her backyard, where she would cook her meals and make coffee. And every morning a new routine would develop where she'd come out and wave to her neighbors, who'd also be at their backyard firepits. The dreamlike quality of her life was omnipresent as she pondered a future without the internet, without washing machines and hair dryers, toasters and vacuum cleaners. She'd heard somewhere, likely on a TV show, that everyone in past eras stank, that even the wealthy ladies and gentlemen rarely bathed or washed their hair. Savages in silk finery.

Lost in her strange but contented reverie, she was startled when her mother opened the screen door and stepped outside. Jackie, too, was in her nightdress, barefoot.

"Feeling better?" Grace asked hopefully, moving *Take Mom to a hotel* to the top of her to-do list.

"Mm-hmm."

Jackie's face was expressionless, her eyes unblinking. She made her way down the short flight of steps to the grass and then headed across the yard in a way that appeared both purposeful and aimless. Was she sleepwalking?

"Where are you going?"

Her mother didn't answer. She traipsed diagonally to the far corner of the yard, where the neighbor's hydrangea bush sprawled over the low rickety fence that marked the boundary between their properties. Grace watched her, uncertain of Jackie's intentions. The bush was heavy with blue-petaled flowers—why hadn't Grace noticed before how pretty they were? Now she thought her mother might have a good idea: the blossoms were so voluminous that they'd only have to cut three to make a beautiful bouquet.

Grace stood, debating if she should get a pair of scissors to cut the stems—or did Jackie plan on simply breaking them off?

"Mom?" The zombielike quality of her mother's locomotion didn't seem normal. Should Grace make more of an effort to "wake" her?

The hydrangea bush looked more immense with Jackie beside it for scale. In her perpetually addled state, Grace envisioned her mother walking into the bush, being engulfed by it—swallowed—and disappearing. What happened next was almost worse.

Jackie stepped into the plant's embrace and started eating the flowers. She ate as a horse would eat, or a giraffe, her mouth eager to graze.

Grace leaped off the steps and ran across the grass. "Mom!"

Without Miguel, Grace might've been unaware of the danger, but she assumed that if hydrangeas were poisonous to cats, they were also toxic to people.

"You can't eat that! Stop it!" She grabbed her mother, yanking her away from the plant.

Jackie pushed back with surprising strength, nearly sending Grace toppling backward.

—she fell softly, gliding on her back toward her huddled tormentors—

For an instant she saw nothing but sky, as if she were lying on the ground.

She gripped her mother's arm and forcibly pulled her. "You're gonna get sick!"

It was almost funny—wasn't her mother already sick? She wrangled Jackie toward the house.

"Get off me you dumb bitch! I'm hungry!" Soggy petals and saliva flew from her mouth.

"I'll get you something to eat." Grace didn't have time to talk sense into her—were the neighbors watching the freak show? She hauled her fuming, snarling, delirious mother up the stairs.

Through the door, into the kitchen, over to the sink. Grace turned on the water and tried to force her mother's head under it.

"Spit it out!" She sloshed handfuls of water in the general direction of her mother's mouth, until finally Jackie spit out the toxic mash.

A tad more alert, Jackie swished the water around, like she'd just finished brushing her teeth. The crisis over, Grace shut off the faucet, breathing hard, glaring at her mother. Jackie glared right back, her face a wet mess.

"You're a piece of shit. Can't even keep the fucking lights on! Too lazy to pay your own bills!"

"Fuck you, Mom, it's a power outage." Grace didn't bother getting angry; clearly Jackie was all kinds of unwell. So much for taking her to a hotel today. "Do you want to go back to bed? I'll bring you a snack and something to drink?"

Jackie's face was a storm of discontent, but she hobbled along when Grace led her—more gently now—back to her room. The house's supply of cool air was dwindling, and it was even stuffier upstairs, so Grace opened a window. Her mother sat with her back against the headboard, legs extended on the bed, arms crossed.

"I'm not gonna lie down," said Jackie. "So you can't smother me."

"Suit yourself. I'll be back in a minute."

Grace accepted her mother's deteriorating condition as only a person who subsisted on nightmares could. Back in the kitchen, she filled her mother's usual shake container with water and deliberated on what to take her to eat. She stared at the fridge, which held most of her mother's precious fruit. Nope. Grace wasn't willing to risk all the new groceries; they'd probably be okay in there for another twelve hours or so. The bananas weren't fully ripe, but they were accessible; she grabbed two from the counter.

Jackie was just as she'd left her, arms crossed, scowling, sitting up in bed. Grace handed her a banana and set the other one on the night-stand, with the water. It was almost comical how pissed off her mother looked, like an elderly toddler determined to win a fight. She yanked down the greenish skin and stuffed the banana in her mouth—still shooting daggers at Grace.

"Guess I'll leave you to your tantrum. Call if you need anything." She was at the head of the stairs before her mother hissed at her.

"How can you be so glib? You act so innocent, like nothing hap-pened." She spoke with such vitriol, such condemnation. Grace was more accustomed to the accusations by now, but the tone of her moth-er's voice sent her nerves aquiver with a prickling of contempt.

She stood at her mother's door. "I thought about it. Like you asked me to do," she said softly.

Her mother scrutinized her. And then the terrible grin of a wicked witch transformed her face. "Oh. I see it now. Ha! You remember. I see you remembering!"

"Fuck off."

"You can live in peace now, when you embrace the truth!" Jackie's eyes had a weird, intense glow.

Grace turned and headed down the stairs.

"You'll thank me later!" her mother called after her. "For setting you free! Maybe you'll return the favor someday—tell someone you love what they really need to hear!"

Grace made a beeline for the kitchen, the back door, the stoop, needing some distance to shut out the sound of her mother cackling. The air wasn't as refreshing as it had been before, the neighborhood not as quiet. Earlier she'd found a moment of calm here, as she took in the day. She wanted it back, but it wasn't the same now. Like so much else, her mother had ruined it.

52

Grace sat on the sofa in her childhood home. The fabric curtains that had once given her sister some privacy had been taken down, but the bed was still in the dining room. It was dark outside, but the living room was brighter now that the ugly twin lamps had been reunited. Mommy left her birthday present on the kitchen table, and Grace had already opened it even though Mommy said they'd celebrate when she got home from work. On previous birthdays Grace and Hope had shared a cake. Mommy promised to bring home a cupcake; Grace wasn't sure if she'd ever get a cake again.

She didn't get the lamp she'd asked for, though maybe it didn't matter now. The gift she received instead made her very, very sad, and a part of her wondered if it was intentional. Or maybe it wasn't. Maybe Mommy just couldn't be bothered, in the weeks since Hope's funeral, to shop for something else. Grace held the zippered pouch on her lap, filled with the eye shadows and lipsticks, eyeliner and concealer, that Hope had so wanted.

"I'm sorry you don't like your present." Out of nowhere, Hope appeared on the couch. Alive and healthy. She wasn't even in her wheelchair.

"It was meant for you." Grace was supposed to be twelve in the dream, but she looked like her adult self. She handed the cosmetic pouch to her sister.

"Thank you," said Hope.

"You're welcome."

"I'm sorry Mommy didn't get you what you wanted."

Grace shrugged. "I have no idea anymore what I want."

"Well, I got you something." Hope pulled a small box with a bow on it from behind her back.

The sisters smiled at each other, and Grace took the box. Something inside the box made a pitiful little squeak. The smile started to slide away from Grace's face before she got the lid fully off. There, nestled atop the tissue paper, was a hamster. It made a scared, tortured noise, and Grace started to cry. The delicate creature was half-crushed. Its back legs weren't working, and there were drops of blood on the tissue paper.

"Why would you give me this?" And now Grace was a child again, newly twelve, weeping.

"It was just a joke, jeez."

Hope reached for the hamster and stood—unassisted—and flung the animal as hard as she could. The hamster's limp body slid down the wall, leaving a thin trail of blood. Grace was glad, she supposed, that it wasn't suffering anymore. But she wanted to crawl into a hole and never come out. Sometimes the world was too cruel, and her sister had a knack for spotlighting the horrors Grace didn't want to see.

"Stop crying, you big baby. Here—here's your real gift." Hope pulled a slightly larger box, with a slightly larger bow, from behind her back.

Grace held it on her lap. She really didn't want to open it. More than ever, she wanted to find that hole—or dig it herself—and curl up with her eyes shut tight. Her heart was going to burst. She felt it ballooning in her chest.

"Go on," Hope urged. "It's just what you always wanted."

What had Grace always wanted? She carefully lifted the lid, slow and steady, as if it were a bomb. Now she was an adult again, gazing into the box—gazing at a human fetus, clean and waxy as a doll. She felt her fury rising, without understanding who or what she was angry at. By all appearances it was sleeping soundly on its tiny blanket, but Grace knew it was dead—or, more accurately, she knew it had never opened its mouth to breathe.

Fearing her sister's mockery, Grace tried to swallow away her tears, but they escaped down her cheeks. Tenderly, she replaced the lid and handed the gift back to Hope.

"You can't return it," Hope said, refusing to take the gift from her. "I'm not being mean to you," she added gently. "This—this embryo—is you, your second chance. You have to try, really try, to be a better person."

"I will," Grace whispered.

Hope nodded. "Do the right thing."

———

Sweaty and hot, Grace kicked the comforter into a ball at the foot of the sofa. Napping wasn't helping, and she didn't want to go back to sleep, but she also didn't want to be awake—not with the electricity still out. Duquesne Light continued to claim the power would be back at one o'clock p.m., never mind that it was after two. She felt antsy now, like she'd had too much caffeine. The most recent dream snaked through her veins. Was it a call to action?

The longer she sat there the faster the snakes went, filling her, until the force of them propelled her to her feet. She jogged upstairs to put on some clothes.

Her mother was awake, apparently lying in wait. "Did ja figure it out yet Grace? Did ja figure it out?"

Jackie, pinned against her headboard, looked like a mannequin that had come to life but couldn't move. Grace ignored her. Went to her room and threw on a comfy T-shirt and a pair of shorts. She had to get out of the house, and though she didn't plan to go far—the backyard—she wanted to look more presentable than she and her mother had looked that morning. In case anyone was watching. Maybe they weren't. Maybe they were all cooped up in their own homes with their own batshit relatives.

She darted into the bathroom to give her hair a quick brush. Coco was in the bathtub, trying to stay cool. Grace turned the water on enough for a constant dribble and watched as the cat held her paw under the drip and then licked it.

"That's very ladylike of you."

"Who are you talking to?" Jackie screeched. "You're not supposed to have people over while we're sick—you might be contagious!"

"Just the cat."

"Cat. Fat cat. Cat with a rat. Hickory dickory fuck, the mouse ran out of luck. The clock struck two, the mouse got the flu, hickory dickory fuck."

"I don't think those are the words, Mom." Grace detoured into Jackie's room and tried to put her hand on her mother's forehead to see if she had a fever; Jackie batted it away. "Can I get you anything?"

"There's nothing to get, is there?"

"Not really."

"Then no. It's so easy to make offers when there's nothing to give."

"Okay . . ." Her mother wasn't well, but she also didn't seem to want Grace's help.

Feeling light and surprisingly graceful, Grace bounded to her bedroom to grab a notebook. She couldn't waste the last of her phone's battery, so she'd have to jot things down the old-fashioned way. And when the electricity came back, she'd be prepared. In the meanwhile, she would draft confessions to every one of her damsels.

Her mother continued experimenting with her nursery rhyme. "Hickory dickory fuck, the mouse ran out of luck. The clock struck four, the mouse tried to roar . . ."

Grace galloped down the steps and out the front door. She strode around the house to the backyard, which felt safer, more private, than the front porch. Notebook in hand, she wrote as she paced. It was possible—probable even—that she looked like a manic person who was off her meds, but she didn't care. For once, she knew exactly what she needed to do.

53

The hard part was figuring out the general template. She wanted to sincerely confess, but she also hoped to convey to each damsel that she genuinely cared about them. It wasn't hard, in the anonymity of her backyard, to write "I'm sorry" in her notebook. They would be angry, hurt, confused . . . but could they accept her apology? Could they see that Grace had been well meaning? Or perhaps it didn't count as an apology if it became more about Grace's motivations than her damsels' sense of betrayal.

Don't overexplain. LuckyJamison or River would give that sort of advice. Wow. It struck her for the first time how fucked up it was that her inner voices had *names*. Grace flipped to a new page and tried a shorter version of the template.

It felt good to write it out. It felt good to write it over and over again. The repetition made it real. *These women trusted you. You're just another internet troll.* A more-than-teensy part of her hoped some of them would still want to be friends.

A jubilant shout broke her concentration. Then she heard more whooping and clapping.

An air conditioner in her neighbor's window roared to life. The power was back! Grace threw her arms up in celebration and raced inside. She plugged her phone in to recharge. It was almost three o'clock. She plugged her laptop in. She turned on everything that had automatically shut off—including the fan in her mother's room. The router took a few minutes to reboot, and Grace impatiently knelt beside it, watching it cycle through a series of blinks. Finally the dots were all aglow and ready to communicate with the world.

She plopped on the sofa with her phone and typed out a master copy of her confession. That, she decided, was the best way: send them all the same "I'm not who you thought I was" admission. The truth wouldn't go down any better with individualized adornments—"What I said about your drawing skills was a hundred percent true," or "I really do want you and your children to be safe and happy." For now, in their shock, they were only going to hear that Preston, Malcolm, SunSoakedSergei didn't exist. She had to anticipate that they would reply, perhaps hatefully. And she wouldn't ghost them. She would accept their anger—and then express something more personal, something positive, even if they didn't believe her.

Thanks to copy and paste, she was able to send the message to all her damsels in a matter of minutes.

———

Grace marched back and forth across the living room, triumphant, high on her virtue. She'd come clean. She wasn't a catfisher anymore. No more dirty little secrets. Someday she'd admit the entire thing to Miguel so she truly wouldn't have anything to hide. This was the new Grace. She pictured the fetus in its gift-wrapped box opening its mouth and inhaling its first breath. Her new self was alive.

Jackie plodded down the stairs. Her nightgown looked misshapen, stretched, like a monster had tried to crawl out of it.

Though nothing between them was really okay, Grace was eager to tell her mother what she'd done. It would probably only earn her some snarky remarks, but Grace was bursting to share her sense of victory. She hadn't ever thought of her hobby as a burden, but she felt so relieved to be free of it; maybe it had hampered her more than she'd realized.

Her mother was in her own little world and rounded the corner into the dining room without acknowledging Grace in any way. A moment later she heard the clattering of knives. The thump of the cutting board landing on the counter. Realizing what was about to happen, Grace raced into the kitchen. As Jackie reached for the refrigerator door, Grace threw herself in front of it, blocking her mother's way.

"Can't open that yet!"

"Get out of the way—I'm starving."

"I can't."

"You're starving me! You haven't given me anything to eat in days!"

"Mom, the power's only been back for a minute, let the refrigerator get cold again. Ten more minutes."

Jackie glared at her, moved in close so they were nose to nose. Her mother's eyes looked cloudier than ever. Her breath stank. How long had it been since she'd brushed her teeth? Grace flattened herself against the door, turning her head aside, but couldn't escape the smell.

"Look at me, Grace. I'm wasting away."

"Why don't you brush your teeth," she suggested. "Wash up a little. And then we can fix a meal."

"You don't want me to eat," her mother snarled. "You don't want me to get better."

"That isn't true. Mom . . ." Grace eased out from under her mother's imprisoning closeness. She gripped Jackie's shoulders, turning her toward the center of the kitchen. "There's something I want to tell you—I think you'll be pleased."

Jackie's demeanor softened. A fluttery smile brightened her pallid face. "Oh? Yes?"

"I told them. All of them. All the women I was lying to. I confessed to them. I told them who I really was. And I apologized." It felt good to say it aloud. First came the words in her notebook, and then DMs to her damsels. But saying it aloud felt like a necessary step toward absolution, like standing up at a twelve-step meeting to admit your addiction.

Her mother's face flickered between hope and confusion. "And?"

"And . . . I needed to do that. To come clean. Start fresh. This is the beginning of a whole new stage in my life."

For a long moment Jackie stood there silently judging her. It didn't dampen Grace's sense of accomplishment; she wasn't expecting her congratulations. She had told her mother because she needed to tell her, not because Jackie wanted to hear it. Grace's joy didn't start to wither until her mother's features crawled downward. Something trembled beneath her skin. She took in a breath, but instead of speaking—or unleashing a cacophony of insults—Jackie spit in her face.

Grace stood there with her mouth agape.

"You're not my daughter." The words came loaded with wrath.

"What—" She smeared the putrid goo off her cheek and nose.

"You think that's what I wanted to hear? You think I came all this way, spent all this energy, gave you all this time—time to sort out your feelings, your thoughts—for *that*? You're pathetic. Pathetic. My God what did I do to deserve a child like you." She turned away, lurched toward the sink. Grace thought Jackie was about to vomit.

"Mom . . ." And then it hit her, the only confession her mother wanted to hear. *Hope.*

A sound emerged: a spark igniting a fuel source. The sound of a burner on a gas stove, whooshing to life, but it came from inside her. The blaze was building. Grace saw herself on a pyre, flames engulfing her feet, climbing upward, scorching her skin. "I didn't . . . ! I'm not going to admit to something that isn't true."

Jackie spun, her gaze steely. "But you know it is true."

"I don't know that! You've been fucking with me!" Grace screeched. "Brainwashing me! Hypnotizing me!"

With a show of dignity, Jackie squared her bony shoulders and stepped toward Grace. "I gave you the truth. It was a gift. A gift you can't accept. But it's a gift you can't give back."

"Mother, you didn't give me a gift. You're fucking with my head!" Grace pounded her own skull as she said it.

"You're unstable, Grace—you're a fucking mess."

"You did this to me!"

"I've known it since the night your sister died."

"Maybe *she* moved the pillow—did you ever think of that? She had a convulsion and—"

"JUST TELL ME WHY YOU DID IT!" her mother screamed, full throttle. "Just tell me, so I know! Was she bossing you around? Teasing you? I know how she was, Grace—it's the reason I could forgive you, because I shouldn't have let it go on like that, leaving her with you. But I deserve to know what happened! What was the *last straw*?"

Grace felt herself slithering out of her body, elongating, transforming into a two-dimensional wraith.

"TELL ME!" her mother demanded.

"*You're* the last straw! You are the last fucking straw!"

Grace watched her physical self seize the knife from Jackie's cutting board.

She watched that other self plunge the knife into her mother's deflated gut.

For an instant she was in her body again, horrified by her hand on the knife as the blade disappeared into her mother's flesh. But then Jackie started laughing. Cackling, like the moment was the funniest she'd ever experienced.

"This, Grace! This is who you really are!" Laughing. And laughing. "It took a while, but we finally got there. Your true self, Grace."

Grace watched from the ceiling, a sliver of herself. Below her, her corpulent form stabbed her mother again. And again. And again.

"Here you are, Grace!" Jackie drooled blood as she cackled. "We did it, my girl! Truth wins in the end!"

The knife broke, and still Jackie stood, demented in her laughter, deranged in her pride. Grace watched as the earthbound part of her grabbed another knife and kept trying, desperate for her mother to *shut up*.

It was taking longer than Grace's conscience could bear. She allowed herself to float away, out of the room, out of the house, toward the perfect blue of a faraway sky.

54

The phone rang. Grace jolted into a sitting position. She didn't remember lying down on her bed. What time was it? She must have fallen asleep but perhaps not for long—it was still sunny outside. Her head ached. She reached for her phone and saw a collage of Band-Aids on her hand. How had she gotten hurt?

By the time she could stay upright without feeling dizzy, the phone had stopped ringing. Someone left a message. Grace massaged her scalp. She couldn't remember what day it was or what she'd been doing before she came upstairs to her room.

Holding the phone in her left, uninjured hand, she checked her voice mail. It was from the hospital. Her body stiffened, bracing for bad news, as the message started to play. A moment later she shot to her feet as if she'd been zapped off the bed by a cattle prod. What she was hearing couldn't be true. Her heart throbbed, and her mouth went dry. She needed a drink of water but not until she'd played the message again.

". . . we were able to remove his breathing tube a couple of hours ago, and he's been breathing okay on his own. We'll keep monitoring him, but if he's still doing this well in the morning we'll transfer him back to a regular room."

Grace screamed, jumping up and down. "Halle-fucking-lujah! Oh my God!" She did a crazy dance, throwing her arms around, squealing. "Yes yes yes yes!"

Coco slunk through the doorway, eyeing Grace with cautious curiosity.

She scooped the cat into her arms. "Your daddy's getting better! He's getting better!"

After more than enough hugs and kisses, Coco twisted her body away, ready to jump down. That's when Grace noticed her dirty paws.

"What have you been getting into?" Coco fled down the stairs. Grace knew she needed to pursue her, see what mess the cat had made. But she sat on the edge of her bed, taking a moment to fully process the nurse's message.

The last thing she clearly remembered was confessing to all of her damsels, and then uttering the admission aloud to her mother. A chill danced across her skin.

"Oh my God." She'd had a dream. *When?* Her sister had told her to do the right thing. And now Grace had. And now Miguel was off the ventilator.

She clamped a hand over her mouth, her throat heaving with sobs. After weeks of crushing self-doubt, she'd done something right. And maybe, in the cosmic process, helped to save her best friend.

———

"Coco?" Grace followed muddy cat prints down the steps. She racked her brain, trying to figure out what Coco could've gotten into. It looked like the cat had waded through a puddle of ketchup, but that wasn't possible. Though even as she thought it, she pictured her mother in a frenzied act of revenge, tossing Grace's food out of the refrigerator. With the way things had been recently, it was a little too easy to imagine unhinged Jackie laughing as she squirted ketchup onto the floor.

Grace tracked the little footprints to the dining room, where they headed into the kitchen.

Full stop.

Her pulse skipped a beat or three. Her flesh contracted around her bones.

There was no mistaking what she saw. Blood. Her mother. Dead.

Brutally dead. Don't-bother-checking-for-a-pulse dead.

Coco meowed. Brushed against Grace's leg. Sashayed into the living room, indifferent to the catastrophe.

Grace understood now: it was blood on the cat's feet. From where she stood mid–dining room, she could see the pattern of thicker paw prints around her mother's body. Coco must have checked it out, sniffed around. *Did cats have a taste for blood?*

Gagging, Grace bolted upstairs, reaching the toilet just in time. There wasn't much in her stomach, but it all came up. Her throat burned. The residue in her mouth tasted sulfuric.

She crawled to the top step and huddled there, face in her hands. Her heart couldn't find its rhythm; it jittered in her chest. The air smelled entirely of her mother—the floral rot, oxidized blood, and . . . bad breath.

She remembered Jackie yelling in her face. Spitting in her face. Laughing. Laughing and laughing. Grace shut her eyes but couldn't stop seeing. Everything.

Truth. That's what her mother believed was the path to salvation, or bliss. Grace nodded and knew the truth. She'd killed her mother.

Deep breath in. Out.

She'd killed her mother, but Miguel was doing better. If they moved him out of intensive care in the morning, she might even believe she'd done the right thing.

In the meanwhile, she went downstairs to deal with the mess.

———

She FaceTimed with Miguel the next afternoon.

"I'm so glad to see you, lovey. You look better." She felt jubilant. Actions had consequences, and she was *right*.

"You look terrible, no offense." His voice was hoarse. "You're getting too thin."

Grace shrugged. "I'm on the mend." She nibbled a handful of Jackie's blueberries.

They FaceTimed every day. Miguel was weak but holding steady. He asked after Jackie, and Grace decided this was not the moment for a tell-all. For now, her job was to take care of Coco—until Miguel was home and could do it himself. She had no illusions about the repercussions of her guilt, but Coco wouldn't have anyone if Grace was hauled off to prison. She'd explain it all later, if she could. It was possible he'd never understand, never want to see her again, but for now he and Coco needed her and she wouldn't let them down.

She made no effort to dispose of her mother's body, but she didn't want to look at it. Jackie inhabited a corner on the dining room floor, beneath the comforter from her bed. The smell got worse and worse, and Coco started acting more skittish. Grace might have suffered through the stench on her own, but after a week or so she asked Miguel if she and the cat could stay at his apartment for a few days.

"I just need a little break from my mother."

"Sure," he said, sitting up in his hospital bed. "Better do it now, 'cause I might be going home soon."

55

Coco was happy to be back in familiar territory. She settled in as if she'd never been away, the interlude at Grace's all but forgotten. Grace cleaned Miguel's apartment. Laundered the bedding and towels. Ordered in groceries so he'd have everything he needed when he got home. They were counting the days. Their chats had gotten really short; they were both just waiting for Miguel's release.

Finally, Grace got the call. She packed the few things she'd brought into her duffel bag. When it was time to say goodbye, she found Coco napping on her perch by the living room window.

"I might not see you again," she whispered, cradling the cat in her arms. The cat blinked sleepy eyes at her. Grace kissed her head. "Give Miguel some cuddles, okay? I love you."

Hesitating at the door, she looked at the apartment one last time. Perhaps Miguel wouldn't notice the work she'd done to make his homecoming perfect, but that didn't matter. This was what she'd want to come home to. Everything in its place. His fur baby looked out the window, waiting for him.

———

As she pulled her car into the hospital driveway, Miguel was already outside, sitting on a bench with his plastic bag of belongings. They waved madly at each other as she stopped at the curb. Before he got into the car, Grace slipped on a face mask.

"Lovey!" Miguel cried.

They embraced in the front seat, the long, tight hug of love and fear and relief.

"Ready to go home?"

"So ready."

She saw him studying her as she checked the mirrors and drove away.

"I'm not contagious anymore," he said. "If that's what you're concerned about."

"No, I'm concerned I might have something. I think my mom had some weird—I don't know, not the virus."

He nodded, but she felt his gaze. "Are you okay, Grace? You look . . ."

What did she look like? Like a person with resolve? Or did he see something less noble.

She was glad for the face mask; it hid the way she pressed her lips together to keep from crying. A clock was winding down. She wasn't sure what her future held.

"It's been difficult, but . . . I'm optimistic. You and Coco are okay, that's what matters."

"You matter too. Still having those nightmares?"

A noise that was half sob, half laugh escaped before she could stop it. "No. They finally stopped. That's one good thing. There's just been a lot on my mind."

"Yeah." He sighed. "I'm so glad to get home, sleep in my own bed, see my baby girl. But . . . I don't even want to think about what's next. It could be a while before I can work again."

"I love your cat—she's the best."

Grace needed a minute to figure out how to say what she'd been thinking about for days. She felt nervous in Miguel's presence. There was so much he didn't know, and she wasn't ready to tell him. She kept her focus on the road so she wouldn't have to make eye contact. "Listen, I might have to go away for a while—a little thing with my mom. I'll tell you everything later, I promise, but you don't need my whole saga right now."

"Is your mom okay? What's going on?"

"I have to accept . . . I have to take responsibility. But I'd like it if you lived in my house—if you want to. I used the last of my savings to pay the mortgage for the next few months. So, except for utilities, it would be free for a while. Then after . . . I don't think it's much different than your rent."

"How long are you gonna be gone? What about Jackie?"

"My mom won't be living there anymore." She turned her head away so he couldn't see the tears welling. "I'm not sure how long I'll be away. Longer than I'd like."

"Seriously, what's going on? Where are you going? You're kind of freaking me out."

"Not today, okay? I'll tell you, but I just want you to enjoy your first day of freedom. I just wanted you to know you can stay in my house if you want to, for as long as you like, whether I'm there or not."

"I'd rather you were there. But . . . it would be nice to have a little yard, a porch."

"Washer and dryer? Air-conditioning?" A spark of humor returned as she tried to sell him on the idea. "Walking distance to the supermarket?"

Miguel laughed. "Okay. I'll consider it. Thank you."

She parked in front of his building and got out to give him a hug.

"Sure you don't want to come in for a bit?" he asked.

"I'm sure you need some alone time. And kitty cuddles. I stocked your fridge."

"Thank you, Grace. I love you."

"I love you. Give Coco some kisses from me."

"I will." She watched him head into his apartment. "See you later!" he called.

She waved in return, too choked up to speak. It might be a long time before she saw him again.

———

She hauled the moving boxes out of the basement. Ignored the comforter, and the decomposing heap beneath it, as she carried the boxes through the dining room and took them upstairs. Later someone—maybe everyone—was going to question her priorities, but Grace didn't want to leave this task for Miguel, should he decide to move in. She packed up all of Jackie's things.

The furniture was too large and heavy to move by herself, but Miguel might find a way to make use of it. She wrote DONATE on all the boxes with a fat Sharpie. It was the best she could do to ready the room for a new occupant. The rest of the house was tidy, but she did a quick dusting and mopping.

She hoped someone—the police or the coroner—would appreciate that she hadn't tampered with the evidence. Tucked in with Jackie's corpse were the knives. After she called nine one one, they would come and haul the body away. The kitchen floor and walls still showed faint smudges that she didn't think looked too much like blood. Anyone with a good imagination could think she'd dropped a pot of coffee or a jar of spaghetti sauce.

The last thing on her to-do list was a long, hot shower. She had no idea what her impending living conditions would be like. This could be the end of the life luxuries she'd always known.

Clean and dressed, she finally called nine one one and told the dispatcher her mother was dead. And yes, she was sure her mother wasn't breathing and didn't have a pulse.

"It's too late for that."

———

Only now did Grace start to get nervous, knowing the police were on their way. Only now did she fully appreciate how strange it all looked.

The minutes ticked by, and she didn't know if they were going to arrive in three minutes or thirty, but she started to panic. She paced, light headed as her blood zigzagged chaotically through her chest. There was so much to explain, and so little of it would make sense without everything that came before it. Should she start with her sister? Losing her job? Jackie's arrival? Her mother's accusation?

Grace had worked herself into hysterics by the time the two uniformed officers approached her door. She told them the only thing that made sense in that moment, the one thing that explained the chain of events.

"I had to do it! She was contagious!"

EPILOGUE

Grace had quickly become Silas's favorite patient. He met with her almost every day and only rarely had she been too morose to communicate. Most of the time she was eager to tell the next chapter of her story, keen that he—"someone, anyone"—should understand the entwined chain of events. "I'm not crazy" was one of her frequent refrains—a message with a double edge for someone who might otherwise be in prison. Torrance wasn't exactly a spa, but it offered more liberties and compassionate care than the alternative.

Today she sat with a plastic bowl of apple slices. He hoped eventually she'd gain a little weight, make more of an effort with her overall health, but for now she was still eating mostly fruit. She was in an especially good mood because her friend Miguel had just moved into her house. Silas would dissect that relationship at a later time; he wasn't sure what it said about Grace's best friend that he'd come around to accepting her explanation so readily.

"Thank you for sharing so much with me," he said, as the story finally reached the moment of her arrest. It had taken several weeks for Grace to tell the whole thing from beginning to end.

"Thank you for listening."

Another reason he liked her: she was capable of performing all the societal rituals of polite interaction. The fact that in her everyday appearance and behavior she showed no signs of overt deviance made her case all the trickier. She was either profoundly delusional or a cunning sociopath. He was leaning toward the former, primarily because her emotions seemed more spontaneous and genuine than what he typically witnessed with the sociopaths.

"So Grace, where do we go from here?"

Her eyes widened and she looked frightened. "Doesn't it make sense now? That you know the whole thing, everything that happened? I didn't *want* to kill my mother."

"And yet you admit to killing her."

"I wanted to kill the confusion, the doubt she brought into my life. That was a really bad day . . ."

"You snapped."

Grace nodded.

"Do you really believe that there's some sort of physical illness that makes people obsessed with the truth?"

She shrugged. "I wouldn't have. But she talked about it. I still don't know what her husband Robert died of. And I never really knew what was wrong with my mother—sometimes it seemed like everything was wrong with her, and sometimes she seemed fine. Not fine, okayish. Even when she was being really nice, it was confusing."

"I understand. You had a really hard time with her."

Grace nodded, more subdued than when her session had started. "I'd never felt so off balance in my life."

"Can we talk a little about your sister? It sounds like your mother was obsessed with getting you to tell her what happened the night Hope died."

"I really don't think I killed my sister."

"You don't *think*?"

"She was right, that I'd blocked a lot of it out. And what I remember now are the nightmares I had, so . . ."

"You've hinted at . . . You think your mother had something to do with your nightmares?"

Grace nodded. Then shook her head. "I don't know. Sometimes I thought that."

"Can you see how it would bother your mom, to leave one daughter in care of the other? And then one night the worst possible thing happened, and Jackie wasn't there. She never knew exactly what happened."

"I didn't know she'd felt that way, for all those years. I thought there was a simple explanation—my fault for being negligent, but not . . ." She rested her elbows on her knees and gazed at the floor, distraught.

"Perhaps the simple explanation for your mother is she'd spent too long obsessing about the what-ifs, imagining every scenario. And no matter what she spun around in her head, she could never know the truth of what really happened that night. Does that seem possible to you?"

"Maybe. But I don't think that explains everything."

Now it was Silas's turn to nod. He closed his notebook. "Why don't we stop here for today. I think you're making very good progress. How do you feel about everything?"

She turned her head toward the window and the slightly dystopian landscape. "I think you don't really get it. I hope to get my life back someday. But that's not gonna happen until you believe me."

"Maybe not yet. But we're getting there, okay?"

Grace wore a sad smile as she got up to leave. After Silas closed the door behind her, he sat at his desk to summarize his notes. She really was such an exciting case; every session gave him so much to digest.

On the one hand, she was so reasonable. So articulate. On the other hand . . . Soon he wanted to start working with her to recover the memories of her sister's death. It would reveal a lot—to both of them. And, ironically, it wasn't impossible that Grace's mother would be proven right in the end: the truth might set Grace free. He would be quite proud of himself if someday, with his assistance, she could integrate back into society.

Silas leaned back in his chair and stretched, wishing he had time for a catnap before his next session started. As a rule, he never shared anything personal with his patients. It almost made him wince—or shudder—to imagine how Grace would react if she knew about the troubles he was having.

He hadn't been sleeping well for a few weeks now. His nights were plagued by the strangest dreams. And his imagination, well schooled in the depraved and the macabre, was revealing things he wasn't sure he could ever unsee.

Acknowledgments

I started writing *Mothered* in April 2020. We still believed in the first half of 2020 that the best parts of humanity could yet prevail and we would course correct our social and environmental wrongs. There was a golden moment of optimism when we hoped this difficult time could inspire a holistic renaissance. And then the moment passed. Selfishness and ignorance won, and at some point that positivity started to sour and then rot, and what was left was a simmering sense of doom.

It was in that decline of optimism that I wrote much of *Mothered*, and it became impossible to shut out the realities of the world I was living in. Unlike my previous books, *Mothered* was written in a start-and-stop manner where I didn't write for weeks—sometimes months—before returning to the story. This was necessitated by the confusing mental toll of learning how to process and live in a pandemic, as well as needing time to deal with my mother's death from COVID-19.

When it was all said and done, this was a book that I very much enjoyed writing, and the things I learned by changing up my writing process have been beneficial. Upon declaring it "finished," I asked a few people if they'd like to read this "batshit crazy" thing I'd written, and I'm grateful to John Stage, Deborah Stage, and Brooke Dorsch for eagerly agreeing.

My agents, Stephen Barbara and Claire Friedman, have been dedicated supporters of this project, and I can't thank them enough. And of course, this wouldn't be a book in readers' hands without the unwavering passion of my editor, Liz Pearsons. Immense thanks to her and the entire Thomas & Mercer team: Gracie Doyle, Sarah Shaw, Rachael Herbert, Olga Grlic, and Jarrod Taylor. And special thanks to the eagle-eyed copyeditor Alicia Lea and proofreader Elyse Lyon.

Given the difficulty of living alone through a pandemic, I would be remiss in my gratitude if I didn't credit my cat, Tilly-Leguin, for keeping me sane with her warm and fuzzy companionship. While the rest of us were wondering what the hell was going on, my cat was living her best life in our new house, watching squirrels and birds and deer out the window and running like a lunatic up and down the stairs. She is the best nap buddy ever. And in the spirit of managing #PandemicLife, I also owe thanks to Carrie Mitchell, teacher and choreographer extraordinaire, and the virtual Happy Tappers Club. What do you do when you're alone in a new house during a pandemic? Take up tap dancing!

I couldn't continue to publish books without the support of readers, librarians, and enthusiastic booksellers. Thank you to Pamela Klinger-Horn for her early and supportive presence in my career. Thank you to my friends at my local bookstores: Mystery Lovers Bookshop, Riverstone Books, Penguin Bookshop, and White Whale Bookstore. And last but not least, thank you to my fellow authors for generously blurbing my books (I'm pretty sure I haven't thanked you enough!).

My brain broke sometime in 2020 . . . I'm sure I'm forgetting to thank someone—is it you?

About the Author

Photo © 2017 Gabrianna Dacko

Zoje Stage's debut novel, *Baby Teeth*, was a *USA Today* and international bestseller. It was nominated for a Bram Stoker Award and named one of the best books of the year by *Forbes Magazine*, *Library Journal*, *PopSugar*, Barnes & Noble, Bloody Disgusting, and BookBub. Her follow-up novel, *Wonderland*, was described in a starred review from Booklist as "a beautifully choreographed and astonishing second novel." And with her third book, *Getaway*, the *New York Times* declared her "a writer with a gift for the lyrical and the frightening." When Zoje isn't writing, reading, or streaming documentaries, she can be found in her mini dance studio, tap dancing. She lives in Pittsburgh with her cat.